Poison

Amanda Caret

Contents

Chapter One   1

Chapter Two   7

Chapter Three   12

Chapter Four   17

Chapter Five   22

Chapter Six   26

Chapter Seven   30

Chapter Eight   35

Chapter Nine   39

Chapter Ten   44

Chapter Eleven   49

Chapter Twelve   53

Chapter Thirteen   57

Chapter Fourteen   61

Chapter Fifteen   65

Chapter Sixteen   69

Chapter Seventeen   73

Chapter Eighteen   77

Chapter Nineteen   83

Chapter Twenty   88

Chapter Twenty-One   95

Chapter Twenty-Two   99

Chapter Twenty-Three   104

Chapter Twenty-Four   110

Chapter Twenty-Five   117

Chapter Twenty-Six   121

Chapter Twenty-Seven   128

Chapter Twenty-Eight   136

Chapter Twenty-Nine   144

Chapter Thirty   153

Chapter Thirty-One   158

Chapter Thirty- Two   164

Chapter Thirty - Three   168

Chapter Thirty-Four   174

Chapter Thirty-Five   181

Chapter Thirty-Six   188

Chapter Thirty-Seven   196

Chapter Thirty-Eight   204

Chapter Thirty-Nine   210

Chapter Forty   215

Chapter Forty-One   222

Chapter Forty-Two   231

Chapter Forty-Three   238

Chapter Forty-Four   248

Chapter Forty-Five   253

Chapter Forty-Six   260

Chapter Forty-Seven   266

Epiloque   273

Chapter One

Catalina's POV

The girls bitched and groaned as I stepped out of the car. We were completely lost in the middle of bum-fuck-no where. We had no other choice but to pull over and ask someone for some help. I figured a pub would be a hell of a lot safer than some strange house.

"Are you coming in with me or not?" I stalked towards the entrance as soon as all their heads shook. It was only a pud, they had nothing to worry about; they were just being a bunch of pussies.

The wooden door flung open as I barged my way through and all eyes turned to me. I scanned the room a couple of times to find that I was the only woman standing on the premise; fabulous. My eyes locked with the bartender and I stalked forward to confront him. By this time of night I wanted out of my tight clothes and into comfy ones.

"I'm lost." I stated as he handed me a water. His brown eyes shined with amusement as he looked up at him.

"Oh sweetheart, I know. You're the first woman that's walked in here in ages. Well the first real woman; the prostitutes don't count." The man beside me chuckled as he put his glass of beer up to his mouth.

"Oh she's a woman alright." He grumbled as I turned towards him.

"Try and be a gentlemen for two seconds of your pathetic life." The words hissed through my teeth as I motioned for him to get up. Without looking at me his arm shot out and he pulled me into his lap.

"Happy princess, we've compromised. Now don't wiggle too much or we'll be upstairs before you know it."

I gaped at him as I leaned over the bar. His lap was oddly comfortable and his torso against my back was rock hard, but somehow cozy.

"Where ya' going beautiful?" The bartender asked as he poured another drink.

"I'm just trying to get to a motel; but I need some gas, too. I just need directions."

"I can't do better than that." The bartender smirked as he looked past me at the man v under me. "Robert can show you the way, it's time for him to leave anyway."

"Are you kicking me out again?" So called 'Robert' huffed from behind me.

"Yes, I'm cutting you off. You need some sleep, not more whiskey."

"You're a fuckin' ass," he grunted. "But I'll be a gentlemen and show the lady the way."

"There's gas behind the building, it's not a pump but there's at least a few gallons."

"Thank you." I shook the bartenders hand and hopped off Robert's lap.

A part of me was a little concerned about following this man even tho I was lost. He looked rough; with tattoos covering his arms and diamonds in his ears. Robert was talk and muscular, taking up a lot of room and almost to the ceiling; I jumped back when he stood.

"Jesus, you're tall." I gasped as he moved in front of me. His black leather jacket was placed over his fitted black v-neck. Roberts pants jingled as he moved his upper body causing my eyes to travel down to his pockets where a chain hung from two dark denim belt loops. Black leather boots coveted his feet as they stomped against the wooden floors.

My eyes locked with his bright blue ones as he looked down at me. "Six-five, sweetheart."

"Jesus," I repeated as he led me to the door. When we came outside the girls had the cabin light on and were locked up in the car.

"So you aren't alone." He chuckled as he met all the wide eyes.

"It would appear so."

"I'll go get the gas and fill your car up, than you'll follow me."

~

The girls all gave me an expecting look when I closed the driver door behind me. "What?" I shrugged my shoulders as Robert's black Harley roared to life.

"Of all men to lead the way you choose a biker? He's gonna chop us to pieces." Jessica complained from the back seat.

"He's not gonna chop us to pieces, don't be so judgmental." I shot back as I pulled onto the main road behind him.

"Well my death better not be in vain, someone needs to fuck him." Rosie grumbled. All eyes landed on her as I continued to drive twenty over the speed-limit.

"Coming from the virgin." Jessica countered.

Robert wouldn't be a bad fuck. You could easily grab onto his beard and pull him in for a kiss. His body would completely take over yours and his voice alone could leave you squirming.

"No one needs to fuck Robert. I'm sure someone wants to fuck him." I grumbled as we turned into another dark road.

"So who's gonna?" Mary questioned.

"I'm looking to loose it," Rosie grumbled "but I don't know if I could handle that much man."

"I'm sure Catalina wouldn't mind taking a ride." My mouth fell open at Mary's bold response, but I couldn't fully deny it. Robert is a very attractive man, who wouldn't want to experience that with him.

"I didn't come here to get laid, I can here to go to a friends wedding." I hissed through my teeth.

"Which you can bring a plus one to." Rosie added.

"I'm not being a man I don't even know to a friends wedding!" What had gotten into them.

"You're bringing him to our motel." Jessica giggled.

I punched the radio and cranked up Foo Fighters to block them out. I wouldn't have this discussion. It's not like I chose to get lost, it just happened. Robert just happened to be friendly with the bartender and he just happened to be at the bar. I couldn't bring him to the wedding, I probably wouldn't see him ever again. I'd thank him, maybe hand him a twenty and he'd be on his way.

~

I began to worry that he wasn't brining us to a motel and he was bringing us somewhere else. We had been on the road for an hour now and scenarios were beginning to form in my head. The bickering of the girls had long stopped as they'd drifted off into a nap and I was left in the dead silent. The radio had long been turned off so I could hear myself think.

Five more minutes passed before I saw a bright red sign for the Marriott Hotel. So he was being truthful and I wasn't going to die tonight. I didn't ask for a hotel, I asked for a motel. The girls and I had enough for two rooms at Motel 6; we didn't have money for the Marriott.

I parked the car and walked over to where Robert was taking off his helmet. "Thank you so much." I fished out my wallet and went to hand him a twenty. He held his palm up and shook his head.

"It's on me." Robert got off his bike and started to walk towards the hotel.

"What do you mean?" I hollered after him. My eyes darted between him and the car; which had the driver door open and all the girls sleeping. I raced forward, grabbed the keys, shut and locked the doors and raced back towards Robert. When I reached him in the lobby he was already thanking the man behind the desk.

"What are you doing?" I asked out of breath.

"Getting rooms."

"Room's'?" I dragged out the 's' with bewilderment.

"Yes, two rooms for you girl's'," he mimicked me "A room for me. I don't feel like driving back this late and it's suppose to snow."

"How much do we owe you?" Not sure if we'll be able to pay you back, but I can pretend for a little while. One of the girls can call up one of their parents and ask for a little more and then we'll pay them back. I'd call mom, but she's got dads bills to handle.

"On me, If I need a favor I'm sure you'll follow through."

Oh lord. What kind of favor did he have in mind?

We turned towards a man's voice that was becoming closer to us. My stomach jumped to my throat the moment the words left his lips.

"Hey what are you doin' here, Reaper?"

Reaper? As in the Grim Reaper?

Chapter Two

Catalina's POV

Dear lord, I had allowed a psycho to show us the way to a hotel. I'd let said psycho pay for our rooms and now I owed said psycho. I mean who goes by the nickname Reaper unless they were a psycho!

"Wh-" Robert cut me off before I could finish my sentence.

"I'm the Vice President of an M.C. We all have street names, I'll let mine explain itself. No I won't hurt you, I'm intrigued by you." He grumbled a hiss as we walked to the car.

"Intrigued? Why would anyone be intrigued by me?"

"You got the class of a queen-mouth of a trucker and body of an hourglass, what man wouldn't be intrigued by you?" He shrugged as he nodded in my side window to wake the girls. They all jumped from their sleeping positions and high-tailed it to get their things. Robert grabbed mine and lead us back into the hotel.

"So you wanna fuck me?" I spoke under my breath as he opened his door.

He turned back to me with mischief in his bright blue eyes. "Oh baby, I'd bend you the fuck over." He stepped into his room, handed me my bag and closed the door.

I turned to the girls all gaping at me. "Looks like we know who's gotta fuck him." Rosie giggled.

"Shut up."

~

I stood on the balcony overlooking the beautiful pool and the welcoming hot tub. The air was freezing, but the hot tub was calling out to me. It was past hours, far past hours; three in the morning. My brain wouldn't shut down and I couldn't get comfortable, maybe a dip wouldn't be that bad.

I held my towel around my body like a second skin. The air was bitter and freezing, but the steam coming off the tub was too amazing to pass up. My bare feet hit the stone for a second before I was giving up and launching myself into the hot tub. The water was boiling and instantly relaxed my muscles. I was alone for a solid ten minutes before heavy footsteps sounded behind me.

"Not safe for a girl like you in an outfit like that be out here alone." Robert's voice was deep and husky, most likely from sleep. I gave a heavy sigh as a response before turning around to face him. Our eyes locked before I watched them lock with my chest. They gave a little bulge before moving back up to my own. "You definitely shouldn't be out here alone." He grunted under his breath.

"You gonna join?" I asked, eyeing his swim trunks.

"Oh yeah, I brought the goods." He held up a bottle of Jack and slipped in front of me. I moved to the other side of the jacuzzi and gave him a tiny smirk. "Let's play a game."

"What game?" I swallowed as I watched his Adam's apple bob with the sip he took.

"Every sip you take, you say something about yourself." He passed the bottle across to me and cocked an eyebrow.

"Sure you want to do that, wouldn't wanna uncover any bodies."

"Can't easily uncover something that's a story deep, sweetheart." That words never sounded so hot before. His Irish accent added to it, made it sensual and sexy.

I took a swig of my old friend Jack and looked him in the eyes. What was something I wanted to share with this man? What would get me into the least amount of trouble; but then again, did I want the trouble?

"I have a weakness for motorcycles."

"Do you now?" Robert smirked as he took the bottle out of my hands. "I prefer a woman's hair down, makes me think of it a mess on a mattress."

"I took you for a ponytail kind." I whispered.

"Oh yeah, why's that?"

"Gives you something to pull." I grabbed Jack back and held it against my chest by the neck.

"Oh sweetheart, there's plenty to pull."

"I've always wanted to shoot a gun." I smiled as one spreads completely across his face.

"That can be arranged. I'd love to watch."

"What makes you think I'll let you watch?" I countered as he took a few swigs.

"I could get you to allow me to watch plenty of things." Oh the dark promises in that sentence.

I was in a dangerous situation, we'd been playing for far too long. I was completely wasted and he was drunk. My mind was fuzzy and I was sitting in a jacuzzi in the middle of the night with someone who wants to fuck my brains out; someone who goes by the fucking name Reaper.

"How'd you get the name Reaper?" I slurred as we stepped out of the hot tub.

"You don't wanna know." He whispered as he grabbed the bottle.

"Yes I do."

He sh'd me and led me up to the rooms. I stumbled into my door. Robert grabbed the top of my arm and fell into his room. He was trying to steady himself, but we both ended up on our asses. I erupted into a fit of giggles as Robert chuckled underneath me.

"Looks like you's stayin' here tonight." He slurred.

"Looks like it!" He kicked the door closed behind us and scooted further into the room; still on his back, still with me on him. "I need to shower." I grumbled when we made it beside the bed.

"So shower."

I stumbled to my feet and waddled into the bathroom. The shower was marble and a rain shower head. My clothes dropped to the floor once the door was locked and I stepped under the hot water. The complimentary soap smelt like coconuts; I scrubbed it all over my body. Considering this wasn't my soap, I tried hard not to use too much of it. This was Robert's room and he would need soup and shampoo.

After far too long in the shower I got out and wrapped a towel around myself. When I opened the door there was a large shirt hanging on the knob. I slipped it on over my bra and panties and walked out completely drained. Robert was in bed with an arm across his face.

"Last chance to back out." His rough voice filled the quiet room.

"Back out of what?"

"This is a very dangerous game you're getting yourself into."

"Were playing a game?"

"The second you crawl into this bed, it's game over."

"Well who wins?"

"Me, once you're in here you're mine."

Sink or swim.

"Looks like you win then."

Chapter Three

Catalina's POV

When I say I was hung over, I meant I was hung the fuck over. I stretched my arms and legs without opening my eyes to the hotel room. There was an overpowering male scent that blanketed the atmosphere. I was over heated like a polar bear was laying on me. My eyes opened to the beautiful room and landed on the sex God asleep next to me.

"Holy shit." I breathed out as I took in the appearance. My memory was clear until I crawled into bed and than it went blank. His arm shot out and pulled my tiny body into his chest where he nuzzled my hair. I couldn't help my body's response of going completely rigid. I slipped out of bed and quickly dressed into my clothes. The door shut behind me loudly as I raced down to my room. The door swung open with a bang startling Mary.

"Well, well. What do we have here? The same clothes from yesterday? You weren't in your bed when I woke up this morning." Mary smirked towards me as she placed two coffees on the table.

"Shut up," I grumbled as I sipped at the coffee she handed me.

"So tell me all the dirty details." Mary giggled as she bounced down on her bed. I rolled my eyes at her and looked over at the clock. The time was already in my mind, but my eyes strained to stay on hers. What had happened last night? Whatever went down between Robert and I was far more intense than I had expected.

"Nothing rea-" my voice was cut off by the door barging open. Jessica and Rose came tumbling in filling the room with giggles. "What's up with you two?" I grumbled as I took another swig of my drink.

They both shrugged their shoulders before plopping down on the beds. One hand of each of them was warming a Starbucks. "Catalina warmed Robert's bed last night." Mary blurted out. I was covered in chocolate frappe before I could close my eyes.

"When did this happen?" Jessica screamed. "Why aren't you still there?" The girl was gonna spill the little she had left of her drink on the bed if she didn't stop bouncing.

"Last night, nothing really happened. I went down to the hot tub and he followed me. We got super drunk and then crawled to his room. He put me in a shirt and I crawled into bed and then everything's blank; I don't remember the rest. I'm assuming we went to sleep."

"Went to sleep!" Rose huffed. "With that God next to you I'd be doing the Macarena naked!"

"Are you gonna go talk to him? What happened in the morning?" Jessica asked nervously.

"Nothing, I woke up and left. He was still asleep." I shrugged my shoulders. For the second time that morning I had sticky chocolate coffee spit all over me.

~

"We need to go now." I demanded as the girls stood ready to head to the rehearsal dinner. They looked at the clock and nodded their head in agreement. I poked my head outside the hotel room door to make sure the coast was clear. Once I saw the hallway empty I quickly shuffled out of the room and ushered the girls behind me.

I was three steps away. Three from being free from this conversation. A strong, calloused hand wrapped around my exposed arm and pulled me into a concrete wall. I was in so much shit. The girls snickered as they observed the scene unfold before their eyes. There was a huff and then a crouch; I was scooped up and thrown over a shoulder.

"Wait here!" I demanded as the hotel room door shut behind us with a slam. Robert threw me on the bed and placed his hands on his hips.

"Not only did I wake up alone, but you avoid me. That's not working for me, princess." He huffed as a hand racked through his already messy locks.

"I didn't take you for the sentimental type." I bit back at him.

"Oh sweetheart, I'm not. I'd usually be more than glad I don't have to kick the pussy out, but I haven't had my fill of you yet. In fact, never have I ever cuddled up; let alone cuddled up with clothes on." He huffed.

I let out a sigh of relief. "So we didn't..." I trailed off unable to finish the sentence.

"Oh sweetheart, your cunt would know if my cock had been anywhere near it." He chuckled.

"Cocky fucker." I grumbled under my breathe and rolled my eyes. Remind me for future reference that this is a no no.

"In fact sweetheart, the farthest we went was a steamy make-out session." Robert huffed and moved towards me. "We'll be finishing what was started soon, but for right now I'm gonna give you a little glimpse about what happens when someone doesn't respect me." A smirk cast over his features as he stocked forward and sat down. I was placed over his knees before I knew what was happen and a crack was through the air.

I gasped as my mind tried to catch up with what had just happened. Roberts warm breathe was in my ear before I could process. "How'd that feel, sweetheart."

Good.

"Did you just fucking spank me?" I huffed, but my voice died at the end due to his palm rubbing calming circles over my behind.

"Mhm." He hummed as he continued to soothe me. "I really wanna do it again. So tell me, how did it feel?"

"I-I don't know." I whispered as I felt my dress being hiked up. His palm left and then was back with a crack before my body could feel his absence. "Of God." I grunted.

"Like that?" His husky voice sounded so pleased. My head nodded as I pressed my cheeks to one of his thighs.

Crack

Crack

Crack

"That'll do for now." I could hear the grin in his voice. He was pulling me into his lap and kissing my jaw before words came out of my mouth. It had felt good, so foreign.

"I won't roll my eyes." I giggled.

"Oh sweetheart, roll your eyes all you want. That was just an excuse for me to see that pretty little ass of yours." He nipped at my jaw. I looked over at the clock and his eyes followed. "You have somewhere to be, go."

I rose from his lap and straightened myself, walking to the door with him on my trail. Robert spun me around and laid his lips against mine before opening the door.

"I told you, you were mine." A smirk danced across his face.

"I know."

I entered the elevator with my head down. The girls all stood with smug looks on their faces. I had no where to escape and the elevator doors locked me and my red behind in.

Chapter Four

Catalina's POV

"I heard Reaper's in town."

"Did you hear who's here?"

"Guess who paid us a visit."

"I heard one of the guys bumped into him."

"Why's he here?"

"I wonder if someone owes him."

My ears buzzed with the commotion of the rehearsal. Every group of people I walked by were talking about a certain man; a man who hours ago threw me over his knee. It was far past closing, but the party was still going strong and the drinks were still overflowing.

"I wonder who they're talking about." Pondered Jessica. I sent her a smile with a shrug of my shoulders.

"It can't be good if he's here." A women beside us standing with her date hissed. Did the whole fucking state know about him.

"If he's here, then they're all here." A raspy voice hiccuped.

"I need some fresh air." I half smiled to the girls and stumbled my way through the crowd.

The cold air ambushed my exposed skin and forced the bottom of my dress to dance around me. "You shouldn't be out here all by yourself." A deep voice mumbled from behind me. I spun on my heels and faced the man before he could utter another words.

"Relax, I'm not gonna hurt you. Not unless I'm asking for my head on a silver plater." A deep chuckle traveled from within his throat.

"Who are you?" My voice stayed steady as I took a step towards the door.

"Part of a neighboring MC, we have an alliance with The Devil's Disciples."

"The Devil's Disciples?"

Why was this man looking at me like I should know what he's talking about. I've been in town for maybe forty-eight hours.

"Your man's motorcycle club."

"Robert?" I questioned.

"Reaper."

"I'm the Vice President of an M.C. We all have street names, I'll let mine explain itself."

Roberts words from the other night came flooding back to me as I pieced it all together. "Oh of course." I smiled. "I should really be getting back inside."

"Don't let his poison consume you." Were the last words I heard out of the man before the bar door closed and I was encased in chaos.

~

The parking lots were dark, the streets deserted. Shadows were creeping beside me in the night and I was desperately trying to make our way to the hotel. We spent some time at the bar for me to sober up so I was able to drive and the girls were currently giggling their asses off in the car. They were completely oblivious to their surroundings, but something was setting me off. Something was telling my gut that something was going to go wrong. I was gonna end up in a bad place at the wrong time.

A car screeched to a stop a good few miles in front of us on this straight road. My foot hit the brakes to keep us from being any closer to what was happening up there. We were far enough away where if something were to happen they wouldn't have noticed the headlights. We were far enough away to make an escape without any problems. I pulled into a text stop that was to my right before anyone could notice us.

Before us, I watched as the driver door was yanked open and someone was pulled out. "Girls, shut up or we're all gonna die." I hissed into the back set as they all shut their mouths. The doors were locked the lights and car were off and the windows were up. Everyone was in their rightful seat slouched down and the only thing left to do was call him.

"I think we're in danger."

"What? Where are you? What kind of danger?" Robert barked from the other end of the phone.

"A car in front of us was pulled over and someone was yanked out, I can't really see. We pulled over into a text rest and turned everything off and locked everything up."

"Alright, send me your location I'm gonna come to you."

I hung up the phone and dropped a pin for him before slouching back down. I couldn't worry about what would happen when he got here. I needed to worry about getting everyone in this car out of this situation. Why does the gps always being you the worse way possible.

Jessica screamed first followed by all of us as there was a knock on the back window. I looked back to lock eyes with Robert and quickly unlocked the door. He climbed into the crowded backseat and sent me a smile.

"Everything's gonna be fine." He promised. "You did the right thing to pull over, they have no idea your here."

"We didn't-" I began before he finished for me.

"I walked a good distance so that they wouldn't know I was coming." He scanned the girls before looking back at me. "I'm not aligned with them, but I know people thatare. I've already talked to them, they're gonna come from the other direction and then we're gonna leave."

"Thank you." I smiled.

"No problem, sweetheart, but I'm gonna need you to let me in the front seat."

I unbuckled and crawled into the back which meant crawling into Robert. He swapped our position so that he was on top and then maneuvered to the front seat. I watched through the front window as dozens of lights appeared in the distance. The noise was so loud I didn't hear Robert start the car. We pulled off in the other direction and he laid on the gas all the way to his bike.

The air was freezing when I stepped out to get into the front. Robert put his helmet on and walked over to his Harley.

"Follow behind me closely." A single head nod and I was in the car behind him.

~

The girls went scurrying into the lobby as I waited for Robert to be ready. "The guy from last night approached me at the bar." All his movements stopped before he turned to me.

"What'd he say?"

"That he wouldn't hurt me, that your mc and his mc were allies." He nodded his head before stepping closer to me.

"Anything else?" His eyes squinted as he waited for my answer.

"Not to let your poison consume me." His jaw clenched, his eyes became slits and I watched his Adam's apple bob as he gulped. "What does that mean?" I asked after a long period of silence.

"Oh baby, I got an army of skeletons."

Chapter Five

C atalina's POV

"An army of skeletons?" I huffed when he released my arm from his grip. The hotel room door closed silently and left me in a cage with this man. A man who's street name was Reaper. A man who apparently had an army of skeletons in his closet. "What the fuck is that suppose to mean?" I grumbled as I poured myself a drink.

"It means I've done very bad things." He shrugged his shoulders as he discarded his shirt.

"What kinds of things." He looked over at me with a sigh.

"You aren't ready for that answer yet, you'll get it when you're ready."

"How will you know if I'm ready or not?" My arms flew to cross over my chest. Robert's eyes dropped to the now pushed up cleavage that was for his eyes. I watched as he adjusted his pants and huffed out, throwing my arms in the air.

"I'll know."

"I'm not gonna get this outta you am I?" I grumbled over to him. He shook his head once as a smirk spread across his face. I looked down at my dress and heels, then back at the door. What was he expecting out of tonight? "I'm not sleeping with you." An eyebrow shot up at my statement.

"Really?" He took a step towards me.

"Really." I took one back. "I'm not one to sleep around."

"That's not what I was applying." He defended. "Sweetheart, if I needed sex right now, I'd be having sex."

"Oh really." Cocky motherfucker. He nodded his head and advanced towards me. As he advanced, I back up until my bottom his the door. With my eyes locked on his, I slipped out and raced to mine. I slammed the door shut and locked it, turning to face Mary as she was getting in bed.

I gave her a look begging for no questions and slipped into the bathroom. My dress dropped to the floor and my heels clanked against the tile. The steamy hot water poured out of the shower head as I turned the knob. I shimmied out of my panties and yanked off my bra, my feet wiggled out of their confines and I stepped under the water.

The room was cold compared to the steam filled bathroom. The lights had been turned off and Mary had passed out quickly from all the alcohol. I was left to dress in some leggings and an oversized sweatshirt as quietly as possible. Wool socks were pulled onto my feet as I slipped under the covers. From indulging in so much boos that night, I fell quickly too.

My eyes strained to read the numbers on the bedside clock. Mary groaned and threw the pillow over her head. I rose from bed quickly and raced to grab the door handle.

Red Flag

My hand shakily released and I peaked through the peep hole. Robert stood in a pair of sweats and a sweatshirt on the other side. With a sigh of relief I unlocked the door and cracked it open.

"What are you doing? It's three in the morning." I hissed out.

"Let's go on an adventure." He gave me a shy smile. My eyes scanned over his body and back up to his eyes. His hand came darting in and grabbed my wrist, gently pulling me into the dim lit hallway. "Come on,"

I nodded my head as heat raced to my cheeks, his hand trailing down to interlace with mine. He pulled me down the empty hallways into the elevator and around the lobby before we reached our destination.

"A vending machine? This is our adventure?" I gave him a confused look as he pulled the thing from the wall. His hand disappeared into his sweats pocket before emerging with a switch blade. My mouth dropped open as the machine door popped open and his eyes slid to mine.

"What do you want?" He asked his a smirk. My eyes darted around for any bystanders or cameras. "Relax, sweetheart, you're safe." An arm snaked around my waist and pulled me into his body. "What do you want?" His breathe fanned my ear. My eyes were sliding over the items I wanted to eat, but my mouth was sealed. Pain spread through my ass and down my thighs and up my spine. A yelp escaped my lips as I jumped to put space in between us, but his tough hands pulled me back to soothe my aching backside. His hands rubbed and kneed the spanked cheek while his teeth nipped at my ear.

"I expect an answer when I ask you a question, sweetheart. Now, what do you want?" I found myself clutching to him as I pointed out what I desired.

The bed was piled with junk food and he was popping open the beer bottles. I sat Indian style on the bed as my eyes followed him. "That was some adventure." I joked as he walked around the bed. "Is there a reason behind waiting me at three in the morning?"

"I got to smack that ass didn't I?" He teased. I stuck him he middle finger, bad move. Pearly white teeth latched onto the finger with a nip. "You were running from me." He grunted after he released.

"I wa-"

"You were, but you aren't anymore." He commented as he crawled closer. A bag of Doritos crunched in his hands. "I scare you, but you're scared to leave too." I gulped as his face inched closer. How the hell did he know this. He switched out positions in the blink of an eye. His back his the headboard and my breasts were we level for him, a leg bend to hold me closer to his chest. My legs straddled his waist and my arms circled his neck.

"You're terrified of I'll do to you, but you're scared of what you'll do without it."

I avoided his eyes, trying desperately to find an escape; but his hands were so warm. "I'm not scared of you."

"But you are, cause you like the things I do to you. You don't want to like them, but you do. You're scared because you know I can hurt you. The real question is if you'd like it or not."

Chapter Six

C atalina's POV

"I would most definitely not like pain." I seethed at him. I'm not that type of girl, I didn't want to be beaten.

"You were soaked after I spanked you." He smirked up at me as his fingers caressed my sides. They tiptoed under the hoodie I was wearing to reach my bare skin.

I wiggled on his lap as my eyebrows stunned together. That was completely untrue, I was embarrassed. I'm a grown women and he put me over his knee, pulled my panties down and spanked me. "I was not!"

It all happened so quickly. He was sitting on the bed with me over his knee, my sweats and panties were around my ankles. I went to sit up, but his elbow came down between my shoulder blades to hold me in place. His fingers kneed my skin, "Count."

"I will-" my hair was gripped and his lips found my ear.

"Count." His hand left my ass to go flying through the air and make contact with my sensitive skin.

"Sweetheart," Robert warned.

"One." I gulped as I tried to push the stinging to the side. He rubbed the spot for a second before his hand came down on a different part of my bottom. "Two." I choked back on tears.

He hushed me from above and soothed my bottom before continuing. "Three." Smack. "Four." Smack. "Five." - "Ten." I hiccuped as he massaged my bottom.

"Such a pretty pink." He murmured from above me. I blinked my eyes noticing the tears has stopped. "Now let's see," I could hear the smirk on his voice as his hand traveled down my bottom. His fingers found my core with a groan as I squirmed. They made no attempt to enter me, but moved up to rub at my bundle of nerves. "Baby girl, you're soaked. His fingers left me before I was flipped on my front in a very uncomfortable position.

Immediately my legs closed to shield myself from his eyes, but it was too late. He got up and laid me on the bed, the snacks surrounded me. "I'm getting cream for you bottom, then we'll address your situation." He walked back into the main room with a bottle in his hand. "Flip, sweetheart." I did as I was told and rolled over so my backend was exposed to him. Anxiety poked at me and I couldn't help but feeling embarrassed.

I heard the lotion hit his palm and then ecstasy washed over me as he worked the ointment into my rear. "Such a good girl." He murmured as the hoodie I was wearing rode up and exposed my back to him. His lips gently made contact with my spine. After the work was done he stayed with his forehead on my back and his hands on my hips.

I slid over to my front and looked up at him widely. Where'd we go from here? I had no idea what direction I needed and yet I'd follow which ever way he pointed.

"God, you're stunning." He kissed at the corner of my lips. I could feel the heat racing to my cheeks as I pulled the hoodie to cover my lower region. "I can fix that," He smiled down at me. "But only if you want me to."

I swallowed the lump in my throat as I looked up into his green eyes. His full lips were beckoning for me to kiss them. Robert leaned down till our lips were brushing each other's, "I think you want me." He whispered, each word making his lips connect with mine. This teasing had to stop, I closed the distant and latched onto his bottom lip. His free hand flew to my thigh and pulled me over him. I was under Rob in no time, my hoodie hiked up from his exploring.

"Close your eyes." He whispered as another kiss was laid on my lips. My eyes fluttered shut after hearing the demand and waited patiently. A gasp flew out of my mouth when I felt him press against me bare. Hot, hard skin to hot, wet skin. "Open." Another whisper in my ear. My legs spread wider than they were before to give him more room. A deep chuckle filled the room as he brushed hair out of my face. "Your eyes, sweetheart. Thank you for the beautiful display, though."

Embarrassed, I turned my head to the side quickly only to have him grab my chin to kiss me. "There's nothing to be ashamed of."

"I said I don't sleep around." I peeped. He leaned further into me and laid kisses all over my face.

"I know, sweetheart. I won't penetrate." My hands ran up his muscular arms to his face.

"I mean I don't do any-" I cut myself short as I explored his face. He was nodding his head; he knew. My hips moved to make my position more comfortable, but in the process I rubbed against him. The moan slipped out of my mouth before I could stop it. His eyes closed above me before I slowly felt him begin to move. Roberts head flew back as he grunted.

"Take the hoodie off." He grunted when he looked back down at me. I hesitated, I'd be even more exposed than I was right now. "Baby," his voice wavered from holding himself still. I sat up and slipped it over my head, the icy air hitting my chest immediately. A shiver raced down my spine as I watched him discard his shirt. He dragged himself up my body, his chest rubbing at my hard nipples. His hips bumped and pushed against mine, I turned my head to bite at his wrist that was at the side of my face. "Feel good?" He grunted as he quickened his pace. Sex without penetration was a lot better than one would think.

"Uhuh." I hissed as it washed over me quickly. I flung my body towards him as I quivered.

"Shit baby," he jumped quickly to the bedside where tissues sat. I was still in his arms when he slipped one tissue covered hand in between us to catch his release. We stayed in the moment for a few minutes before he threw the tissues away. The comforter was pulled back and he slipped the both of us inside.

"I have to be at a wedding today." I yawned into his chest.

"We have to be at a wedding today."

Chapter Seven

Catalina's POV

I was burning alive or so it felt. A shear coat of sweat was latching onto my skin making me clammy. A hard chest was pressed tightly to my back causing the most heat. My eyes fluttered open to take in my surroundings.

The blanket was at my waist and there was a strong, muscular arm wrapped around my torso to my shoulder. I looked down to see that the wrist watch read noon; my breaks were pushed up and my nipples were rocks. Robert's arm veins popped as he took a handful of breast and gave a light squeeze.

I flung up and wrapped the blankets around myself; startling him awake. A hand ran calmingly down my spine as the other wiped at his eyes. "Babe, it's alright." His husky morning voice filled the air. It wasn't alright, nothing was alright. I had been easy, I had let him make me orgasm. I had let him spank me.

Robert reached up and pulled me to him, my chest against his chest. His fingers gripped the blanket I was using to shield myself and pulled it from between us. They raced down my arm over my sides and down to the middle of my thigh; where they pulled my leg over his hip. His hands landed on my bottom to pull me flush against him; bare skin to bare skin.

"Don't hide from me." He whispered against my lips. His teeth catching my bottom one and sucking it into his mouth. I could feel his cock against my center and my nipples against his chest, but his tongue was distracting me. I pulled away before it could go on any longer.

"I need to go get ready for the wedding." I mumbled as my eyes cast down to his chest. My embarrassment was too high at the moment.

"I'll be ready in ten minutes." Robert grumbled into my hair. My eyes bugged out of my head as I looked up at him.

"What?" I practically screamed. "You aren't coming."

"Yes, I am."

"No you aren't, you aren't invited. You don't even know the people getting married!" I pulled away an inch so I could look into his eyes.

"I'm coming and that's final." He seethed. I shook my head no, but he stopped me. "Do you want what happened last night to happen again. You don't have any idea where you are, you have no protection and you're a group of young women. A few clubs around here don't give two flying fucks about if you're a person of not. All they'll see is pussy. So I'm coming and you can bitch and moan all you want, but you'll thank me when you get home safe and sound."

I opened my mouth to protest once more, but all I turned out to be was a gaping fish. He was right and I hated it. If I brought him it would raise questions, questions I wasn't ready to answer. People around here knew Robert, but they knew him as Reaper. I couldn't voice these concerns, they were too personal. It would come off as if I was embarrassed of him.

"Go get your stuff and Coke get ready in here." He huffed out a sigh and turned towards the bathroom. The door closed with him inside and the jets of the water pouring out filled the room. Grumbling to myself, I stalked over to my real room grabbed my shit.

"Hey, what are you doing?" Mary eyes my things.

"Robert's coming." I hissed out. A massive smirk came over Mary's features. "Stop giving me that look!" I yelled at her.

"I knew it was gonna happen." She smiled.

"He's coming as strictly a body guard." I huffed as I slammed the door shut. This couldn't be happening...

He was still in the shower when I got in the room so I stripped and joined him. If I wanted to be ready on time I'd have to shower now. His brows raised as I stepped in and turned my back to him. "No funny business, we can't be late."

The three girls were shoved in the back seat, I was shot gun and Robert somehow managed to get to drive. The ceremony was quick, happy and romantic. The after party however was a different story. It went on for hours and was loud and rambunctious. All eyes were on Robert and I, we were the talk of the party. Even the bride and groom were talking about us. Whispers were going around about The Reaper being here. It was a whole lot of unwanted attention.

"Her parents are so religious, how is she with him?"

"I figured she'd be waiting till marriage."

"There's no way she's still a virgin, not with Reaper."

"Her parents must be so ashamed."

I hastily walked to the parking lot, needing some silence and air. His scent followed close behind. "Don't listen to them." He murmured.

"Kinda hard not to," my shoulders shrugged in the cold air. His jacket was draped over me as he pulled me to his side.

"I didn't know your parents were that religious."

"Yup, the whole nine yards. They must feel like they've done wrong." My humorless laugh echoed in the night air.

"Was my cock inside you?" I blushed deeply from his question, but my head shook no. "My fingers?" No. "Tongue?" No again. "Then you're still a virgin."

"Not in all the senses." I countered.

"There was no penetration, as far as I'm concerned you're a virgin. Besides, it felt too good to pass up." I looked up at him. "Let's go."

"I'm gonna get in the car."

"I'll get the girls." He hollered over his shoulder as I slide into the passenger seat. I pulled his jacket off my shoulders and placed it over my lap, jamming the keys in the ignition.

Robert came out with his swayed, biker walk with the girls following closely behind. He slipped into the drivers seat and slammed the door shut.

The drive back to the hotel was quiet, the girls were whispering in the back seat and Robert's eyes were glued to the road. Instead of parking he pulled up front and unlocked the doors. The girls slipped out without any question, but something was up.

"What's going on?" I whispered to him.

"Get out of the car, sweetheart. Go to my room and I'll be back soon."

"Where are you-"

"The less you know, the safer you are." He closed the door and sped out of the parking lot.

Chapter Eight

Catalina's POV

I waited in his room for two hours before I had given up. My car was parked in the lot, but the Harley that was suppose to be next to it was vacant. I shuffled into my room and looked around at half my things. What I needed to do was pack, but how could I manage with Mary sleeping in the bed.

One ear bud blasted some tunes while I quietly gathered all my things and placed them in my luggage. I was done by the time my phone buzzed in my bra.

Robert : Where are you?

Me : Where were you?

Robert : Come to my room or I'll come get you.

"Fucking bastard," I mumbled under my breathe as I walked down the hall to his door. I jiggled the door handle a few times before it was pulled open and a very tired Reaper appeared. "Where were you?" I hissed.

He grabbed my arm and pulled me inside, locking the door behind him. "The MC needed me."

"For?" I crossed my arms over my chest and raised an eyebrow. He didn't answer, just locked the door and dragged me towards the bathroom. Warm steam was already fogging the room, my eyes shot to his.

"We're taking a bath." He demanded.

"No we're-" he silenced me by tugging at my yogas and panties. They hit the ground before I could let out a scream. "Oh my-" His hoodie was tugged over my head effectively shutting me up. My hands scrambled to cover myself from him, but it was no use. He scooped me up after he was naked and slid us into the tub. My back hit his bent knees as he forced me to straddle him. "Who do you think you are!" I seethed at him.

He placed his hands behind his head and leaned back. "You'll release your tits and relax when you realize how silly you're being. Sweetheart, that's nothing I haven't seen or touched. Honestly, id be more worried about my cock nestled between your pussy lips." My mouth gaped at his closed eyes.

Unfortunately he was right, everything he said was true. My hands fell from my chest and I leaned into his chest, nestling my face into his neck. He released a sigh as I snuggled closer, his breathed turned to fan my ear and his hands rubbed up and down my sides.

"How easy it would be to slip inside." He teased as he rotated my hips with his calloused hands.

"I leave tomorrow." I couldn't help but blurt out. He needed to know that I wasn't going to do anything. I needed to be able to leave without any problems tomorrow morning, my heart couldn't stay here. "You've been an exceptional person." I whispered into his neck. The truth was he had, he gotten me here safe, paid for beautiful hotel rooms along with other things.

"Save the speech, sweetheart." He huffed, "I don't want it. If you'd let me I'd spend our last night fucking the shit outta you, so be grateful and be quiet." With a nod I snuggled into his chest and closed my eyes, little did I know that'd be the part of that day.

My phone alarm went off bright and early creating a very grouchy Rob. I crawled over his body to reach it, straddling him in the process. "Now that's a good thing to see first thing." He chuckled as his hand came up and flicked a hardened nipple. "Did you have a nice wet dream 'cause I know you weren't cold."

My face reddened as I scurried into the bathroom. I grabbed all my things and tossed them into my suitcases. He laid in bed while I ran around and picked up my belongings in the bedroom. "We gonna have one more moment?"

"I'm not chopping your damn morning wood, asshole." He smirked at my snarky response, slowly rising to his knees. His hands were wrapped around my waist before I could protest and I was dragged on the bed. My hair sprawled across the pillows as he pushed my knees to the mattress. One warm, rough finger gently glided across my exposed slit.

"See sweetheart, I'm the one who clothed you last night and I didn't see any use for panties. You were the one with the wet dream who ground up against me in your sleep causing my problem."

"Please," I begged as he continued to tease me. The plea hadn't been meant to slip past my lips, but I'd seemed to lost control. I watched in wonder as he slipped his sweats to his knees. Boxers were nonexistent and his cock sprung to full attention. I screamed out when he grabbed himself by the base and smacked it against me.

"Again, beg me again." He ordered as he continued to smack against my center.

"Please."

"Please what?" His smirk was across his entire god damn face and I've never wanted to smack someone so much in my entire life.

"Please!" I screamed as my hands shot to my face. Tears were forming behind my eyes and he was pushing me somewhere I didn't know.

His presence was closer than the last moment and his breath was one me. "Baby, it's alright. You did good sweetheart, look at me." My hands grabbed at his hair and as soon as our eyes locked he was against me. I was sensitive and close and it didn't take long at all for me to reach the edge. Before I knew it I was screaming and he was right behind me.

"We were suppose to leave a half hour ago." Mary complained as Rob packed the trunk with our things.

"I'm so sorry you have a long drive with that one." Robert yelled from behind the car. I rolled my eyes as I climbed into the drivers seat. The girls pulled into the car quickly and quietly, thanking him as they got seated. There was a hulking figure in my door before I had the chance to shut it. "You're a hell of a girl," he whispered in my ear. "You're different than most, don't let anyone change that. You're gonna make some man very happy one day. I've never done this, but thank you for your time." He pulled away quickly.

I wanted to say something to him, anything really. He closed the door, tapped the hood and walked to his bike before I had the chance. So I pulled out onto the road with the feeling of him still between my legs and his poison still in my veins.

Chapter Nine

Catalina's POV

Life was weird without him. I could still feel him in my sleep, still hear him. The bed was never as warm as it had been and I still longed for his strong arms. Considering it'd been one whole month since we said our goodbye, hopefully I would stop cringing every time I heard his name. Mom and Dad had been weird when I'd returned, it was like they knew i had done something.

I walked into the house from the cold, stomping snow off of my boots in the process. Usually I stop in once everyday or two to check up on things, but the moment I walked in something was wrong. The homey feeling was replaced with an ominous edge and the silence could cut someone.

"Mom? Dad?" I hissed into the open air, my gut was telling me to go return to my apartment, but how could I leave them?

"They've gone out for a bite to eat." A deep, husky voice whispered back. My feet scrambled me back towards the front door without taking my eyes off the room. My mind scrambled to place the voice, but I was coming up blank. I didn't know this person and they were in my parents home. "You should have stayed away." They chuckled darkly. My back should have hit the door, but instead it hit a rock wall of a chest.

I jumped forward only to be pulled back. A hand wrapped under my breast and the other grabbed at my thigh. My breath had long gone away from me and left my body scrambling. I could feel him breathing on me. "So sorry 'bout this." He spun around and smashed me to the door grabbing a chunk of hair and slamming my head against it. I was flung to the floor before I could catch myself and then flung into the coffee table. The glass shattered under my weight and pierced my skin all over. He wasn't done and I knew it, my hands clawed at the carpet trying to pull myself away from him, but it was useless. The intruder grabbed the hem of my pants and flung me into the cabinets. My body hit the floor once again and this time he took it upon himself to kick me. My vision was going black and I knew what was coming, but my body couldn't stay awake any longer to watch.

~

The beeping of a machine woke me from my blank state. My head was pounding and black dots were clouding my vision. I didn't want the flashes to come back, but the scene was unfolding over and over again in my mind. The room was as white as a fucking ghost and there were flowers everywhere.

"Good to know I'm loved." I mumbled as the smell overwhelmed my senses. A hiccup sounded throughout the room and sobs followed.

"Oh sweetheart, thank god." My mother grabbed at me. My eyes darted over to her tear stained face and I sighed.

"You're safe." The door opened and footsteps were heard walking towards the bed. My eyes didn't leave my mother as she held my face in her hands. I thought it was my father that had walked into the room, but my mothers eyes said differently. She jumped back from me and then towards me.

"I'll scream!" She warned, my eyes darted towards the approaching person and tears hit my eyes.

"Why are you here?" I hiccuped as he proceeded towards me and gently grabbed my hand.

"I took care of it." He whispered to me.

"Who are you?" My mother cried as she took in Robert's appearance.

"What do you mean, you took care of it?" A tear rolled down my cheek and he wiped it away.

His eyes darted to my mother and then back to mine, silently telling me he couldn't tell me in front of her. "Mom, can you give us a moment?"

I nodded my head as she walked out the door and left the two of us alone. His lips brushed against mine when I turned my head back to him. They were velvety soft and wet just as I remembered them.

"I took care of it." He whispered to me as his hand brushed back my hair.

"Took care of what? How did you even know this went down?" My eyes darted back and forth from each of his.

"You think I'd just throw you out to the wolves, other clubs know who you are now." He sweeper under my eye. "You pulled up on something they didn't want you to see, they weren't just gonna let you walk."

"But I'm alive." I countered.

"You wouldn't be if it weren't for the club members I sent to check on you. The guy was running late for his shift, that's why this happened."

My mind races back to his first statement. "What do you mean you took care of it?" I whispered up to him.

"Don't ask that question, just know you don't have to worry about that man again." Robert looked away from me.

I grabbed his chin and brought his eyes back to mine. "I've been good, I haven't tried to peak into whatever it is you don't want me to peak into, but this is personal. What do you mean? Give me the real answer and not some half assed bullshit."

"God I forgot why I was drawn to you." He sighed and sat on the bed next to me. I watched him fish out his iPhone and scroll through a few numbers.

"Who's bulldog?" I whispered into his shoulder as he hit FaceTime. The phone ran twice before a burly man with an underbite answered the phone. There was no greeting between the two, bulldog simply awaited more orders.

"Show us." He demanded into the phone and a faint yes Reaper sounded back. My breath was knocked out of me as I took in my attacker, hung from the ceiling by his wrists and his toes barely touching the floor. He was left in his boxer briefs and numerous trails of dried blood caked to his body.

"This happened because of me?" I hiccuped as my eyes locked with Robs' jaw.

"Your parents were his original targets." He huffed back to him. "If your call where we go from here."

My parents who had done nothing, nothing what so ever. They hadn't even seen what had went down.

"Kill him, slowly."

Chapter Ten

- -

Catalina's POV

Hospitals were never my thing, they made me crazy and paranoid.. Never mind the fact that I felt as dirty as a pig, I hadn't showered in days. I was a fall risk and had on itchy, yellow socks. The gown was uncomfortable and a disgusting green checkered pattern. Robert sat in the recliner beside me and my mother sat bickering with my father on the other side of my bed.

Rosie walked in with a bottle of Sprite and her eyes took in the room. Her mouth dropped open as words stumbled out. "Hey Mrs.- oh Rob- ugh Mr." The mouth closed before continuing. "Well, this is awkward."

"Hello, Rosie." My parents answered at the same time. Robert grunted without truly looking towards her.

"How's the patient doing?" She smiled at everyone in the room and handed over the Sprite. Robert intercepted the pass off and took it within his hands. I looked towards him confused as he twisted the top and then handed it back to me.

"Thank you." I whispered as I took my first sip and Rosie beamed at us. "I've been better." I answered her previous question.

"The doctors said her injuries could have killed her." My father muttered.

"Did they catch him?" Rosie gasped as she took a seat in a chair at the end of my bed. I stole a glance towards Robert who kept perfectly silent. No emotion was readable on his face what so ever, but his eyes drifted to mine. Could everyone else in the room read our silent conversation?

A nurse shuffled into the room with a clip board. "How are we doing today?" She smiled at me.

"I would die for a shower." I grumbled as I flicked at the scratchy blanket over me.

"I'm sure you would, unfortunately we don't allow our patients to shower. It's strictly for guests who are staying overnight with the patient." She shrugged.

I huffed as my eyes rolled. "You're saying I can't shower?"

"Sorry sweetheart, you're a fall risk." Once again my gaze drifted toward the bulk of a man beside me. His eyes locked with mine and with a single nod I knew he'd help me.

"What if I had help? I'd even use a shower seat." I begged, but my mother interrupted. "Oh sweetheart, I'm not sure I'm strong enough to truly help you."

"You don't need to be." I stated as Rosie choked on her drink. The nurses eyes drifted towards Robert who had shifted closer to me.

"You'd stay seated?" she whispered. I gave her a curt nod. "I'm really not-"

"Nothing would happen to her." Robert cut in the nurses sentence.

"Oh no-" my father tried to say.

"Dad, stop it. I'm tired and I'm not gonna sleep well until I semi clean. Please, you and mom head home and get some rest."

"We'll come back with some clothes for you." My mother patted my fathers leg.

"I don't want tight clothes." I told them "I just want to be comfy."

"I have that covered." Robert stated as he rose from the chair. My father went to further protest what was going on, but my mother stopped him. They rose together and walked out the door.

The nurse played with her own fingers as she nervously looked between the two doors. "Please make this very quick, I like my job."

"It will be." Robert threw his keys towards Rosie and instructed her to go to his car and grab his duffle bag. The nurse shuffled out of the room along with her and closed the door tight. I watched as Rob walked into the bathroom to turn the water on before I got in there. My feet his the floor and he was beside me, both hands on me.

The bathroom was just as white as the rest of this god forsaken place. I could already feel the warmth as the steam rolled out and into the closed room. Robert shuffled out of his own clothes much to my surprise. Ever so gently I was released from mine.

"You don't have to stay here you know." I gasped as the hot water hit my bruised skin. Nothing has felt this good in a long time. Robert stepped into the tiny shower with me fully naked, his body so close our shins were touching. I'd mentally blocked out what it'd been like to have him this close to me, but physically my body would always remember.

"Yes I do." He grumbled as he grabbed some shampoo and dug into my hair, gently massaging my scalp as I all but moaned. "You're my responsibility." His foot jabbed at the base of each of mine, pushing in between my legs so that he could have better access to my hair. I had told myself it wouldn't be sexual or I wouldn't get turned on, but my body was a god damn drought and it wanted to get rained on. "I got you into this mess and I'll already get you outta it." Once the water ran clean he tied my hair on the top of my head and grabbed the body soup. All areas because his favorites were covered completely with suds. "Does it hurt to stand? I need to get the backs of your thighs and I can't do that with you sitting."

"I can stand." I hiccuped as I slowly rose to my feet using Robs shoulder and the handrail. His fingers traveled over my thighs once more and moved to the back. He was on his knees in front of me, his eyes searching my face for something. His fingers hit the curve of my ass and I looked down meeting his eyes. Ever so slowly he brought his hand in front of me eye level with him. I couldn't stop the moan that did sped as he began to rub the subs around my center. Front all the way to my back before he rose to his feet and his hands came up to my breasts.

"I'm gonna shave you." His fingers pulled at my hard nipples.

"No you're not." I protested embarrassed. This sexy man was no going to shave me.

"Yes I am. Imagine how refreshing that'll feel." I was shaking my head before he could finish. "There's nothing to be embarrassed about little one."

"Why do you want to?" I fiddled with my fingers as I whispered the question.

"Because I know what it's like to be in a hospital for this long and I know how much I wanted to trim my balls. I also know that you walk around bare down here so this has gotta drive you crazy."

"Why were you in the hospital?" My eyes locked with his as I used his chest to steady me.

"Another story for another time." He whispered as he leaned down and kissed me. So I'd have to come back to it later on.

Chapter Eleven

Catalina's POV

How stupid does one have to be to have gotten ones self into what I just have...

Allowing tall dark and fuck me to shave me was a big mistake on my part. The recliner was yanked into the bathroom along with a regular chair and he had a towel wrapped around his lower half. He had privileged me with one of his very large hoodies, but I still say naked from the waist down. My face was a god damn tomato and I was patiently waiting to feel myself get nicked. The sting never came and my face never settled down, but Robert was as casual as ever. When he had finished the task and I was completely hot and bothered he pat me down with a warm towel.

"I'd pound you right now if we were in different circumstances, but I could still get us off just the same." His eyes twinkled with lust as he looked down at his new masterpiece.

"I'm sure my bruised ribs would really appreciate that." I rolled my eyes as I pulled the hood onto my head to hide my face. My legs were still open and under his restraint and my face would stay a god damn red pepper until I was released. Maybe even after he unlatched himself from me would my embarrassment stay.

"No your ribs wouldn't enjoy it, but my freshly shaved pussy would." This needed to stop, my face felt like it was going to melt off. I believe that sweat actually started to roll down my arms and then magic happened. Robert threw his head back and laughed like no ones business. His hands actually flew to his stomach he couldn't control himself. When he finally did settle down he leaned over me. His hand brushed my cheek as he removed the hood and kissed me. "How much longer are you gonna make me wait?"

"As long as I see fit." I whispered back against his lips.

"I've never wanted something this badly before. I've never been denied something I've asked for." He breathed as he brought me up into his arms and carried me out of the bathroom.

"Well then good, it's unhealthy for someone to never hear the word no." I whispered into his neck. He snorted "I don't like the word." He grumbled as he placed me back on the hospital bed. I watched him rummage through a duffle bag before pulling out a pair of silky cheeksters. "I'd put you in a thing or leave you bare, but I'm sure you'd be more comfortable with these."

"Are those mine?" The question slipped my lips before I could stop it and he stopped in his tracks. An eyebrow rose as his eyes searched mine and then he proceeded towards me. His head was between my legs before I could protest but he didn't move, just locked eyes with me. I watched him take a big sniff and then sniff the panties.

"Yeah, I believe they belong to you. It's not like I got them out of your drawer or anything." He rolled his eyes and spread my lower lips with two fingers, gently laying a kiss on me. I gasped and he moved back, kneeling to pull the panties up my legs. "My eyes haven't even landed on another women since they've met yours." He whispered as his lands trailed down my calves.

"I know." I whispered from behind his hoodie. "How do you know?" His voice was just as hushed as mine. It was as if we were speaking something forbidden and we didn't want it to touch anyone else's ears.

"If you had, you wouldn't be here. You wouldn't have saved me and the man wouldn't have gone after me." I pulled the hoodie up to look at some stitches that trailer down my side. "Yet, no regret courses through me."

"The regret would save you. It'd make your mind decide that you needed me gone. Your life could go back to normal." His fingers traced around the backs of my knees.

"I've never been normal, I've never fully fit in. Twenty-two years and I finally feel at peace."

"Twenty-six years and I finally feel like I'm suppose to make it home." I looked up at him in confusion. "What does that mean?"

"It means someone would be pissed if I could myself killed." A tiny smirk fell over his face.

"The M.C would care. You guys are like family." I countered. This man meant more to a lot more people than he believed.

"Brothers." Robert agreed as he rose from the bed to put clothing on. I finally was able to close my legs and when I did Rose walked in.

"The police are here." She spoke as she handed over a muffin. Robert was quietly putting his belt on before she noticed him. When her eyes finally met his body hers froze completely. "How was your shower?" She gulped as her eyes met mine.

"Refreshing." I rolled mine at her and broke off a piece of muffin, handing it over to Rob as he came and sat beside me.

"Tell them she's asleep." He ordered. "They don't need to question her right now."

"Lie to them? They're cops!" She gasped. "Rose, go." Robert spoke once more and she was stumbling out the door to speak to the police.

"I'm gonna get interviewed at some point." My eyes searched his for what to do. The man that had done this was long gone and the police didn't need to know who's order it was. I wouldn't survive a moment in jail, they'd chew me up and spit me out.

"You'll say you don't remember. That everything's fuzzy and you can't even remember how big the person was." He shuffled closer to hold my hand. "When they ask why you might have been a target say I don't know. Say that maybe you walked into the wrong place at the wrong time. No details sweetheart, none. The man that did this is dead and it won't happen again."

"And they won't-"

"Nothing points back to us."

Chapter Twelve

- -

Catalina's POV

"Where do we go from here?" I asked Robert as we sat in the kitchen of my parents house. I knew he couldn't stay here forever. He had a home and a club to get back to. Him being here for my transition home was enough, I couldn't ask for much more.

Roses lips pressed against the rim of his beer bottle, his eyes drifting to mine. Roberts shoulders dropped as his eyes scanned my face. "I don't fit here." My teeth gripped my lip as his words sunk. He wanted to go home. I knew he would, but some part of me that's buried deep was hoping he wouldn't. I couldn't ask him to stay and I knew that.

"You don't want to fit here." I whispered as I looked down at my lap. He could fit anywhere he wanted or at least that's what I wanted to tell myself.

"How could I fit here?" He countered my statement. His eyes locked on his beer as he brought it to his mouth once again. It was three-fourths gone and he'd need another soon enough.

"With me." My father walked into the kitchen and eyed Robert. "When are you heading out?" He questioned as he grabbed his own beer. Roberts eyes never left mine, instead of answering he finished his beer. I rose from my seat and grabbed another, opening it and handing it to him. "Dad I think mom needed your help outside." I looked towards him with pleading eyes.

"Your mothers upstairs and she doesn't need me. When do you head out Robert?" His eyes looked past me and at him. My stomach jumped to my throat as I looked towards my father. Why was he doing this to me? I wanted him to stay with me, why couldn't he stay with me. I didn't feel safe without him near me. Did he even want me with him?

"Tonight." Roberts deep voice filled the silent air. I spun toward him on my heels, my eyes bugged out. The words almost couldn't get out of my mouth, they couldn't form.

"Tonight!" I gasped out. In my head we had more time than this. Ice blue eyes flickered towards mine as my voice reached his ears. He nodded at me once before looking towards my father.

"I have duties, babe. I need to get back. The guys have been asking where I've been." My father hide a smug smile behind his hand as he coughed.

"Can you give us a minute?" My father shrugged his shoulders and waltzed out of the room. Robert shifted in his seat to look towards me fully. The lump in my throat slipped down once my father was out of ear shot, I could talk to Robert if I was the two of us. "You have to go back."

He nodded his head. "I know that." His hand reached out to gesture me over to him. I straddled his lap and locked my fingers behind his neck playing with his hairline. Bright blues eyes looked up into mine, "Am I gonna be okay here?" I whispered down to him.

"You tell me." He whispered back.

"I don't know," I shrugged my shoulders. "You've become my protection." His eyes fell to my lips and then traveled back up to my face. A calloused hand came up to wipe the hair out of my face.

"Me staying is only making you need more protection." His chest heaved as he looked down at our lap. "It's not safe for me to be anywhere near you. Do you know that? Are you aware of the kind of person I am. People like me don't end up with people like you."

"You aren't the kind of person you think you are." I tried to counter.

"Sugar, you don't know or have seen the things I've done or do." He chuckled as he leaned back in the chair. I went to open my mouth but his eyes shut me down. Nothing I was going to say could change his mind and he had made that clear. He rose from his seat bringing me along with him and walked us out to his car. The bike was back at the club house, I'm sure he missed riding it.

We stood at the trunk of his SUV, standing side by side staring at his bags. The world around us was cold and the wind bitter, but my shoulder that was pressed up against his arm was warm. I could feel his arm muscles flexing underneath his long sleeved shirt. "What if another comes to get me."

"They won't. No president will want another member of his club killed over some girl. The faster I get away from you the safer you'll be."

"Why would they come at me in the first place." I rubbed at my arms that could feel the wind nipping at them.

"They think you mean something to me." My eyes darted towards him without moving my head. His wording was harsh, but brutally honest. "Only way to change that is act like you don't." Robert threw his last duffle bag into the trunk and slammed it shut. I followed him as he got into the driver seat.

"So this is it." I faked a smile and shrugged. He gave me a curt head nod as his right hand gripped the wheel.

"I gotta head out." He grunted as he looked towards me. "Do yourself a favor and learn how to shoot a gun, okay?" I nodded, wishing that he'd just teach me himself. "Heart or head is the best place to aim otherwise it's messy."

These were gonna be his last words to me? This was gonna be our last conversation? "So this is it for good?"

"Yes." was his curt reply to me. "Step away from the car, sugar."

"Entirely?" My heart skipped,

"Yes." Robert pulled out of the driveway and hit the gas, speeding down the road and back to his home.

Chapter Thirteen

Catalina's POV

"How are you feeling today?" I sat on the leather couch in the same fucking boring room with the same God damn brick wall of a women. Stacy sat cross legged in front of me in her leather chair in her plan tan pencil skirt.

"I feel like I've felt for the past three months, like a living breathing target. Every time I step into that house it's like I can't fucking breathe." I rubbed at my knees, trying to release some of the anxiety that was built up inside of me.

I missed Robert... A lot.

My lips were sealed about that thought. As far as Stacy knows Robert doesn't exist. My attack was random, just someone trying to rob the house. As far as she knows the attacker hasn't been caught either. That on the other hand would stay forever the same. The world would think the man was random and disappeared. Police weren't even able to figure out who the guy was, they don't know what he looks like or anything of the sorts.

Robert and I hadn't spoke since the day he pulled out of my driveway. I had tried to call him one or twice, but after having them declined I gave up. He was off living his life and he made himself clear. He didn't want to be apart of mine. I still don't know if it was to protect me or to protect himself from having someone cling to him.

Whichever it was, I was tired of waiting around for him. I needed to get the fuck outta this town and the hell outta sweatpants. I missed my girls and how bold I was. The handgun that was sitting pretty in my purse surely helped a little with my confidence. I had went to the range, had learned the ins and outs of that. I was an armed and ready girl and my favorite were moving targets.

"Any better than previous days?" Stacy tried with me.

"Now that I'm armed a little. I still have the flashes and the panic attacks. My body will completely shut down on me and my mind will go blank."

"Your black outs." She nodded as her pen scribbled something down on the clipboard. "Ever think of moving?"

"Are you asking me to run from my problems?" My foot tapped against the hardwood. Cherry wood with boring walls and no decorations.

"No, I'm trying to help with your hysterical outbursts and it's been months. It seems that nothing we talk about works and even medication can't seem to settle your mind."

"We're done here." I rose from my seat, the leather squeaking underneath me. "I don't want to run from my problems," I eyes all her awards and degrees hanging on the wall framed. "I don't want to fucking have problems, but here I am. I don't know how to fix me. Frankly, I'm not sure I can be fixed or that I even want to be. I'm going out with my friends and I'm talking to people I don't know. My every day life has turned into doing exactly what you tell me to do and I'm fucking tired of it. I'm tired of it all.

I'd try some color next time or maybe some paintings, your office is bland kind of like your personality."

The door shit gently behind me as I walked down the hall and out of the building. That women has fed me nothing but god damn bullshit for months now and my parents were paying way too much money for that. They were the ones that insisted I come to see her, insisted that I give her my ear for a few sessions. All she's done is make me livid.

My phone rang as I was pulling onto the main road. "Hello darling!" My mothers cheerful voice filled the car as I took a left turn.

"Hi mamma."

"I just got off the phone with your father, are you going to be home for supper?" With a sigh I stopped before pulling onto the street that would lead to my home.

"I'm almost home. What's up?" Something was off in her tone of voice and I couldn't put my finger on it.

"Oh nothing darling you'll see when you pull in." I ended the call and took a few more turns, finally pulling into the driveway and parking the car. In front of me was a giant moving van.

"You've got to be fucking with me right now." My shoulders sagged as I walked to the front porch. "Did Stacy get to you too?" I asked my parents as I walked up to the front porch. "Why are you moving?"

"We darling, we're moving." My father corrected me.

"You can't just pick up my life and move me, I'm not a child anymore." I glanced around at the empty house.

"We have all your things and you haven't lived in your apartment for months; we sold it."

"Excuse me?" I huffed. "You can't just sell my things!"

It was a losing battle and I knew it. They told me we were moving because my fathers mother was getting older and needed to be cared for. She had bought a mansion for all of us to move in together. The destination was unknown to me. I was ushered into my own car and told to follow. They had everything I owned packed away in their van.

I'd strangle the both of them right now if it was an option, but that wouldn't go over well. After numerous gas stops and miles away from the girls, we pulled into a cute little diner to eat dinner. I slammed the driver door of my car and looked towards my parents. The wind ripped around us bringing specks of snow with it. The large line trees made it darker than it actually was outside.

"Rosie, I don't wanna fucking move." I hissed into my phone.

"Oh hush honey, maybe you'll meet someone. The girls and I will come in a week to see you. If the house is nice enough well all move in." She giggled on the other end.

"I've never seen so many motorcycles or tucks." I looked towards the line of Harley's parked in a row.

"Well that seems to be what you're into nowadays."

"Shut up, I gotta go I'll talk to you later." I hung up the phone and shoved it in my back pocket.

Welcome to RedRose

Welcome my ass, I huffed at the sign. I thought my days wouldn't get any worse.

Chapter Fourteen

Catalina's POV

CONGRATS YOU SURVIVED A WEEK! Xoxo

I read the group chat for the girls an rolled my eyes. My car rolled to a stop at a red light on the outskirts of town. I'd gone for a drive needing my music and some time to myself. Twenty-two years old and my parents were still dictating my entire life. I needed out of that house and fast.

My new mission was to find a dirt cheap apartment just so I could get away... Oh and a job. Out of the corner of my eye a bar caught my attention. "Why not." I whispered to myself as I took a sharp turn and pulled into the parking lot.

It was loud and messy, but there was only one guy behind the bar. I straightened out my jacket and scarf and made my way over to the bartender.

He double glanced at me before fully looking up. "How can I help you?"

"I'm looking for work." I shouted above all the men talking.

"Well you're the classiest hooker I've ever met." He looked me up and down a few times. "I'm not a hooker, jackass. I'm looking to bust tables or work behind the bar."

If his eyes popped any farther out of his head they'd surely fall out. "Oh god I'm so sorry, it's just that every women that walks in here's a hooker. This bar doesn't attract the civilized lady's. No offense to the hookers or anything." He stumbled over his words while I stood unamused. My eyebrows raised once at him. "I can't hire you, little lady"

"Then give me your manager." My hands landed on the edge of the bar.

"I am the manager. You gotta go through the owner."

"And who may that be?" My patience was running thin.

His eyes darted around. "Jess, but I don't think I'd be smart to send you over to his place."

I rolled my eyes. "What's the address?" He shook his head at me. "Come on I can handle it, give me the address."

"Down the road take a left, all the way down that road and then a right, then all the way down that road. It's a club house."

He was joking. I pulled up to a gate with guards, two very large men who glanced at each other when they looked at me. The gate flung open when I told them who I was looking for and why. I tried to be polite and ring the doorbell, but a women answered who was wearing a thong. Her nipples were pierced and she eyed me like a piece of candy. "I'm here for Jess."

"Aren't we all sweetheart." She licked her lips and held the door farther open. I took my steps inside and let her lead me to an office. She opened the door to another three women completely naked. A big burly man was sitting in the chair behind the desk. "She says she's here for you, baby." His brown eyes dashed to me, racking up and down my body.

"Aren't they all?" He snickered and ushered me forward. The closer I got it became clear that one of the women was under his desk showing him a good time.

"I'm here about the bar." I spoke out. He turned towards me with surprise. "I'd like a job there."

"You're hired, start tomorrow."

"Thank you." I turned towards the door and got ready to leave.

"That's it? You aren't here to join?"

"No I'll pass on this one." I turned my back and walked out after hearing a muffled moan. Numerous men hung around; watching tv and drinking beer. Besides the females in Jess's room there were none. The house was clean and surprisingly decorative. I walked down the impressive staircase to a living room which held the front door. My hand reached for the handle as it was turned and swung open. The edge of the wooden door hit the center of my nose sending me backwards to the floor. Thankfully my ass cushioned most of my fall and there was only a minor bump to my head, but it was enough for a headache.

"Jesus fuck." We spoke at the same time. "What the." My eyes locked with his crystal blues ones before I could look away. He grabbed me by my elbows and pulled me to my feet, my hands firmly gripping his black long sleeved shirt.

"What are you doing here?" His voice was gravelly and he had a week of scurf on his jaw and around his mouth. My breathing was uneven and embarrassingly loud as I looked up at him. Why couldn't I talk all of a sudden. My eyes darted around us and my body tried to shimmy away from his. I slipped free when he wasn't expecting it and booked it for the door. My car was a few feet away from me when I was engulfed by arms.

A hand was on the side of my head, pressing it against his chest. "Please tell me why you're here?" Robert's voice was soft into my hair.

"Why do you care." I seethed through gritted teeth.

"You were safe."

"Well, I was moved!"

He held me at arms length and looked me over. "How did you find the clubhouse? Why are you here?"

I huffed out a breath, a stray piece of my hair flying up. "I need a fucking job."

"No job that you could get in there is a job for you." His teeth clamped together as he spoke through them. I could smell his whiskey scented breath with a hint of chocolate. "You have no right." I came back. Who did he think he was talking to. "I have every right." His nose was inches from mine. The tips of my toes burned from leaning on them so I wasn't so towered. His hand snaked to the back of my neck while the other gripped my hip. "No women of mine will be working anywhere near whores or bastards." The grip on my neck was firm and held me close enough so his lips bridged mine when he spoke.

"I don't belong to you, Reaper." I swallowed the lump on my throat. "You belonged to me the second you walked into that fucking bar."

Chapter Fifteen

Catalina's POV

Long story short, I didn't get the job. No job, no apartment and I was going insane. The phone dialed twice before I heard his husky voice on the other end. "You scare everyone out of hiring me, I can't afford an apartment and I can't live in this house anymore. Something needs to give and I need out."

I heard a sigh before an answer. "I know somewhere rent free." He offered. I could see him on my head running his hand down his face in frustration. I'd given the man a hard for the last two weeks I've been here. We haven't really seen each other besides a few times, I refused every time he asked.

"What's the catch?"

"You'll be living with me." He chuckled over the phone. Red flags, bad idea don't do it.

"Honey, come help me make dinner for the family." My mother hollered from the kitchen.

"Do I get my own room?" I grunted into my hand.

"If you please." Robert sounded unhappy about this request. As if i would sleep in the same bed as him... again. "I'll move in right now."

"I'll come get you, pack your things." The other line went dead.

I looked outside my window into the driveway, a black SUV had backed in and popped the trunk. How much did he think I had? I looked around at my four or five boxes sitting next to the bedroom door. I heard the doorbell, heard my fathers protest and heard footsteps pounding up the stairs. Robert took up the entire space of my doorway in ripped jeans and a black t shirt.

"I should eat you right here just to give him a reason to be even more pissed." My face crimsoned at the comment. "How likely is that to happen?" He huffed, his eyes racking up and down my body. I couldn't answer, my mouth open and closed like a fish.

"There's a gun and kitchen knives in the house, I don't think that's a very good idea."I rubbed at the base of my neck. Was it hot in here or was it just me? Something told me that there would be a lot of conversations like this once I was moved in. He chuckled and shook his head, what was so funny? "Can we just get going with this." Three trips up and back down with boxes and my parents stood dumbfounded with each one. "I'm just too old to live here anymore." I had told them as I was shutting the front door. My father was grabbing his keys.

"Step on the gas."

Luckily, dad had been unsuccessful with trailing us. My phone rang so much I finally turned it off. Rob was hauling all the boxes inside as quickly as possible. It had decided to downpour half way through the drive here. The house was amazing and surprisingly big. The decor was even perfect. "My mother." He had explained when I asked him about it.

My room was the closest thing to a master as you could get without actually getting a master bedroom. Once again it was absolutely beautiful and I changed little to the cream and browns. Ocean blues decorated the rest of the room to give color, the bed was orgasmic. Never in my life had I laid on something so comfortable... well maybe once, but people don't count.

I discarded all my clothing and peaked into my new bathroom. The shower reminded me of rain and it was built with stones. The flow of color pleased me completely. My feet moved back to the bedroom where I searched for a towel. Instead, I found a gulping Reaper standing in my doorway drinking me in. My hands flew to cover myself. "I was bringing the last box up for you." I nodded, awkwardly standing in front of him. He walked out of the room and as I was beginning to relax my body he came back. "You kinda need towels." His body inched towards mine. I was offered a towel as he walked past and put the rest in the bathroom. My skin prickled as he came back and walked up to me. His chest pressing into my back. A hand sneaked around and gripped at my ribs. "Say yes." His husky whisper was in my ear as he nipped at it. I could feel his hard nestling in between my cheeks. His hand moved up and grazed the underside of my breast causing me to groan. I heard the belt buckle come undone, heard it fall to the floor with his pants. When I felt him against my towel again it was different. "Tell me." He ordered, still at my ear his teeth nipping.

My head was nodding before my brain could catch up, "Y-yes." The towel was yanked away from my body and tossed to the ground. His cock pressed in between my butt heels as his fingers found a nipple. He walked our body's towards the bed and push me onto my stomach while he hovered over me. A palm cams down on my left cheek as he pulled my hips towards the edge of the bed. I felt his body leave from over me and then his cool breath in between my legs. I waited, but nothing came. My body registered him down there, but then he was gone. My body was being pulled up the bed, his arm sneaking under me to pull my body towards his. His head hit the pillow and he flipped me around to face him. My leg was pulled over his hip so we were nuzzled together. He was perfectly pressed between my legs and his eyes scrunched at the feeling.

"I didn't ask this of you to use you." He rubbed his nose against mine. "I missed you." His lips brushed mine when he spoke, fingers tracing up and down my spine.

"You left me." My body shrunk thinking back to it. Reaper pulled me closer to him, kissing my forehead and holding my body. "I won't do it again." I held up my pinky asking him to promise. His was easily twice my size but they twisted together anyway.

I guess pinky-promises was sill a legit way.

Chapter Sixteen

- -

Catalina's POV

Life living with Robert was something different. I was on my own, but also not. We bickered about what to have for dinner and such. Somehow we always managed to be sitting with out knees touching by the time dinner was in the table. "I want to work." I had demanded one night as we ate pasta. His eyes flashed to mine before going back to his plate.

"I just don't trust." He had mumbled as another fork full entered his mouth. We had this conversation almost every night. When it was time to sleep I stayed in my own bed, but almost every night he snuck in and and spooned me from behind. Every night he graced my bed I slept better and there was always a moment right before I fully fell asleep he'd kiss me behind my ear.

The grocery store was oddly crowded as we walked through the produce section. He was dressed in a pair of dark grey sweatpants and his usual skin tight black t. I had somehow managed to race out of the house in his oversized hoodie and leggings. His hand tingled my lower back as we walked and I only looked towards him when he squeezed. "Do not move." He seethed in my ear as his eyes darted to someone across the isle. I looked up in a panic, his hand brushing my cheek before his eyes reassured me. His body moved away from mine and towards the man that had been watching us shop. I could tell by the body language that this was Reaper speaking. Everyone cowered away from the two speaking as I stood a bystander.

Rob can hulking towards me grabbing my wallet and my coffee from the cart and looking around "Put your hood up and look at your feet when you walk, hold my hand." He ordered. I did as I was told, leaving the cart behind we walked out and into the car speeding off towards home.

"What was that?" I gulped as I looked in the rear view of the car.

"Nothing important." He stated firmly as he pressed on the gas.

"Nothi-" I started before I was rudely cut off.

"I'd tell you if you needed to know." Robert glanced at me. I'd open my mouth and talk back if I thought it would get me anywhere, but I knew when enough talking was enough with Robert. He was hard headed and stubborn, the only way he was going to tell me was if he wanted to.

We pulled into the house and I waited for him to get out. I looped my arm around his as we walked up the steps. What I wanted was to cuddle up, get him into the comfy state he goes into when it's the two of us. What I wanted was the movie and comfortable clothes, what I got was the opposite.

I opened our front door which lead to the leaving room, an odd show in my way. I looked up to the archway that showed the kitchen. My eyes locked first with the naked women and then to our kitchen table in which she was laying. Not only was she on full view, but she was having a grand ole time with herself. My mouth dropped completely and I froze in my place. Robert moved beside me as he took in the sight.

"You brought a friend?" She smiled. Who the fuck was this bitch.

"Candy," You've got to be shitting me. This women went by the name Candy, fitting. My eyes jumped to Robert who was standing staring towards the women. "How'd you get in? You can stop that." Her hand fell to her side and she shrugged her shoulder.

"The spare key."

How should I be reacting to this situation? I felt as if I should be storming over to her and throwing a blanket over her naked body. That I should be kicking her out and screaming. Instead I reacted with a pang in my chest. Tears pilling up in my eyes, waiting to fall at any moment. My eyes stayed trained on Robert who had taken far too long to kick her out. It felt like a betrayal almost, so I excused myself.

"I'll be upstairs." With that I swiftly moved up the stairs and into my room. The moment the door latched closed a few tears spilled. My fingers angrily wiped them away from my cheeks, what a silly naive girl I must be. To come live in a house of a man and not expect him to just want what he can get. Yet what he's gotten is not fully what he's wanted. I've yet to give him what he truly desires and maybe that's why my heart and mind chose to believe that he saw more.

My body settled only when it was submerged in a warm bubble bath. My mind and heart still scrambled even as I told them not to. There was a rapping at my door that signaled someone knocking. I wanted to tell him to get lost, that he took way too long to come and find me. Instead the door was opening and Robs body was standing in it.

"You ran off on me." His shoulder pressed against the frame as he used it to keep him up.

"No, I was just giving you some privacy." I defended as covered myself from his view. The bubbles of the tub blocked most of his view anyway. His eyebrows drew together and he unlocked his arms from over his chest as he proceeded towards me.

"I didn't need it, I gathered her clothes and handed them back to her. I asked her to put them on and then took the key she used to get in. I put it in a different place so that we wouldn't have another incident."

"You can fuck whoever you want Robert, it's not my decision. If you want that women you can have her. We aren't in a relationship." I tried to keep my voice as steady as I possibly could. The last thing I wanted was for it to crack while I was preaching to him.

"Who I want to fuck is you and I don't want that women. If I wanted that women I'd be downstairs pounding it. What I want is you, so here I am. You're up here in a bath pretending not to be upset, but you are because I belong to you just as much as you belong to me. Don't forget that. I'll be in the living room waiting when you're ready." With that he walked out of the bathroom doorway, stripping his clothing.

Chapter Seventeen

- -

Catalina's POV

My body was pruned when I hauled myself out of the tub. So many people were ransacking my mind. I hadn't talked to my family in probably a week or two, the man from the store who was dead locked on me and now a bitch named Candy. I don't know who the hell she thought she was, but to come into someone's house, strip of your clothing and bring yourself towards climax on their dining room table was surely something.

Wool socks hit the wooden steps as I made my way down the stairs and into the kitchen. Robert was sitting in a pair of black sweats, his shirt no where to be found. My eyes racked up and down his body as his eyes drifted shut. I tried to look away, but I couldn't get his words out of my head.

I belong to you just as much as you belong to me.

Prove it, why hasn't he given me anything else. Maybe it was me, maybe I wasn't the one that was giving enough. I was keeping him at arms length. He was close, but I didn't let him too close to protect myself. My mind was telling me to go to him, but my eyes were looking at our dining room table that was in the corner of my sight.

Then again, how could I open up to a man that kept me in the dark? Yet, at the exact same time let me into a life that he wasn't preparing to let someone into.

My eyes drifted past the dinning room table and into the kitchen where he stood with a beer in his hand peering out the window. The counter looked small compared to his hulking size, hell everything looked small. "I thought you were going to be waiting in the living room?" I half awkwardly laughed, feeling silly about the way I had acted earlier.

"I thought you were gonna let yourself wither away to nothing in that god damn tub." His deep voice pulled me closer.

"I thought about it," He turned to face me, a fresh shirt stretched over his chest and his sweatpants covering his strong thighs. "I remembered how hungry I was and how good of a cook you were; thought I'd come down for a quick bite first."

His eyes lingered away from mine and to the mouth of his bottle before he placed it in the sink. The fridge door opened and his hands offered me an iced one and held another close to him. He clearly had something to say and I could see the wheels turning on how he wanted to word it.

"I would never disrespect you by bringing another women into our house, I may be trouble and a biker but no women should have to deal with that. Maybe we're in a relationship, maybe we aren't. Either way I have enough respect for the other person living here not to pull that shit. If we aren't in a relationship then why would I make a housemate listen to that all night long? If we're in a relationship, I have morals. Adultery, lucky for you isn't something I do."

"I know, I thought about it in the tub. It seems like something you would pull, but I know better or at least I was hoping that that wouldn't be something you would do to me." He had moved closer to me during his speech and in the process taken my beer from my hands. A warm hand wrapped around my waist and pulled me close enough to pick up.

"I should have joined you in that tub."

"No, you would have taken up to much room and I wouldn't have been able to relax the way I wanted to." I fluffed his hair with my fingers.

"Oh trust me, you would have relaxed straight into me. Just like you're going to relax into me tonight when you fall asleep in my bed." A dark smile promised me that there wasn't exactly a choice in the matter, not that I'd protest entirely.

"You sound so sure." I tried my best to tease back. The moment was over within a minute as glass shattering in the other room had Robert hauling me up the stairs and into his bedroom. He was crouched in my face with both hands on my shoulders.

"Listen to me, put pants and shoes on that you can move in. The shirt you're in is fine, you can pack a small bag. Get the cash that's in the closet, that'll need it's own bag. You have five minutes."

"Where are you going?" I panicked.

"That was an order." A gun was in a dresser drawer and he locked the bedroom door and stood defensive. I moved as quickly as I could only grabbing what I needed. When I knelt down to get the cash I froze almost completely. This man had enough cash to buy a million dollar house and multiple cars stashed away in his closet. "Catalina, now!" He barked at me.

He grabbed my wrist and ordered me to stay behind him as he slowly cracked open the bedroom door. We had made it through the upstairs hallway and to the living room. Every window in here was intact which left his office the place they must have entered. He ushered me out the door and into the car before ripping out of the driveway. "Head down."

"Where are we going?" I whispered from his lap.

"Someplace that's gonna keep you safe." his fingers slide through my hair trying to calm my racing heart. Was my body shaking? Was I forgetting to breath or was I breathing too loudly? "I'm gonna take you to the club-house, I have my own room there where we're gonna crash for a few days. I've already sent guys back to my house to take care of whoever broke in."

"You don't do it yourself?"

He sighed, "If it's who I think it is there would be too many. I could have handled it if you weren't there, but they're aware of your presence and someone would have been sent to find you."

"Hey Reaper?" I smiled from my weird angle, hair falling in my face when I looked up at him driving.

"What Kitten?" His eye's connected with him for a moment before they were back on the road.

"You're not such a bad guy." A deep chuckled resonated from his chest.

"Got a few people that would say differently, sweet thing."

Chapter Eighteen

Catalina's POV

The clubhouse was a mad house, nothing was sacred in this place. Women were running around naked and men were chasing after then completely nude. In this place given birth names were not what you were referred to by. Robert was called Reaper so often that sometimes I found myself doing it. Although for me, I liked to humanize him so calling him Robert was almost always the way I referred to him. I think that it became something that was important to him, that he didn't have to be the Reaper all the time.

I stood in the kitchen trying to make a cup of coffee without getting involved in anything that was going on around me, but it was very hard. I was a guest in this house and that was very clear. People liked to observe what I was doing, how I moved and ate and drank. My entire day was basically on display to everyone in the house and I'm not entirely sure how it made me feel.

Robert walked into the kitchen, jeans and a fitted t-shirt like usual, his body came up behind mine and caged me between him and the counter. "Morning." he kissed my exposed neck. I poured two mugs of coffee and pulled at my long sleeve, something felt very off today and it was getting to me.

"Good morning." I whispered back to him. "The house is extra loud today, something must be in the air.

"Yes it is, I like the leggings though." I could feel his smile against my smile. It made me warm inside, made the hairs on me rise and stand to attention. He had been driving me nuts, but in an amazing way. We shared the same room and same bed, yet nothing happened between us since we've been staying here. My will was wearing on me and it was very clear that Robert could read that.

"All these women running around naked and you've noticed my leggings." I giggled as his fingertips grazed my hips casually.

"I noticed the duck boots too and the long sleeve that looks very nice."

"Now you're just kissing up, here's your coffee." I turned in his arms and pushed his mug between us.

Two men were sitting at the island silently watching our exchange. I watched one set of eyes up down what Robert had just talked about. The other watched my hand as Robert touched mine to grab his coffee. They exchanged a glance, but no words. Something about them sent a warning sign through my head which wasn't something that happened often. Then again all the men in this house looked like something you should steer clear of, even Robert. He had this look that warned anyone near him that he could snap you in half. I had gotten distracted by his looks, ones that seemed almost unreal. Take your entire imagination to create a perfect man and bam there he was. All wrapped up in an unattainable era of danger. Reapers poison I suppose.

I looked up to Robert staring at the two men who looked back at him and coward. "Since when do you two stay in this house?" He snarled towards them.

"Boss said we could for a little while till we can get on our own two feet." The one who focused on me spoke out in a menacing tone.

"Last time I checked you were unwelcome back here, so explain how you're sitting in the kitchen." Robert side stepped once to stand further in front of me.

"Simple, money and guns."

"Thought you were staying till you can get on your own two feet? If you have money then you're already on your own feet and you no longer need the clubhouse."

"I got her pregnant." The other one spoke out, he seemed safer. His presence didn't effect me as much as the other ones. What had they done to get kicked out of here?

"Of course you did, I told you to stay away from her in the first place. Yet, you fucked around with her anyway. You're so lucky you aren't six feet under right now, but you I don't understand. What the hell are you still doing here?"

Robert sighed as he turned towards me and lead me out of the kitchen. We walked up a staircase and towards a room I had been in before. He opened the door without knocking and he probably should of. We walked into an office that was clearly soundproofed considering that noise when we opened it. There was a desk and a women riding someone behind it. My hands flew to my eyes and I went to walk out, but Robert grabbed me with a big sigh.

"I need to talk to you." He grunted as the noises stopped.

"Ahh Catalina, nice to see you again. Last time your women was here she was asking me for a job at the bar. Such a pleasure."

"I need to talk to you. You decide if Mercy should be in here or not." Robert pulled me to his chest and removed my eyes from my eyes. My mug was still in my hand and I took an awkward gulp as Mercy got off and stood beside the chair facing up. She sized up Robert and then looked towards me with a sultry smile. I shrank towards him to try and remove myself from her line of vision or maybe I was making a claim. Could I claim him like he was mine? Well he kinda was mine? "Kitten stays." okay, I was his.

"What do you need to talk about Robert?" I was taken aback. The only one that I've heard call him by his name in this house is me.

"The two that are sitting in our kitchen that shouldn't be. He got Bennet's little sister pregnant. The other one did shit that's inexcusable!" He seethed.

"She's sixteen, she was aware of her actions."

"He's twenty-six years old and I told him to stay away from her. Bennet was absolutely livid! She's aware, but she wasn't old enough to be aware!" Robert roared and huffed as I squeezed his bicep. His eyes flickered towards mine and down to my lips. "What about her friend, huh? That other shit promised her a fun night and all she got was tied up with ropes and fucking poked and probed at. The dude's a god damn sadist and didn't let her know ahead of time. How is any of that okay? The girl was traumatized when I found her."

"Yes she was, he's not allowed to be with any other women while he's under this roof." He twisted in his swivel chair.

"Somehow that makes up for the fact a young girl was taken advantage of? I thought they weren't allowed under this roof, they aren't part of the MC anymore so why are they still here?" I glanced towards the still naked

Mercy, she seemed a little more unnerved then she was before. Maybe what everyones capable up was finally exposing itself to her. I on the other hand, inched closer and closer to Robert taking a hold of more of him with my hands. He felt safe, like I would be okay as long as he was close to me.

"That is not something that's tolerable in this place. I don't give a shit how much money or how many guns they could offer up, I want them gone. If you have to keep Ken then fine, make him pay by having to be there for his child. The other one has to go. If we let him walk around here then the others will start to think that it's okay. I could give two shits about what they like in the bedroom, but underage girls that don't know what they're getting into doesn't happen under this roof. They have too many loose ends that lead officials here and we don't want that. Take care of it or I will."

"You're right. I'll have someone take care of him and make sure he can't get back in. Ken will be there for every moment his baby mama needs him. If he's not and he makes false promises Bennet can do what he pleases to him."

Robert grabbed my hand and led me out the door and up to our room. He sat down on the end of the bed and put his head in his hand. The other was placed on his thigh as he sat in thought. I walked over and kissed the top of his head, taking his coffee cup and mine out of our room. After entering the empty kitchen I put the mugs in the dishwasher and went to grab something in the fridge for the both of us. I was semi bent over grabbing at some strawberries when a hard body smashed me against it upright. Strawberries in hand I froze as a hand was on the front of my thigh and something cold was against my neck.

"Wonder how long it would take to make you my whore?" His voice chilled me.

"I suggest you take the knife against my throat away unless you're ready to accept your death." I swallowed as his hand went sliding closer to somewhere he shouldn't be.

"You're parent's are looking for you, Catalina." With that he pulled away from me and left me shaking.

How did that man know who my parents were, let alone that they were looking for me.

Double Update because I've been away so long! Hope you guys like where this is going! Let me know! Happy holidays! Considering I can write again updates will be sooner than they were.

Chapter Nineteen

- -

Catalina's POV

I raced up the stairs dropping a few fruit on the way back to Robert. The door flung open and slammed shut as I turned around to lock it behind me. He had looked up from his position and looked at me alarmed.

"What just happened." He rose from his place on the bed and fully turned towards me. I rushed him and jumped. My legs snaked around his waist and I grabbed at his shoulders, burying my head in his neck.

"Just sit and let me breathe for a minute." I whispered against his skin. His hands gripped at my hips and rubbed up my back before they went back down. Robert sighed as his hands went up and then down again simultaneously calming the both of us down. "He smashed me against the fridge, grabbed at my thigh, help a knife against my neck and then told me that my parents were looking for me." Robert jumped up with me still clinging to him. He walked all the way over to the door before I was stopping him. "No, no please stop. I want to stay with you right now just leave it alone. He scared me and I need you to be here with me."

"I should go beat the living piss out of the man!" He seethed.

"No." I begged as he tried the door again and I let go of him to hold it closed. My body slid down his as we fought with the wood. I wanted it closed, he needed it open and him out of it. Without thinking I twisted towards him and rose to my tip toes. I grabbed at his face and smashed my lips against his. I just needed him to stop because I couldn't over power him. This was my only defense and it was actually working. His hands slid off the door and grabbed at my lips pulling me closer to him. My fingers grabbed at his hair line as he lifted me into his arms. When he pulled away his lips brushed mine, "That wasn't fair. You used yourself against me and you know how I crave you."

"I needed you to listen to me, what better way then like this?" I shrugged my shoulders as he moved towards our bed. "I needed you here with me and I knew this way you'd stay."

"Once again, that was a cruel way to do it. It feels like weeks since the last time I've kissed you. Although the feeling of you kissing me is much better." He smirked as he sat down and pulled me even closer to his torso.

I snuggled into his neck as I allowed the beating of his heart to calm my own down even more. "I don't understand how he knows my parents." I whispered as I pulled at the collar of his t-shirt. "It doesn't make any sense why people like them would be in contact with someone like him."

"You say that because of what he's done or his sexual preferences." I could feel Robert's wheels turning. Maybe he thought I was judging people who did anything out of the ordinary, but I wasn't. It's none of my business if someone likes it really rough in the bedroom just as long as the other person is okay with it. Maybe Robert thought he was kind of like that man because he's dominant, but he wasn't. Robert was as far away from him as someone could get or at least in my eyes he was.

"It don't care what he likes, I care that the girl wasn't prepared or ready or listened to." I leaned back to look into his eyes, a sign of relief written over his face. "I do want to know how he knows my parents."

"Are you sure he does? I mean he could have just said that they're looking for you to get to you. You are here after all and not with them, maybe he needed a scare tactic." He shrugged his shoulders and laid back on the bed.

"I think the knife against my throat was doing the job just fine." I whispered as a hand rubbed at the spot. He had scared me plenty, but I could have screamed. There were so many people in this house that someone would have been able to get to me in time. What I was really worried about was that they'd hear it and keep going with their lives. Were screams something that happened often around here? I'm certain moans were nothing new.

Robert's entire body tensed under me with the mention of it. I rolled to the side of him and snuggled in his warmth. I just wanted to lay here and take a nap. My eye's closed without permission and I was half asleep when I heard him ask me if I wanted to visit my parents. We would be able to figure out if they were actually communicating with him or not if we talked to them. They would get a chance to properly interact with Robert if we went for a visit. The last few times they had contact with him they weren't exactly thrilled about what was going on. If luck was on my side they would have forgotten that he had helped me shower while I was in the hospital. Then again, when was luck ever on my side? My parents would most likely bring it back up for my father to lecture me about. In my half awake state I told him that I would call them in a few hours and ask them about it.

I woke from my nap feeling refreshed and ready to go again. Robert was fast asleep with an arm behind his head and the other holding me. I snuck out of bed without waking him and grabbed my phone on the bedside table. My mothers voice sounded on the other end after a few rings.

"Catalina how good it is to hear from you." I could practically hear the smile that was on her face at this moment.

"Hi mom, I was thinking about visiting. Any chance you're willing to have dinner tonight or tomorrow?" I turned to look back at Robert who was tossing and turning in his slumber. My mom called to my father asking him about plans. When her voice was in my ear again it was telling me that dinner tonight would be wonderful. Before she had the chance to hang up I told her to be expecting two and that we'd be here for six. I glanced at the clock on wall reading that it was quarter to two in the afternoon. That should give us plenty of time to get ready and have a forty-five minute drive to their home.

We arrived in the afternoon, Robert was dressed casually and still looked sexy as hell. I walked into my parents home and called out to them. They didn't open the door, but I knew that my mother would be in the kitchen preparing whatever food we were going to eat tonight. At least I made it to the threshold of the kitchen. A strange man was standing in front of the counter next to my mother and when a smile that sent chills down my spin made it's way to his lips I spun around. My father was standing behind Robert and ushered us in, he looked down at me as his hand brushed my hip. His eyes squinted as I looked up panicked towards him. I swallowed the lump in my throat when he nodded his head at me and sent a smile towards the people behind me. His gentle hand turned me towards the company as the man stuck a hand towards me.

I looked down at the strangers hand, it was oddly clean for a man. Roberts was callused and rough, one look at them and you knew he was a hands on hard worker. This mans hand looked like he had never touched a tool in his entire life.

My hand fit oddly in his, like we weren't suppose to ever touch and yet he gripped me like a boa. His hand was ice cold and his thumb traced the back of my hand. "It's lovely to meet you Catalina, I'm Alex." His brown eyes shined with something sinister in them and my stomach dropped to the floor. "We'll be getting to know each other very well soon,"

Chapter Twenty

Catalina's POV

Robert side stepped me in order to put some distance between the man and I as we stood in the living room. My mother had handed everyone a beer and ushered us out of her kitchen. Alex made small talk with my father in the corner, but his eyes stayed trained on me and I couldn't shake the feeling that he was up to something. Robert was clearly uneasy as his body refused to relax. He was in a dominating mood and everyone could sense it. The stranger looked onto him with caution, like he was aware that if he took a wrong step he'd be stomped on. I had seen those eyes somewhere and I couldn't place it. It would continue to bother me for the rest of the night.

Dinner was good thanks to my mother, yet eyes stayed trained on me at all times. It felt as if someone has walked into a museum and I was the art work that didn't exactly belong. Roberts blue eyes steadily glanced at this mans brown ones. The tension in the room didn't seem to bother him as he chatted lightly with my father.

"Well Paul, You forgot to tell me about what a beautiful family I would be spending the evening with." His eyes dashed towards mine before racing back to my fathers.

"You can thank Beth for that." My father raised his glass towards my mothering, a loving smile slipping across his face. I looked towards Robert who was bringing his beer to his lips when he stopped. His eyes squinted towards the bottle before placing it on the table and his hand grabbing at some water beside me.

"Robert you don't like the beer I got you? There were so many kinds in the fridge I had to guess which one would suit you the best." My eyes stayed trained on him, from his chest rising and falling softly to a calloused hand rubbing at his scruff.

"The beers fine, I just looked at the time and want to make sure I have a completely clear head for when I drive Catalina and myself home tonight." My mother smiled fondly towards him as she picked up her own glass of wine. Paul on the other hand just raised his beer to his lips and ignore him. Alex glanced down towards Robert's bottle before sending him a forced smile.

"I could get you a glass of water?" He already had a glass raising doubt in my mind. Why was he so insisting that he drank that beer? I rose from my seat and took the bottle in my hands bringing it into the kitchen and pouring it down the sink. When I sat back down in my seat Roberts fingers slipped to my thigh under the table and gave a little squeeze. He was ready to leave and that was clear.

The table was cleared and everything was put in its rightful place before I approached my mother. "I think we're gonna head home, thank you so much for dinner."

"You're leaving already? The night has just begun." She smiled. I could see it in her eyes that she wanted me to stay. Mom and I had always done things together, but my father had a tendency to get in our way and ruin the fun. As an only child he wanted me perfectly molded to his standards and that caused a lot of distance between the two of us. He wants me to strictly follow the religion and beliefs that he did, but I saw differently. Yet he always managed to reign control over my mother, she was never strong enough physically and mentally to overpower him. They had a mostly happy marriage, but my mother loved to experience life and him not so much.

"I'll be back I swear," I promised as I pulled her into a hug. "besides it's very clear that dad doesn't like Robert and it's not fair of me to keep him here any longer. He came, he ate and now it's time to go home." she nodded her head and followed me into the living room. "I think we're gonna head out." I announce to the two men that were sitting on the couch watching the game. Robert was outside starting to car so that it'd be warm when I got in.

"So soon?" Alex rose from his seat slowly.

"I think you should stay." My father pushed as he rose and joined my mother standing. I watched her eyes fall to the floor as he pulled her into his side.

"I think it's time I head home." I countered as I pulled my coat on.

"You are home and you'll stay."

"I'm not a dog, I'm going home and this isn't my home. You moved me out of my home months ago." I walked towards the door as my father spoke again.

"Catalina it's not an-" Robert stepped through the front door and joined us, his hands stretching out towards me. I slipped mine into his and stepped towards him.

"Thank you for dinner," I smiled towards mom and then looked to Alex. "nice meeting you." Robert exchanged a thank you and good-bye and we hurried out the door. He ushered me into my seat and then locked the doors as soon as he was in his. My father was in the doorway putting his coat on when Robert pulled out of the driveway and down the street.

When we got around three blocks away he pulled the car over and opened his door. "Where are you going?" I unbuckled myself and stepped out with him on the side of the road.

"Bastard put shit in my beer." He grumbled as he walked over to the grass and leaned over. I rubbed at his back as I watched him stick two fingers down his throat. The sound of someone throwing up always made me sick. He straightened and looked down at me. "Sorry about that." I gave his bicep a squeeze and him a smile before we headed back to the car. "Compartment in front of you has mouthwash in it, will you get it for me?" He asked as I buckled back up.

I pulled the handle and the thing fell open, yup there was mouthwash and a gun and a knife and a towel. My eyes darted towards him as he sent me a shy smile and shrugged. The mouthwash was in the front and when he was done I put it back and closed the thing. In my head it made complete sense why he carried a gun with him everywhere. Hell, I carried a gun in my purse so it wasn't any different. "Do we get to go home?" I whispered as I curled up half asleep.

"Yeah, Jess sent me a text during dinner saying the house was all set." Thank god, I'd seen enough naked females along with males for a little while. That house made me feel likc I was the weird one because I was wearing clothes.

"Baby, babe we're home." Robert woke me as he pulled my body out of the car and into his arms. Damn this was nice, I didn't even have to walk. It was cold as all holy hell out here though. Before I knew it we were upstairs and I was placed on an amazing mattress, but it wasn't my own.

"This isn't my room." I mumbled as he pulled at my socks.

"Yes it is. The spare room is for guests, you little lady aren't a guest. It's time we slept in here your mattress is way too small for the two of us."

He had a point... shit.

"I like to shower before bed." I whispered up to him as he discarded my pants. My panties were next and when his hands touched my inner thighs I was suddenly wide awake. "What are you doing?" I hiccuped. My legs crossed trying to hide myself, but it was no use.

"Getting you ready for your bath." He shrugged his shoulders as he pushed my legs open. Cold air hit my core making my entire body clench up, his eyes darted as they fell between my legs. When stormy blue ones met mine silently asking for permission I didn't know how to react. I felt one of his hands leave one of my thighs as he kept eye contact. A finger made contact and slid down the middle of me. Before I had any control of it my head was nodding and I was repeatedly telling him yes. His fingers rubbed me in circles making me dizzy, but they slipped lower. "Jesus, baby you're soaked." His fingers rubbed a path around my entrance before one poked at me. My fingers pulled at Roberts shirt trying desperately to get it off of him. I loved the feeling of his skin more than anything. With his other hand he ripped his shirt over his head and threw it across the room, instructing me to do the same. I sat up and flung mine over my head, but my hands slowed at the clasp of my bra. After this I would be completely exposed to the man above me.

His free hand wrapped around the back of my neck and brought my face up to his as he kneeled between my legs. His fingers were still rubbing at me, circled my bundle of nerves and then lower. Roberts lips crashed down onto mine, his tongue slipping into my mouth as his hand left my neck and unclipped my bra. He threw it with the other articles of clothing somewhere on the floor, but he didn't break away from kissing me until I was laying down again. He broke away, trailing kisses down my neck and over my collarbones before moving down my chest. Blue eyes looked up at me when a warm mouth enclosed around a nipple and I screamed out. In the same moment he pushed a single finger in and my back arched towards him. One became two, but he didn't push anymore, instead his thumb worked in unison with his fingers rubbing at me. His mouth was hot and he refused to forget about the left side of my body. "Oh god," I cried as something began to snap in me.

"Not yet baby," Roberts voice was stern as he looked up to me. My eyes shot down to him. Not yet? What did that even mean? He kissed down my body until he was eye level with his fingers. If he wasn't making me feel the way he was I would have been mortified. "Now baby." He whispered as he watched me snap like a rubber band. My back arched and I screamed, what I yelled I don't know. When I settled down Robert was crawling back up my body. His wet fingers sent heat straight to my face, turning me the color of a tomato. My legs closed to try and cover myself, but it was too late. Robert made eye contact with me as he stuck his fingers into his mouth and sucked, his eyes all but rolling into the back of his head. "Shit baby." His voice was husky. He leaned down and kissed me roughly, my taste of his tongue. It was odd to know that, but he didn't seem to care and he was in charge. When he pulled away he leaned down once more to give me a soft kiss and spoke to me, "You ready for that bath now?" I nodded my head. "Mind if I join?" he kissed my nose.

"I was kind of already planning on it." I whispered up to him. A smile broke across my face as he threw me over his shoulder.

Chapter Twenty-One

Catalina's POV

I woke slowly the next morning wrapped up against Robert's warm skin. His breathe was even as he slept peacefully and every time I moved even the slightest bit away from him he pulled me closer. My eyes scanned the room as soft light seeped in through the window. Fluffy snow was falling outside and in my mind I noted what a perfect morning it was. Rob's eyelashes fluttered as his eyes opened slowly. A grin pulled across his face yet he didn't flash me his teeth.

"Good morning," his husky morning voice sent a shiver down my spine, making me nuzzle even closer to him.

"Good morning." I whispered back to him, a smile falling across my own face. His skin was so smooth, maybe it was because he had just woken up or maybe it was the fact that I had far too many feelings towards this man.

"I never thought I'd actually feel this way about waking up and having someone still in my bed." he finished his sentence and gave me a squeeze.

"What are you feeling?" I questions as I nuzzled under his jaw. He smelt of woods, sleep, man and a tint of whiskey.

"Like I need it every morning." He planted a kiss on the top of my head. "Hungry?"

"Very." He pulled away from me and out from under the covers. I watched as he pulled a pair of boxers on and then threw a fresh pair of panties my way. The covers fell off me sending a chill over me, it was freezing out of bed. Robert sent me a warm smile and he grabbed his bathrobe and motioned for me to stand on the bed. I rose and he pulled it onto me, allowing me some coverage so that I wasn't completely nude. "Bra?" I asked for, but the devilish smile told me that was a no. He shook his head once and pulled some wool socks onto my feet.

"I like you this way, open and on view for just me." He scooped me up and I wrapped my legs around his naked torso. The kitchen was colder than the bedroom, but the coffee that he placed in my hands after he put me on the counter made it a little warmer. My chest was exposed, but instead of feeling insecure a sense of comfort was washing over my body. I was completely comfortable sitting on a kitchen counter in nothing but an open robe, lace thong and wool socks. The hulk of a man before me had no problem what-so-ever wearing nothing but boxers in front of me.

"So last night," I gulped as I looked at my creamy morning cup. He was in front of me within seconds, his hands on either side of my face as he pulled me to look at him.

"I'm all ears, tell me whats going on in that head." He kissed my nose and pull away. "Just look me in the eyes when you say what you have to say."

My chest tightened as I looked at him, they were extra bright this morning. "I didn't- that was the- you didn't get-." I sighed as I struggled with the words that I was trying to get out. He knew that I hadn't been with anyone before, but did he know that I meant at all besides a make-out. I hadn't given him anything in return and I feared that that would cause problems between us. If we were going to continue then I needed to know that I meant something to him besides a warm body. He had shown me without words or without directly telling me, but I needed some kind of anything.

"I know, don't worry about me. Last night was about you and trust me I enjoyed it just as much as you." He bit at my bottom lip. "Was last night okay for you?"

"Okay?" My eyebrows raised at the question, my head nodded.

"You were comfortable?" I nodded my head again. My eyes left his for a moment to look down to the floor. I was greeted with the view of his waist in-between my legs instead.

"This is a relationship?" I whispered, Robert let out a small laugh bringing my eyes back up to his.

"Sweetheart, no one else has ever slept in that bed without fucking. I certainly haven't dressed them in my clothes and made them breakfast and served them coffee. This is a relationship baby and you're stuck in it if you like it or not." He smirked as he looked down at my exposed chest. "Eggs for breakfast?" he asked as I let out a small laugh. I nodded my head as I took another sip of my coffee.

Five minutes later and a plate of eggs and bacon were in front of me. Robert and I ate quietly as the snow continued to fall outside. It was coming down quickly now and was covering more and more of the back glass door. Robert pulled a pair of dark sweatpants up his waist that he found laying in the living room. We moved into the living room to cuddle up on the couch for a movie, but half way through there was a knock at the door. I covered myself and tied the robe around me securely, pulling the blanket so I was completely covered. Robert got up and glanced back to make sure that I was all set before opening up the front door.

"Jess," Robert opened the door and allowed him in.

"Robert, Catalina." Jess walked into the living room and then glanced between Robert and I. "The office?" Robert nodded his head and led Jess into his office and closed the door. I sat on the couch and looked towards the closed door and then to the paused movie. They talked in whispered voices so that I wouldn't be able to hear the conversion and when they emerged Robert looked stressed beyond belief. Jess sent me a reassuring smile and then walked out the front door, Robert took his place on the couch after locking the door.

After a few moment's of still being left in the dark I looked up towards him asking the silent question. "You're not the type of women I'm going to be able to leave in the dark are you?" I shook my head no and stayed quiet waiting for him to continue. "The people that broke in, turns out the M.C isn't exactly done with the Devil's Disciples."

Chapter Twenty-Two

- -

R obert's POV

    I slid into the passenger seat of Jess's car, anxiously looking back towards the house which Catalina was still in. This meeting was something not entirely out of the norm, but enough to have some worry coursing through you. We had no idea what was to come, all we knew was that we had been summoned and unless we wanted something even worse to happen it would be best to show up.

"What do you think they're going to want from us?" Jess grumbled from the drivers seat as he ripped down the highway. I shrugged my shoulders as I pulled out my phone, scrolling through messages aimlessly. I stumbled across a picture of Cat, looking at it for a moment before I locked my phone. I didn't like the idea of leaving her alone, but what was I suppose to do. "If they're calling a meeting, then something that can't be accomplished with violence." I whispered back as I put my foot up on the windshield. My body was sore and I had a serious case of blue-balls. I was trying to go the pace she wanted, but with something as sweet as her in bed with me every night it's becoming extremely hard.

"How is she man?" I glanced toward Jess as he pulled into the middle-lane to pass someone going too slow in the left-lane.

"I don't know how to answer that without sounding pussy-whipped." Jessie was a brother, one of the only people that I open up to in my life. I had expected him to ask me this question considering that she was living in my house and I stopped fucking the girls that visited the club-house. He wasn't dumb and neither was I, I knew that he could read me even if I tried to hide it from the guys. I never kept girls around, no matter the beauty or the personality they never stayed because I never let them. I had never wanted to be tied down, didn't even plan on it for the future. Yet here I was, this girl had gotten under my skin. I had tried to shake her, but nothing I did worked.

"So sound pussy-whipped, it's only me in the car." He shrugged his shoulder. "Remember Ruby, damn I loved that women. Great body too, I mean like that women could stop traffic if she wanted to."

I chuckled, remembering Jessie's high school sweetheart. She was practically twice the guys age, but he loved her with everything in him. I chewed on my bottom lip thinking about Catalina and her own body. "She's different, I know that I should stay away but I can't. I tried and she dragged me right back. I feel responsible for her and she refuses to run... yet. She still could, I mean one more break in and maybe she'll run for the hills."

"She seems strong," Jess commented as he pulled off the highway and onto an exit. I nodded my head, she was. "So hows the pussy?" He chuckled. I glanced at him out of the corner of my eye and then turned my head towards the road ahead. Jess glanced at me with a devilish smile, then back at the road, then back at me with an open mouth. "Dude, you're shitting me." His arm flung out to smack me. "You haven't fucked her yet!"

"No, I haven't." I huffed.

"Shit, you really like this girl. Robert the gentlemen." I nodded once as he parked the car in front of the diner that we were suppose to be meeting them at. We both hopped out and locked the car behind us. I touched my gun that was hidden in the waistline of my jeans and under my shirt.

"Hello gentlemen." Juan gave a twisted smile as he gestured for us to sit across from him in the booth. His men were scattered around the diner as a few waitresses served them. It was mostly empty besides us, it made me uneasy.

"Juan, you called us here get to it." Jess spit across the table.

"While you're at it, why don't you hand over some cash to cover the repairs to my house that your mongrels caused." I gave him a forced smile as he took detail of my face.

"I have a proposition, an arrangment so to say." His eyes once again scanned my face. He looked as if he was sizing me up. Jess nodded, silently telling him to go on. "My daughter," his hand pointed towards the door to the kitchen. A tall, caramel skinned young women walked in dressed in a jacket and some sort of dress. Her brown hair lingered on me as she flashed me what was suppose to be sultry smile. I glanced to Jess as his eyes scanned the girl up and down and looked towards Juan who was smiling fondly at the young women. "My Maria," he smiled towards me.

"What's this arrangement and what's in it for us." My focus was on the man in front of me, I didn't want to be here any longer than I had to be. What I really wanted was to get home to Catalina, I wondered if she would have gotten dressed by now or would she still be running around in my hoodie and sweats with her hair on top of her head. I smiled thinking about the image, if she was dressed I'd just have to undress her.

Juan looked towards me with a twisted smile as the girl came to a stop near our booth. She leaned back against the island, her dress lifting until it was uncomfortably short. The girl looked like she belonged in a club not a breakfast diner in the middle of the afternoon. I eyed her out of the corner of my eye, what roll did she play in this.

"We will stop the violence, I believe that our M.C's could work very well together. We would need some kind of insurance for the treaty and what better way than a marriage. It's how they did it back in the day and I've made many well maintained alignments this way in the past. My eldest daughters are happily marriage into other M.C's that we are friendly with. We use it as a way to say truce.

"An arranged marriage, this isn't the eighteen-hundreds. People are forced to marry people they don't want to marry." Jess looked towards Juan like he had lost his mind. "This is your daughter?"

"Si." Juan smiled at her as she wiggled her fingers at us. I looked at her face, this women wasn't old enough for marriage.

"How old is she?" I huffed out as she rubbed one of her legs with the other.

"Sixteen." Juan smiled towards me. I flinched at the look in his eyes, something was off. Jesus Christ, what father signs away his daughter just for his M.C to have closer allies. This was wrong on so many levels. "What father auctions off his daughter." I hissed back at him.

"Auction? No, no you have this all wrong. My daughter picked out who in your M.C she wishes to marry." She walked over to the booth and slid in besides her father. Her heel brushed at my calf from under the table and I did my best to keep my face from looking disgusted. One wrong move and Jess and I could both get shot up. We were packing, but with the entrance of his daughter came more men.

My eye's darted to Jess unsure if he was even actually considering this. I smacked at his arm, getting his attention before raising my brows in silent question. He shrugged his shoulders at me. "Whoever she want's to marry could be asked first. If he says no, he says no end of story we won't go through with it."

I shook my head before looking back at Juan. "What other option is there? There's got to be a better way." He shook his head, telling me that he was offering no other way. "Who the fuck does she even want to marry?" I seethed. I couldn't believe this or figure out how the fuck to get out of this. This meant that the violence wouldn't stop and I feared that they had a target in mind.

"El segadora." he smiled towards me as her foot once again brushed against my leg.

The Reaper.

Chapter Twenty-Three

R obert's POV

    I gulped down the lump in my throat, of all people this stupid sixteen year-old girl could pick she fucking chose me. There's got to be some marbles loose if she went through everyone in the club and picked the guy that was known as the Reaper simply because of the people he's killed. I shook my head and Jess stiffened beside me. His eyes were trained on something I wasn't focusing on, but Juan knew I was denying the request and it wasn't going over well. The bitch stomped her foot as she huffed towards her father, her hands grabbing at me from across the table. I backed away as far as possible without thinking it through.

Juan was pissed and it was spreading throughout his features on his face. "My daughter wants to marry you."

"I won't marry her. She's too young, I'm not interested." I seethed as the metal of my gun skimmed the skin of my back.

"This is a gift to you." He breathed through his teeth. This was not even close to being what I thought it was when I left my house this morning.

The men around us were standing straighter as they examined the situation. The girl's eyes were teary as she looked to me pleading.

"Your daughter can have her pick at any other man in our club. Anyone she wants that wants her back and trust me there will be plenty of men that want her." I tried to reason, but tears fell from her eyes.

"She wants you, she wants your rank, your face, your body, you. She wants you." Juan seethed as he sat up higher.

"Anyone else." Jess tried as he glanced around the room.

"It's that women isn't it. She is standing in the way of my daughter!" He gestured to a man to walk over to the table with his phone out. My spine tingled as the phone faced me, it was on FaceTime and there was a women sitting at a coffee table with her friend. Jesus Christ I was going to kill everyone in this god damn motherfucking room. My body raised completely over the table as I grabbed the man that was holding the phone. My eyes darted to Juan, as rage took over. "Call him off, tell him to get the fuck away from my god damn women."

"He has a gun." Juan smiled up to me. "Marry my daughter and the women walks free."

"You're making a huge mistake." I smiled down at him "A huge fucking mistake." I grinned as my eyes drifted to his daughter. I jumped before anyone could react. I was out of the booth with my hand around the girls throat and my gun to her head. All guns were pointed towards me as I stood perfectly calm. Jess had his gun towards Juan as we all stood perfectly silent. Maria was crying in my arms begging me to put the gun down, but I couldn't hear her. All I could see was Catalina sitting with Mary and some armed man filming her.

"Here's what's going to happen." my eyes landed on Juan as he sat still looking towards his daughter. "You can shoot me, but that means I shoot your daughter. You even take a step towards my women and I shoot your daughter. You harm Jess and I shoot your daughter. You see anything you do results in me killing your daughter. You ever come near my home again, I shoot your daughter. If any single one of your men even look towards my women again, I'll hunt you down and shoot your fucking daughter. So this is how this is going to go, Jess and I are gonna walk out here and I'm gonna take your daughter with me until we're in the car, then I'm gonna let her go and your M.C and our M.C will never interact with each other again. This all ends here, any more violence on your end results in every single one of your daughters ending up dead. I'll send their fucking body parts to you in the mail. This meeting is over, do we have a deal?"

Juan swallowed loudly as he glanced towards his daughters face. He had thought his extra men would prevent something like this happening. He had thought this all out and it had went the exact opposite way then he had planned. He contacted a man named Reaper and expected something not to go wrong...

I started for the door with Maria still in my arms, my gun still to her head. Jess followed still ready to fire behind me and we made it to the car in record time. When I got into the drivers seat and Jess in the passenger I pushed Maria away from the vehicle and stepped on the gas.

The phone rang three times too long before I could hear her voice. "He-"

"Go home right now. Get in your car, lock the doors and go home right now. I want all the doors locked and you in the bedroom, don't leave until I come and get you." I could hear her rushing around as she apologized to Mary and left. The car door slammed shut and I heard the locks before the engine started.

"What's going on?" She sounded terrified as she spoke into the phone, but I knew she was doing everything that I had told her to.

"Call me when you're in the bedroom, I'll be home soon." I told her before we hung up. Jess looked at me out of the corner of his eye, his chest heaving.

"We have a long ride home." He stated as he glanced at how fast I was going.

"You nervous for some speed? Usually it's just bikes, even more dangerous to be going faster than I'm going at the moment." I looked at him as he nodded his head. For the first time in years I watched Jess buckle his seatbelt. A smirk fell over my face as I pushed the gas petal to the floor determined to cut this time in half.

When I pulled into the driveway the sky was dark and so was the house. It looked as if no one was home and I couldn't tell if that was comforting or nerve-wracking. Jess flashed me a nervous glance as we both rushed up the front steps. Everything around us was silent, it was like everyone was watching as I unlocked the door and made my way in. Jess took out his gun and readied it in case something was to happen.

"Search the first floor with me and then we'll go upstairs." Jess nodded at the demand and split off to the back rooms of the first floor. The living room was intact and clear so I moved to the dining room and kitchen. The basement was the way I left it and no one had been in it besides me three days ago. When I got back up from checking my rooms Jess met me at the bottom of the stairs waiting to go up. "Check all the other rooms, I'm going in to get her."

I knocked on the bedroom door, but there was no answer from the other side. Once more as I called out to her, I jingled the door handle before I heard any movement on the other side. It sounded like the bathroom door had unlocked and opened. I called out to her once more before I heard footsteps rushing towards the bedroom door. She flung it open, stress clearly written all over her face. She didn't say anything and when I tried all the words got stuck in my throat. Instead I held my gun away from my body and opened my other arm as she rushed me. Her arms snaked up around my neck as she rose of her tip-toes, burying her face in the crook of my neck. My free hand wrapped around her tightly, wanting to comfort her as much as possible without putting her near the gun in my left hand. Jess came around the corner and gently took the gun as I wrapped both arms around her and pulled her up further. Jess nodded to me as I continued to hold her, signaling that everything was all set. I nodded at him once, a silent thank you between the two of us.

"Come on, you're safe now lets get you something to eat."

I got her to kitchen, but she clung to me and was completely silent. Jess opened the fridge as I sat down at the island and pulled her into my lap. Her eyes were glossed over as she stared off at my shoulder. I brushed her hair out of her face and glanced at Jess before grabbing at her chin bringing her eyes to mine. "I'm sorry," I whispered to her as her eyes flickered at me. She nodded her head once before leaning forward and putting her forehead against mine. "What did you see?" Jess put some soup on the stove and I watched as he prepared grilled cheese sandwiches.

"Just a huge man with a gun filming me," she gulped as she continued. "that and you on the phone pretty much did me in." I repeated to her that she was safe once again as Jess placed in front of us food. We ate in silence, my hand rubbing up and down her back trying to comfort her the best I could. I wasn't exactly sure how to do all this, hell I didn't even know if I was doing it right.

When we were all finished and the dishes were in the dishwasher Jess bid his goodbyes before coming up to me. "I'm gonna put people outside the house all night to keep an eye on things while you guys get some sleep."

"Thank you." I slapped his back as he head to the door.

"Just take care of your women." He smiled as he shut the door behind him. His engine roared before either of us spoke.

"Do you want me to tell you what happened today?" I walked up and positioned myself in-between her legs as she sat at the island. My hands ran up her thighs as I drew her attention to my eyes.

She was shaking her head. "I want you to distract me."

Chapter Twenty-Four

C atalina's POV

A part of me was terrified of the beast that I had just released. Robert's chest was heaving as he pinned me down and kissed me deeply. I on the other hand was pretty sure that my breathing had stopped all together, then again maybe it had the first time I'd looked at this man. His hands were everywhere and I was trying my best to keep up with him but falling short. He pulled away from me suddenly, panting like he was sprinting a marathon. His eyes squeezed shut as he took a deep breath and slipped a hand underneath me to bring me closer to him.

"Bare with me, I'm not used to being gentle." He whispered, his face so close to mine his lips brushed me every time a word came out. I nodded my head, my fingers racking through the hair on the back of his head. When he looked at me again, a stormy sea had taken over his usually light blue eyes. "I'm gonna be gentle with you." He promised as he placed a soft kiss on my lips.

He leaned back on the heels of his feet in-between my legs. My breath caught in my throat the moment I fully took him in, it's not like this was the first time I had looked at him but for some reason this felt entirely different.

"You're gonna fucking break me." I had meant to whisper more to myself, hell the words weren't even suppose to be said out loud. I'll blame it on the fact that I was extremely nervous and couldn't figure out how to handle myself.

A deep chuckle rose form his throat as he threw his head back, "You'll be okay." he smirked down at me. An eyebrow rose as I watched him roll the condom on and then what I liked to call jelly. "You're plenty wet, but I wanna make this as painless as possible." He told me as his face came back over mine. One of his hands by my head and the other wandering over one of my thighs.

My breath caught once again in my throat as the tip of him poked me and pushed in. My eyes scrunched shut the hand next to my face brushed my hair out of the way and held the side of my head. His lips came down on mine and gently tried to get me to kiss him back and once I had he pushed in further. My hands shot out to grab onto him tightly, my nails racking down his back and digging into the back of his neck. He pushed slowly more and more until I could fully feel his skin against my pelvic bone. His hips were nestled against my thighs as they wrapped around him. I didn't want to move, every movement sent a sharp pain through me. His fingers brushed my hair away from my face over and over again as he breathed out a quiet moan. My eyes shot open to look at his face, to try and anchor myself to something. I was getting too caught up in how uncomfortable it was. My body felt too full, too stretched that I feared if he moved an inch I'd completely rip.

A gentle smile crossed his face as he realized my eyes were open and they met his. His other hand coming up to lace with mine. Our eyes connected as he stayed completely frozen in his position, constantly searching my face for any indication that it was okay for him to move. I could feel my body squeeze around him, the look coming over his face making every part of me hotter than it already was. His throat moved as he gulped and then smirked down at me. "I'm gonna blow a load if you do that again." My face heated up at his words, I still wasn't used to them no matter how often he spoke to me like this. He moved slowly, steadily increasing to a smooth pace and I threw my head back.

It was well worth it, he held my body tightly to him as he did all the work. I had expected mostly pain and only a small amount of pleasure the first time, but now that he was moving it was the opposite. I tried to stop the moans from escaping from my throat, they were load and foreign to my ears. "You like that?" He grunted at me and as I nodded his mouth invaded mine. Rob gently leaned away from me when he broke the kiss, his hand gripping at my hip as I moved with him. I watched as his other grazed over my breasts and down my stomach until his hand was resting over my pelvis bone. His thumb touched the top of my slit before moving in-between and instancing hitting my bundle of nerves. My back arched completely off the bed when he started to circle it while still moving in and out of me. It happened a lot faster than I had thought I would, hell I hadn't even really expected to at all. I came undone all over him and he leaned back and watched before he lost his shit.

My chest was heaving when he pulled the protection off and threw it in the wastebasket beside the bed. He rubbed himself against me a few times before leaning down and grabbing me. I still hadn't fully come back around when he lowered the both of us into the warm bathtub. A hiss left my lips as the water went past my hips. When I finally looked down at the man underneath me, Robert's eyes were closed and his chest was rising and falling steadily. One eye opened slightly to peak at me before he sent me a tiny smile and brought water up my body. His hands pulled me against his chest, my head finding his neck to rest against under his jaw.

There were a few moments before either of us spoke to each other, he was rubbing water up and down my back and my fingers were dancing across his chest. "Feel good?" his voice was quiet in the bathroom. I nodded my head numerous times, "God yes."

"I meant the tub, little lady." he kissed my forehead as his arms wrapped around me and squeezed tightly.

"Yeah, it does." I blushed when he looked down at me. We talked aimlessly until the water ran cold and it was time to get out. Robert wrapped me in a towel before carefully drying the both of us off and then dressed me in an oversized fleece that he had in the closet.

"I say no panties." He smirked as he pulled me back over to the bed in nothing but a pair of sweats. His boxers had been left behind when he pulled them up his legs and he refused to let me put on anything that would cover me up too much. I straddled his waist as he sat propped up against the headboard and pillows. Between my thighs was sore and throbbed every time he laid a hand anywhere near it, but in a way it felt good. The material of the sweatpants was too rough against my exposed, overly sensitive core so he pulled me a few inches further up him so his skin was against me.

My fingers traced random patterns over his skin as I looked at him, "Will you tell me how you got the name?" I whispered to him. His eyes darted to mine with a very standoffish look taking over them. His hands that were holding my hips gave them a squeeze before he responded.

"This is what you want to talk about?" His tone was sharp and it caused me to look to my lap.

"You said you'd tell me when you thought I was ready, I think I'm ready." I mumbled back to him. Maybe I shouldn't have brought this up.

"I don't think you're ready." He countered in the same tone. It must have been wrong of me to think that he wouldn't be curt after everything that had happened. I tucked stray hair behind my ear and looked towards the closet as I pulled at the fleece trying to find some coverage in it. I heard Robert sigh and pull me to his chest. "Im sorry, baby. I'm sorry. It's a rough topic that brings back bad memorizes." He kissed my forehead over and over again.

"It's okay, nevermin-" he cut me off before I could finish. "I don't want to ruin tonight." He whispered into my hair. "But if you want to know, I'll tell you."

I nodded my head and laid a kiss on his lips, I understood. The backs of my fingers brushed under his cheek bones as he looked back at me. I nodded my head signaling for him to continue with what he was going to say. "You're a lot like my mom, she was pure class and her family was religious when she met my father. My dad was the president of the M.C when they started going out. Her father didn't like him at all, in fact tried everything in his power to keep them apart. My mother was stubborn and none of that kept my father from falling deeply in love with her. It's kind of funny how history repeats itself." His eyes flashed to mine before he looked away.

My heart pounded as I tried to remind myself that he hadn't said them to me. He had just spoken that history repeats itself, he must have been talking about my father not likely him and trying to keep up apart.

"They got married and my father stayed the president of the M.C, Devil's Disciples goes all the way to my great great great grandfather, each of them were presidents passing it down to their first born son or whichever they thought could do a better job. I had an older brother who was suppose to have Jess's spot right now. You can ask around about how I got my name, there's different stories but this is the real reason. I was around fifteen when my brother turned twenty, he pretty much had it all. The white picket fence, the beautiful bride and the baby on the way. My parents were so proud of him and he was so ready to take over for my father, but dad wanted him to wait until at least a year after the baby was born."

I ran my fingers through his hair as he spoke, "My brother and his wife were heading to her cabin one weekend, the snow was bad and it was suppose to be a complete secret. The M.C wanted them to be safe during their travel and that involved no one knowing that they were going, but my father and mother. My brother told his best friend who slipped it to some guy in the club, turns out the guy was a mole and told the club he was actually working with. My father had enemies that would do anything to beat him into the ground. They were driving on a bridge and it was icy, a car came speeding by them too close and my brother swerved just enough. They hit a patch and lost control of their car sending them over the side. The impact of the frozen water under them killed them both instantly."

My eyes glossed over as I watched him struggle with the story. It wasn't me who wasn't ready to hear it, it was him. "My father went mad in the short months after his oldest son death, my mother could hardly bare being alive and he was no help to her. Instead of being there for his own family he threw himself into the club, basically left us on our own. When my dad realized how insanely mad he had gone he gave the position as president over to his vice, which is Jess's dad. I've never seen my mother beg anyone for anything besides the day she begged my father to stay. He was wasted off his ass and was going to go knocking on the door of the M.C that had killed my brother. She begged like her life depended on it and maybe in a way it did. He walked out, bastard was died before he even got there. Drunk drove way too fast into a god damn tree. I think that's when I lost all respect for him. My mom needed him, hell I fucking needed him and he focused only on revenge."

He leaned forward to kiss me roughly before he continued. "I spent the next month planning something that I was never going to tell my mother about. There wasn't any room for mistakes and I was well aware of that. One night I went and while the entire M.C was in the club house having a meeting on the top floor, I lit the bitch on fire. In all of history a club has never went out of extinction as fast as that one did. They never came back from that. Anyone that hadn't been in the clubhouse ran as far as they could in the opposite direction. My mom only found out about it a few years ago when one of the guys was drunk and told her the story."

"I'm so sorry." I whispered as a tear fell down my cheek. If I had been sane I probably would have been running, but this man had me and I couldn't shake him.

"Still want to be with me?" he whispered as his eyes were glossy. I nodded my head and pulled his face towards mine. A normal person wouldn't have been able to touch him, but I was pulling him closer to me and letting him kiss me like there was no tomorrow. Maybe I had some marbles loose upstairs or maybe like he had said, history was repeating itself. His father had done some awful things and yet his mother had fallen head over heels...

Chapter Twenty-Five

Catalina's POV

I was standing in the corner, a place I had put myself to try and move out of the spot light. Robert had a meeting at the club and insisted that I go with him. He was currently sitting to the right of Jess who was at the head of the table. The important people were sitting in chairs around the table or so I believed. Everyone else was standing around the other end with arms folded and biceps bulging. I shifted uncomfortable as eyes continued to dart back to me.

"As you all know, the meeting didn't go as planned. Juan gave us an impossible offer that could't be fulfilled." Jess had said once he silenced the room.

Robert's eyes drifted around as he took a deep breath, I hadn't asked what had went down. I suppose we had been too wrapped up in each other the last three days that my mind hadn't wondered there. It had all been about exploring each other and getting comfortable. I had learned more about this man than I thought I would in the course of only days. My eyes racked over his broad shoulders as he leaned back in the chair. A young man walked over and handed me a foldable one so that I could rest, I thanked him quietly as Jess continued to talk.

"What was so impossible?" Someone shook their head further down the table. The head all turned towards him.

"An arranged marriage," I watched as Jess glanced towards Robert. My mind slowly working out all the pieces. "Juan had let his daughter pick someone from D.D. that she wanted to marry."

"Who," someone else piped in. My eyes locked on the beast of a man that I had a claim to. There was no one else, no other person I would have picked if it was my choice. A lump got stuck in my throat as Jess told the room that she had wanted the Reaper's hand in marriage. His eye's darted back to me, but no words came out of his mouth. Our eye contact stayed as Jess continued on with what had went down and I shook my head at him. What was his answer, would he do it if it meant it was best for his club. A part of me tore in half as I realized that I had no control over the outcome of this. I was a bystander caught in the crossfire and I was going to have to deal with whatever the choice was. Hell, I already had and if it involved my safety I don't doubt he would pick whichever left me standing. He shook his head as he looked at me, the answer was no.

His attention was called to the table when an older member spoke out that he had to marry her if it meant a new alliance. Robert spun with cold eye's as he looked to the man, "I have to do nothing, the answer is no."

"It's what's best for the M.C., Robert." he countered. Robert rose from his chair and leaned over the table towards him.

"My answer is final, I would not expect any of you men to be forced into a marriage as I would not be expected to. The girl was underage and my answer is no."

"It's not a choice, if your father was alive-" Robert's knuckles hit the cherry wood of the table silencing the old man.

"My father is far deeper than six feet so his opinion is irrelevant, the answer is no and that's final. Find your place before I put you in it." Chills shot across my entire body at the man that had just taken dominance of the room. Everyone was silent as they eye'd each other, not another word came from the older gentlemen that was now slowly sitting back down. "I'm fact, I'm making my claim."

Claim? What was he claiming?

All eyes shifted to me and Robert nodded, his arm extending backwards. His hand opened to me and I silently rose and walked into him. Jess smiled at me when I met his eye, but he was the only one.

"Fool," The old man shook his head at the action.

"The only fool here is anyone who doesn't already know that we can take down that pathetic M.C with an eighth of our force. They stand no chance against us and they're fully aware of that. Trust me when I tell you that I believe we won't be hearing from them again until someone serious arises." Jess rose to stand beside Robert with me in the middle. His hands grazed the table as he dismissed, but no one rose until they were both sitting. When it was only the three of us left in the room, I was pulled into his lap as he looked to his President.

"That man is trying to test me." Robert seethed as he looked towards the shut door, "He's been falling farther and farther out of place as the days go on." Jess nodded, mumbling that he was aware and he'd handle it. We were told to go home and more than willing to listen. The clubhouse was barely in the rear view when Robert glanced towards me with that look in his eyes. "What did you claim in there?" My hand found his in the middle of the two seats. "You."

"What does that mean now?" This didn't make sense, it felt animalistic.

"In D.D. we value the women that the men claim, it means just that. That that's their women no one lays a finger on them and everyone is to protect them. They basically become a part of the M.C and they're the most protected members. Everyone will now recognize that you belong to me and I belong to you. Think of it has a wolf finding a mate for life."

For life

The phrase didn't go unnoticed on my behalf. We got into the house and when I turned to look at him the front door was locked and he was discarding the top half of his clothes. "How sore are you?" His eyes met mine when I answered that it was only a little. "Take it off." I gulped as I pulled the sweater over my head and then released my bra. His eyes traveled across my chest before moving down to my pants as he waited. I discarded my leggings and panties in one go and stood completely bare in the middle of our living room. It always took a moment to get comfortable with myself like this, but I knew he needed something different this time. At this moment in time it was my choice, my move. He had left the playing field completely open for my next attack and it was staring me down. I wasn't dumb, I knew what I would be releasing inside this man. I had an idea of the monster that would be unleashed.

The front door was to my back and I could easily walk out it at this very minute, but instead I found myself walking towards this man. Butt fucking naked and I was making my move... towards him. For some reason a sense of trust and longing had taken over my body. I had never felt what I feel towards this person to anyone else and if this is what he needed than I wanted to give it to him. I just prayed that I'd be strong enough to endure it... I suppose we were going to find out.

Chapter Twenty-Six

- -

Catalina's POV

It was official, I was lost in this mans spell and I couldn't do jack shit about it. I stood on the mattress of our bed over him, his hips beneath me. His t-shirt was too big, but soft and smelt like him. He insisted I wear it to bed after last night, told me that it would remind me how much I meant to him. My ass was sore and red, my wrists looked like I had worn a hair tie around them all day that was too tight. Yet my insides were still on fire and even the mere thought of last night sparked something inside me that I couldn't settle down. His hands had been everywhere, followed by his mouth. He was rough, I was denied and spanked and pushed to limits I didn't know I had.

Yet, here I was. Willingly looking down onto this god of a man and not running for the hills. I had known he was dominant, but I had no idea how much he craved it the way he did.

"Oh baby, this is only the beginning."

His words ran back through my mind as my teeth pulled at my bottom lip.

"Count, if you miss one I'll add two more." His hand flung up and down, all calculated in speed, strength and distance. The bite to my ass was something I was on the fence about. He had done this a few times before, but it seemed very different this time. Something about him seemed free, more confident. Deep down I knew that he was certain I wasn't going anywhere. I wasn't sure if it was because I didn't want to or that he wouldn't let me go without a fight. I stood no chance either way...

My weight shifted between each of my legs, each time that side of his hips dipped. Between my thighs ached from all that he was, but yet I wanted more... needed more. He had been what I asked him to be but there was another side to him. I knew deep down that I was going to have to pull that part out kicking and screaming, but I wanted to. Something inside me told me that I was different to him and even though words hadn't reassured me yet I wanted to stay to hear them. I watched as his eye lashes fluttered as he rose from his slumber. This man was majestic and terrifying all at once. A deep grumbled gross from his abdomen as he stretched and the blankets rolled off his hips and below them. I stood from above staring at the body part of this man that I hadn't expected to even think about wanting to see... let alone do things to. I dropped to my knees and shimmied down the bed until I was face to face with him. He had done so many things and I knew that all men loved a good blow, but I had never done this before. Maybe, I was finding strength in the fact that he was asleep and I could worry all I wanted without him knowing,

"Get up here," he ordered without lifting his head from his pillow. Shit, I guess he was up. "Now Catalina." I crawled up the length of his body until I was straddling his waist and my fingers were able to get twisted in his bedhead. My body was shaky and now that he was up and his eyes were open a whole new level of anxiety was washing over me. When he was asleep everything could be exactly how I wanted it to be, he couldn't randomly blind side me if he wasn't awake. "Stop that." He huffed as his hand raked through my hair and pulled my forehead to his lips.

"Stop what?" I questioned. My eyes flashed to his bright blue ones before looking down to where his neck met his chest.

"I know what's going through that little head of yours right now, so stop it. You're staying right here with me." His lips came down and met mine, teeth pulling my bottom lip into his mouth as he nibbled on it before sucking and releasing it. "As for your red fucking lips that I love, I want them around my cock but that can wait for a later date when you're more comfortable."

My face most likely matched a rose at this point... scratch that, santa's suit was closer to the color of my face just by the heat I could feel all over it. I rolled my hips once against his to get his attention, a smirk coming over his face as the realization that I wasn't wearing panties washed over him. In the blink of an eye he had flipped me over and nestled himself between my thighs. His hand ran down before taking the hem of his shirt and lifting it up above my breast, my nipples hardening in the cold morning air. I watched as his hand traveled down my body to his own where he gripped himself at the base and rubbed himself between me. My head flung back as he hit my soft spot, but he froze. "Watch." was his only command as he continued his movements. "God, no one has ever been this wet for me before." I held my breath as he pushed into me a hiss coming through his teeth before both of his fists were beside my head holding him up. "Feels like you were fucking made for me, baby." My chest rose and fell rapidly as i held onto his bicep. "Please," I almost didn't recognize my desperate plea for him to move. A smile he tried to hide fell over his face before he shook his head. He stopped moving completely forcing my eyes to his to search his face. "Last night I was rough and you were such a good girl, you took everything in stride and listened so closely. I'm proud of you for that, I'm proud of us for that; for working so well together and I want to thank you.

Last night I fucked you, I'm not gonna fuck you right now." I swallowed the lump in my throat as I looked up at him. "Right now I'll make love to you."

"A big difference," I whispered more to myself than to him.

"Yes, but just in the way I handle your body. My feelings towards you are the exact same no matter how we do this." I leaned up to kiss him, bringing him down to me so that I didn't have to stretch.

"Show me, baby." I whispered as I let him take over my body once again.

~

Robbie and I stood in the living room as I talked to my mother on the phone. She had called me urgently telling me that my grandmother had fallen ill and that I needed to come see her. His arm wrapped around my waist as I tried to calm my hysteric mother over the phone. A part of me knew that I needed to go and another wanted to stay here in the safety of my home. I tried to get information of her condition out of the crying woman on the other end, but it was no use. They were heading to the hospital and they expected me to be there in the next thirty minutes. I was positive my father was behind all the orders and I'm sure that he was only making all of this worse by the way he was handling it. Robert walked into the kitchen to grab something before coming back when I got off the phone.

"I know you have to go." He sighed as he came over and pulled me into his embrace. "I was kind go hoping that we could spend a few days in our own little bubble, but I won't stop you from going to see her."

I needed to ask him to go with me. Something deep inside was terrified that if I walked into that hospital alone that I was never going to see him again, maybe it all had to do with how my father treated us the last time we were there. "Come on, I'll drive." He grabbed his jacket and put it on before holding mine out for me, I stood a moment staring at him. "My father the last time you saw him," I trailed off unwilling to finish the sentence that made me want to hurl. "I can handle myself with your father, baby. Let's just get you to your grandmother and deal with everything there. Besides, I won't be able to think straight if I sent you there alone."

The car ride was short with his driving and when we walked up to the women at the desk her eyes racked over him. Something came over me as I grabbed onto his bicep to hold him close to me, wanting some sort of claim over this man. His eyes met mine as the same arm wrapped around my waist and pulled me closer while he spoke to the women who was now looking at me. She directed us to the appropriate room and then went back to work.

"Remember last time we were at a hospital?" he whispered into my ear before we entered the room. Of course I remembered the last time we were at the hospital. I haven't seen him in forever and there he was in all his glory. From that moment on I knew that I needed to have him in my life, but this wasn't the moment he was thinking of. In his mind he was thinking of having to help me shower because I was unable to. His mind went there instead, but possibly only because I hadn't relieved to him what I was thinking yet. A blush creeped over my cheeks as the thought came to mind as we entered the room.

My grandmother looked completely fine, in fact she looked annoyed. Her arms were folded politely in her lap and she was absentmindedly looking out the window near her. My mother had planted herself in a chair and her eyes were trained on the floor. My father... my father was pacing until we walked in and he froze.

His eyes racked Rob's before moving to me again accusingly. My eyes darted towards my mother in an attempt to break the uncomfortable staring contest. Grandmother looked over to me and sighed once before mumbling that I didn't need to come. I gave her a gentle smile and walked over to sit next to my mother who was shaking her own head. "Are you going to fill me in?" I whispered to mom who sniffled. She rose from her seat and walked out into the hall and I followed. While we were out there Robert took my seat in silence.

"She's dying, stage four and it's spreading." I nodded my head as I got choked up. I wasn't close to her, but she was still my grandmother. My eyes darted past my mothers shoulder where a familiar face was walking towards us. There was no real reason why this man was walking towards me, but it sent a sinister feeling through my body. Something wasn't right and I could feel it deep in my bones. Reaper must have had a radar for it because his frame filled the door before sidestepping and gentle pulling me behind him. Alex stopped to grab my mothers shoulders in an embrace from behind. Yet the entire time he gave some support his eyes looked past Reaper to me. We all walked back into the hospital room where Alex walked over and shook my fathers hand, exchanging a half hug. My hand landed in the middle of Robbie's back as I anchored myself to him. I was uncomfortable and he could sense it. My mothers voice filled the room as she looked at us.

"Would you mind running and getting us all something to eat, I'll give you some money." My mothers eyes looked to Reaper. He looked to me, but wasn't going to say no. With the nod of a head he took the money and headed to the cafe that was on the first floor. My father was the next to speak and he was asking Alex to speak with him in the hallway. Mom asked me to stay with her and her mother-in-law. I didn't know how to say no so I didn't, but it send shivers down my spine to be separated from Robert with Alex in the same building.

I sat down next to mom as she talked to grandmother, but my ears were trained to the hallway. I wanted to know what was being said that had to be said in the hallway. My fathers voice was muffled, but I could hear Alex faintly. The only thing that stuck out in his words was something that froze me completely.

He promised my father, "Be patient, it's almost time and then everything will be done quickly."

Chapter Twenty-Seven

Catalina's POV

It was my turn to talk in a whispered voice as I stopped Robert before he entered back into the hospital room. Everyone was sitting in there surrounding the bed that my grandmother was sleeping in. She didn't want any of us there and she was making it painfully clear. Robert ushered me out of the door way and across the hall where he leaned against the wall to listen to me.

"I don't feel safe," my chest heaved as I looked towards the room that Alex and my father were sitting in. Robert moved closer when the words left my mouth, his eyebrows furrowing together.

"Did something happen?" His hand slipped to my waist and pulled me closer to him. I nodded my head and gripped at his bicep.

"Alex and my father where whispering in the hallway. Alex said something about it almost being time and that once it was everything would be done quickly." He brushed a strand of hair out of my face and glanced towards the door. Alex was a clear shot from the hallway sitting perfectly straight in his chair. When Robert locked eyes with him his hand shot up and to the back of my neck before he leaned down. As his lips locked with mine on the rougher side my hand found his shirt and fisted it. He was staking his claim and I was going to let him. His tongue poked to enter my mouth and without a second thought I granted him access as he pulled me closer to his body. When he pulled away I was heaving trying to catch my breath and the heat of my body had turned way up. "We're going home."

He left my side to bring my mother what she had asked for and when he handed it to her he turned without another word and grabbed my jacket. I grabbed at his extended hand and we walked to the elevator without another word. Robert checked his phone while we were going down and then rushed us both to the car and out of the freezing weather.

I locked the front door behind us as we walked into the house and took off our coats. "I liked our bubble." I mumbled to myself as I took my shoes off. Robert turned back towards me with a soft smile on his face. "Movie?" he asked when he came back into the living room. I nodded my head and hit the couch. I watched as he stripped of the t-shirt he was wearing and down to his boxers. This man lived to not wear clothes and I couldn't find it in me to complain. He pushed his way in behind me before pulling my back to his chest and settling down.

"Am I safe?" I whispered as I pulled the blanket up to my chin. I felt safe with him, he had a way of making me feel like I never needed to worry. Yet, the fact he made me feel this way made me feel like I might be missing something that I should be feeling. What if I was in danger and would feel it if he wasn't here, but because he was was completely blind to it?

His lips pressed against my temple as he sighed. "I'll keep you safe," He whispered into my hair after breathing me in. "And if I can't do it single handedly than the entire club will help me." I nodded my head as I pushed back against him getting closer.

"What was his name?" As I spoke the words I could all but feel his hand on my thigh, the cold knife against my throat. Robert sighed once more from behind me as his mind went exactly where mine was. "Mike." He hissed through his teeth as his grip on me tightened. "Are you going to ask me what he did to that girl?" I nodded my head, turning my body towards his so I could look at him. "Fuckin' sliced her up is what he did. Tied her down and did whatever he wanted to her." I rubbed the back of his neck as he spoke. "They had been talking for a while, but he didn't give her any insight on what he was really after. She went to him with the plan to fuck and he took advantage of that. Bastard should be behind bars or fucking dead. Give me fucking ten minutes with the shit-head and see what comes out of it." I gulped as his chest heaved and the only way I knew to calm him was to place a hand on his chest and continue to rub at the back of his neck. He gulped before looking down at my collar, his eyes dashing up to mine. "If he ever comes near you again I'll bury him alive." I nodded once and gently pecked his lips.

"Movie?" I whispered before kissing at his jaw. If I wasn't careful with how I handled this I had a feeling he was going to get up and go find this guy. "What about the older guy in the club, the one that didn't want you to claim me. The one that wanted you to marry that girl." My own blood boiled even mentioning the idea of Robert in an arranged marriage.

"Billy, he was in the club when my father was President. That fuckin' bastard." He shook his head clearly not going to go any further into detail about Billy. I nodded my head and kissed him once more before snuggling into his chest and looking towards the television. Something was going on behind our backs and I wanted to know what it was. Everyone seemed shady and I was more on edge than I had been when our house got broken into. Juan's M.C. wasn't done with the Reaper and I could feel it. Alex needed to disappear and Billy and Mike were up to no good right under our noses. I just hoped I wasn't the only one seeing this and that Robert and

Jess were clued in on what the fuck was going on in the Devil's Disciples. As of right now I was going to enjoy my night back in our bubble with Robert because with everything going on I needed to feel safe and secure for at least tonight. Who knows what tomorrow brings...

I must have fallen asleep somewhere after five minutes into the movie because when my eyes opened again there were credits on the screen. Robert had another beer that was mostly empty and he was lazily playing with my hair from his spot. He also had sweatpants on instead of just boxers so I knew he had gotten up at some point during my slumber. His face had stress written all over it and I noticed that when his phone went off he had silenced it. God only knew what trouble had been brewed in the last two hours with the club. Yet as I took in the sight in front of me my body heated up without any problems. I could bring us back into the bubble that we had had before and I knew he wouldn't mind it. So I thought, maybe, that I would.

Sinking to the floor in front of him wasn't entirely thought through, yet here I was. His breathing had already increased slightly and he was eyeing my mouth with question. I knew he knew exactly what I was planning to do and I didn't know if that settled my nerves or made it worse. Yet, I gulped and shuffled forward either way, my eyes casting downward and away from him. He was an understanding man and instead of keeping his grip his eyelids closed and he rested his head on against the back of the couch. My fingers found their way to his waistband and before I could stop myself I was yanking them down and out of my own way. Fully, one swift push and he was bare in front of me and had absolutely no problem or shame with it. He was soft when I gripped him and instead of silence he filled the air with grunts of approval.

Maybe it was a strange way of confidence or an overwhelming urge to please the man in front of me, but when my mouth lowered my eyes stayed open. In fact, my eyes even searched out his just to see him. When his locked with mine I went in fully, there was no longer anything that held me back. Instead I was ready and wanting and his satisfied eyes only egged me on.

His hand buried itself with a moan as he let go and I released with a pop, sitting back and looking at him. I watched as he gulped down whatever was stuck in his throat and then pulled me towards him quickly. Into his lap and back onto the couch, a hand was at my neck and the other on the side of my face and he was kissing me. Kissing me like he had won the lottery and I didn't know how to react at all.

"I wasn't expecting that." His deep voice hit against my lips as a smile broke over my face.

"Neither was I, but I liked it." I kissed him once more before moving slightly further away so we weren't breathing into each others mouths. His eyes scanned my face before his eyebrows pulled together in the middle. An odd look coming over him and a part of me began to panic. What if it was all over for him now, he came to realization that this wasn't what he was telling me this was. Yet, his grip on my tightened to where I was squirming. His eyes came back to me before he spoke again. "What is it?" I asked desperately.

"Funny how one thing can change everything." he mumbled as his hands slid up my waist. "Guess we can thank the gas guzzler you call a car."

A smile broke over my face. "Coming from the man whose second car is a tank."

~

Pop

I hadn't expected the club to get in the way of anything the next day, yet Rob was called in to help get some guys that weren't suppose to be there out. He told me to stop by for lunch so he could see me and I went over and out of the safety of our home not thinking twice. I was greeted warming, but with cation when I walked in. Like normal there was grown naked people running around of both sexes. In fact, someone was having a great time on the couch and someone else was watching. The last time I was here they were a little more presentable than this, but I chose to ignore and go find the man that had been on my mind all morning. When I walked up to the office the door was cracked open and I could hear the voices coming out.

"Just consider it." A voice spoke through the crack. He sounded desperate, like it was something he needed. "She's a sub, she's perfect for you. I've watched a video of her, she's well trained you wouldn't have to do anything. You can't honestly tell me you're interested in fully training the one you have at home. The last time you did that by the time you were done you didn't want her anymore. This women wants to be your wife... YOUR-

"Enough!" Reaper's voice was loud and demanding, he was done listening to whatever this person had to say. The club was still on him about this arranged marriage... "I've made my claim."

"You've made a mistake and we'll forgive you for it."

I decided that it was time I come in. The last thing I wanted was to have someone walk up and find me silently listening in on this conversation. He was going to say something before his eyes locked and me and when they did his mouth closed. An apologetic expression washed over his face as he eyed the bag of lunch I was holding. The same older man that had made a fuss at the meeting was making a fuss now. He even went as far to have the video he had referred to on the screen of his laptop facing the room.

"Scandy video. I brought lunch." I looked at the bag as I walked it over to the desk and placed it in-between Reaper's hands. His knuckled were turning white as he pushed them against the desk to hold himself up.

"Get out." he seethed and for a split second I was almost scared of him, my feet hurried towards the door. "Catalina!" he barked and I turned towards him slowly. "Not you, him. Come here." I eyed the man as I walked back over to mine. He exited from the room taking his sweet time as he looked at me. When it was the two of us again he looked at me with disappointment. "I wouldn't ever dismiss you like that, you should know that."

I shrugged my shoulders. "I wasn't sure." My hands fiddled together as I sat in one of the chairs. "The club isn't happy with you." I whispered under my breath to him.

"No, my father's old friends aren't happy with me. The rest of the club doesn't give a fuck." I shrugged, "I suppose." I answered back. I rose from my chair and began towards the door. "Where are you going?"

"I don't wanna stay here right now."

"I shouldn't be leaving that's why I asked you to come to me." He looked down at the food and back to me.

"I'm not asking you to leave, I just don't want to stay." I sent him a weak smile and opened the office door and stepped out. "Call me when you're on your way home." His mouth hung open as I closed the door and started down the hallway. I made it to the front door before there was an arm around my waist.

"Don't even give a man a moment to get his keys and his coat before you leave him." Rob leaned down and gave me no other choice but to kiss him. When he kissed me he did it forcefully, yet gently. The message was clear and received. I nodded my head when he pulled away and then went to my tip toes and pulled his face back towards mine. "Don't listen to him, please." he whispered against my lips when I pulled away from him. "That's not what I want."

"What do you want?" I whispered up as I ran my fingers through his scruff.

"I've never wanted someone the way I want you, Catalina." He sighed loudly as I looked up at him. Then his eyes closed and he looked like he had something on the tip of his tongue. "I'm in love with you and I need you to know that."

Chapter Twenty-Eight

C atalina's POV

"I love you too." I whispered against his nose as I held his head in my hands while his eyes drifted close. It was alarming how warm and cozy he made our bed, but he did and I now found myself unable to sleep without him. IIis lips twitched at the corners before his breathe evened out and he fell asleep.

I slid out of bed in the middle of the night unable to rest my eyes and settle down. My teeth caught my bottom lip in a hold as I looked down at him before walking out of the room. There was a message on my phone from the girls that I had missed, a group chat going off like a siren. I messaged quickly that I was up and asked what they were all up to. Instantly I got a reply from Rose saying that she wished she was being dicked down. I rolled my eyes and continued on my journey to the fridge, my favorite place in the middle of the night. Well then I'm looking for food that is, my other favorite place was under the hulk. There was a message from my mother asking to see me the next day for brunch. With a lump in my throat I quickly replied that if it was just her I'd be there. Robbie would hopefully not be angry with me for excepting the invitation. This time was different,

I had a feeling I needed to go and so I would. I grabbed a glass of water and went back upstairs to curl up in bed. When I crawled in and settled down, he instancing wrapped an arm around me and pulled me into the warmth of his body. My eyes shut almost instantly and I was fast asleep in moments.

The next morning was quiet, Robbie was dressed in sweats at the kitchen table drinking coffee when I walked downstairs. He was deep in thought where I couldn't reach him, but I didn't mind. There was so much going on that I would let him take a moment for himself without interrupting. When I poured myself a cup and looked back at him his eyes were trailing over me in a soft caressing gesture. "May I ask?" I smiled as I took a sip of the steaming coffee.

"You always do, I was thinking about you actually. Why the hell did you chose me out of all the men?" He eyed me from the corner and my heart melted for the man in front of me. I shrugged my shoulders gently and smiled at him. "Sometimes you don't get to chose, the world chooses for you. But I chose you because I saw the man that you are and knew that I would be cherished and loved."

"From the motorcycle riding, M.C member, and dominant, that's what you saw?" He chuckled. I giggled, he had a point there, most people would have run the other way.

"The perfect man." I joked back with him, yet I wasn't actually joking. "Thank you for it." He whispered as he rose and came to kiss me good morning. I smiled up at him and then glanced to the clock, I needed to leave to meet my mother. He knew his and with a hesitant nod walked me to my car. When I was in and buckled he kissed me against this time with more aggression. His hand tapped the hood as he stepped back and watched me back out. The cafe I was headed to was closer to my house than hers, but she made the time anyway. She was sitting in a typical outfit for my mother and for a moment my heart ached with how separated we had been recently...

"You love him." She whispered an hour into our visit with each other. I looked down into my latte nodding my head at the statement. "More than I thought I could love a person." I whispered back. "If only you knew the man that he is, you'd love him too." She nodded sadly before speaking, "Sadly, I don't see myself having the chance to get close to the man that you're ending up with. Your father won't let that happen."

My eyes glanced to her before I replied, " You know the decision that that will force me to make don't you? I don't think you're going to like the outcome of it either. Robbie is my future and I didn't know it was going to happen, but I've realized that he's a very large part of my life."

"Of course I know what your decision is going to be, I was just like you. It's your turn to create a life for yourself. I just hope that you don't make the wrong one and have regrets..." I tuned my mothers voice out as a face caught my attention a ways behind her. A face that always managed to sent chills down my spine. Alex was down a few shops sitting at a table outside a bagel joint. Yet, instead of his attention being on me like it always is when we're in the same place, his attention was elsewhere on someone else. In sky high heels and skin tight pants walked over the girl that had demanded Robert's hand in marriage. Alex rose from his chair and greeted her warmly before pulling her chair out and pushing it in when she was in it. What were they doing together and suddenly my life seemed to have a lot more going on than settling down and pulling my shit together. In fact my shit seemed to be doing the opposite, it seemed to be unraveling with every day that went by. I looked back to my mother quickly, feeling the immediate need to leave this very open area. I wanted to be home, I needed to be. A quick glance showed that they were just having coffee and chatting, but I'm sure it involved nothing but trouble. Maybe they would marry each other and get out of our lives.

"This has been lovely, but we really need to go. " I started to rise from my chair when my phone went off. My finger slid over his face as I accepted the call and placed my phone to my ear.

"Don't get up. The last thing we need is for him to notice if he knows that you're already there. The door to the cafe is directly behind you and I'm inside."

"How did you know?" I whispered into the phone as my mother gave me a puzzled look.

"Someone from the M.C was here, making sure that nothing happened. I want you to get up from your chair slowly with your back towards him and walk into the cafe." I nodded and hung up the phone. My mom was sitting across from me with a very anxious expression. "What's going on? Why do you have to go so suddenly."

"Does Dad know that you're here right now?" I asked her before I did what I was told. She looked at me with a confused expression before speaking, "Well of course I told him where I was going." A wave of sadness hit me as I nodded my head and rose. "If you follow me inside do it quietly." I warned as I turned my back and slipped in through the door. Robbie was standing a ways back towards the counter and he walked towards me quickly. Mom followed me in like I knew she was going to. When his arm slipped around my waist and he placed a kiss on my forehead I turned back towards my mother.

"I don't understand," She cut herself off before the end of her sentence.

"Your husband doesn't like me very much. That I can understand, but in the process he's forcing your daughter to cross paths with some question-able people. People who interact with people who are dangerous and she's not well liked by. Maybe he can sleep at night knowing that, but I can't and until he no longer places her in harms way as a possibility to get rid of me neither of you will be seeing her again. I have no problem with you, but as long as you report to your husband you're endangering your daughter too." He looked at me with saddened, hard eyes as he grumbled, " Come on baby, it's time to go home."

My eyes stayed trained on my mother's, who was looking at me in a whole new light. I could see that she was either on the verge of tears or burning this entire place down. My arms reached out and brought her into an embrace before pulling away and grabbing Robbie's hand. He ushered me quickly out the back door where the car was waiting. Jess stepped out and gave me a small smile before telling us he was going to bring my mother to her car. I nodded my head and slid into the passenger seat as he got into the driver side. When the car was locked his eyes met mine before he spoke.

"I'm sorry," He started before I stopped him with my hand.

"I know that it had to be done. It was dangerous and clearly Alex shouldn't be trusted if he's associating himself with her. This seems to just keep getting even more complicated."

Jess walked back out the door and ushered Robbie to get in the backseat, so we both moved. He placed himself behind Jess who got in and immediately began to drive. Robbie's hand grabbed my jaw and pulled my lips up to his while we sat in the back seat. "I made a decision today, and it's not something that you're going to like." I pulled away from him but his grip on my face stayed. "I booked you a flight, my mother lives in Florida, I want you to get on that plane and go down there."

"With you." I stated as I pulled farther away against his resist to pull me back. He sighed and swallowed what was in his throat. "I'm not going without you."

"Yes you are, I'll be behind you by three weeks. My mother needs help and I'd go and be with her if I could, but I can't. We're going to try and make some leg way with this whole Alex situation and I can't have you here while I do that."

"Yes, you can!" I raised my voice in protest as tears sprung to my eyes.

"No, I can't." He shook his head and I repeated myself before being interrupted. "The answer is no baby."

"Why, why can't I be here?" I pushed against his chest. His hands found their way on either side of my face as he held me in place.

"Because they're trying to take you away from me and if I keep you here and look away from one second they might be sneaky enough to do it! No one, I mean no one, is going to take you away from me. Certainly not that motherfucker who wants god knows what from you. The safest place for you right now is with my mother. No one will know that you're there and when they figure out you aren't here they won't be able to find you!" by the time he was done talking his chest was heaving.

"Don't do this." I begged, but I knew that it was happening if I liked it or not. Jess wasn't headed towards the house and by this time I knew exactly where we were headed. When he meant he booked a flight, he meant you're getting on a plane tonight. I pulled at the base of his neck and at the long sleeve shirt that was covering him.

"You think I wanna leave you? This kills me, but I'll do it because it means you're safe. I promise I'll come, I promise and my mothers very excited to meet you." I cast my eyes down into my lap and let my hands fall from around him. Instantly he pulled me into his embrace and held me like a cobra.

The airport was crowded as normal, but I couldn't remember the last time I was on a plane. "I don't have any of my things. I should go home." Jess came in the door dragging a suitcase behind him and a carryon in his clutch. I looked up to Robbie and threw my arms around his neck. When I pulled away my fingers dug into his scruff and I pulled him down to me, his lips were soft and my tongue slipped between his lips before his pushed mine back into my mouth and invaded. My fingers grabbed at his hair as he pulled me tighter to his body, when we pulled away he buried his face in my neck. The plane was boarding and I didn't have anymore time, I pulled away and quickly gave Jess a hug before grabbing my things and walking away from them. I wasn't planning to look back because I didn't want to get upset, but I heard his voice call me out of the crowd.

"Catalina," He yelled after me. I turned slightly to look over my shoulder at him. When his eyes met mine he sighed. "Three weeks, I love you."

I nodded and with anger and fear boiling inside me, I boarded the plane.

'

When the plane touched down in Florida I was exhausted. I hadn't thought on how I was going to even find his mother and he hadn't told me. A quick text message told him that we had landed and that I was making my way out of the airport. When I got my luggage I was walking through and there was a friendly looking women standing with a name card. She had dirty blonde hair that fell down her shoulders in waves and bright blue eyes.

I walked towards her and didn't say a word. She spoke first, "Catalina?" I nodded my head.

"Hi,"

"Oh honey, I'm sorry he shipped you all the way out here by yourself." She brought me into an embrace and squeezed. "You can call me Stacy, come on lets go get you settled." I threw my suitcase into the trunk of her jeep and hoped into the passenger seat. She was giving me a side glance while I was sitting and the ride was silent and awkward. "I'm sure you're exhausted, but can I tell you how happy I am that you're here. So Robert found someone and he must plan on keeping you a while if you're here with me. He loves you so much from what I can tell on the phone, he's so worried and already so upset to have you away from him. I guess whatever is going on must be serious because to separate himself from you it a move he only takes when he feels someones safety is in danger."

"Yeah, our life kinda spun out of control pretty fast. I'm sorry we're meeting under these circumstances." I looked towards her to see her glancing at me with a smile on her face.

"Oh sweetheart, don't worry about it. Besides it's bringing my boy down to see me and I have a feeling you might be here for awhile. I have a room all set up for you."

When we walked into the house, I instantly felt at home. She walked me around showing the place with a fully cooked meal awaiting. We ate together and then had a glass of wine before she showed me the room I'd be staying with.

"I hope you don't mind Robert's room." She smiled as he opened the door. "This is where he stays when he visits."

"No, this is perfect." I nodded my head and walked in. She bid me good-night and shut the door. I flew myself into his bed and was met with his smell which put me right to sleep.

Chapter Twenty-Nine

Catalina's POV

Being around so much of Robbie without him there was a very unsettling feeling. His mother was a gem, in fact I felt closer to her in these last weeks than I did with my own mother but that might have to do with the fact that my father had her under his control. For the most part the weather had been absolute shit and I mean shit. It was cold instead of warm and rained for most of the day. The four weeks had been spent in doors trying to keep myself busy. He was a week late and I was utterly pissed at him. Although he was due to land in today, his mother was overboard about it. She cleaned the entire house from top to bottom yesterday and then spent the night trying to figure out what she wanted to cook. I sat in the kitchen at the table on the phone with him during his layover. He was midway here, just changing planes and then within an hour he'd be at the same airport I was at.

"I know Cat, I know." He huffed from the other end as I heard him thank someone. "I'm sorry." I sat silent on the other end having nothing to say back to him. I knew he was sorry that he was a week late, I knew that he was doing everything he could, but I also hadn't been expecting being shipped off to a different state for a month. "You can take it out of me later." He mumbled into the phone.

"What makes you think that that's happening?"

"Because I've missed you." He spoke as if that solved everything.

"Yeah well doesn't mean that's happening." I crossed my arms and leaned further back in the chair.

"We'll see about that." I could practically see the smirk across his face just from his voice.

"I'm hanging up." I hissed as I pulled the phone away from my ear, but not soon enough to miss the I love you he shot through the other end. I ended the call and sighed placing my hands over my face.

Stacy walked in and took one look at me before speaking, "You must have just gotten off the phone with my son." She chuckled as she filled a vase with water and plopped some flowers in it. I nodded once before looking at her.

"How'd you know?" I grumbled, taking a sip of the water that was sitting in front of me magically.

She rolled her eyes. "You're forgetting who had to deal with him his entire life. I mimicked that face throughout his childhood." She smiled towards me before grabbing her purse. "Are you going to come to the airport with me or would you like to stay here?" I rose from my seat and put the glass in the sink before grabbing my rain jacket.

"If I don't want to face his wrath, I better come with you." I gave her a smile as we walked out of the house and got into the car.

The car ride was long, longer than I remembered it being. It may have had something to do with how nervous I was to see him again, I had missed him. It also could have been the fact that I was dreading seeing him at the same time because at least if he was away from me I could remain mad.

We grabbed a coffee on the way and made chitchat to occupy ourselves, but when we got there Stacy quieted down. "I haven't seen him in months." she whispered as we stood waiting for the passengers of the flight to walk out to be greeted. "What if he looks different." She panicked to herself before I turned towards her.

"He doesn't," I whispered back to calm her nerves. "still looks like Robbie. He doesn't seem to change often." A sigh followed my statement.

"Oh he's changed, after all you're standing here with me." she folded her hands together in front of her as she stood clutching her purse. The flood of people soon began and after ten minutes Robbie walked out in the crowd. His hair and scruff had grown out a little, but besides that he was the same. You could spot him out of a crowd in seconds, mostly because people tended to stay a little further away from him. Jeans, boots, and a tee, you'd never think that he was landing in Florida. Stacy sucked in a breath as she took him in walking towards us and my heart started to race. Suddenly, my hands were very interesting and I couldn't bring myself to look away from them. His presence was overwhelming, powerful, and dominating, something that I wasn't used to lately.

When he was in front of us he threw his bags down to the floor and embraced his mother, but I looked up to see him looking at me over her shoulder. Immediately my eyes found the floor again and I tucked my hair. His hands on my waist startled me and he pressed me into his chest with my arms between us. One hand found the back of my head as he held me tightly to him and I caved. My arms slipped up and around his neck and I shoved my face in the crook of it and inhaled. He didn't say anything to either us, just let go slowly but not fully and picked his bags back up. We followed him to the car and then he got into the drivers seat and I slipped into the back. We sat in silence, his exhaustion written all over his face and he glanced at me in the rear view every ten minutes.

The house was smaller with him in it and it was clear as they interacted that Stacy loved that he was here. "Did you handle whatever it was that was causing you troubles?" she asked him as we ate an early dinner. He shook his head and swallowed before answering.

"No," his eyes trailed to me. "He disappeared two weeks after I got you out of town."

That made me uneasy. The rest of dinner was light and I left the two of them to socialize as I went to shower. I turned the shower on and hung the two towels that I would need on the rack before discarding the top half of my clothes. It hadn't even occurred to me that I might of have a visitor. I stood back up after discarding the bottom half of clothing and there was a hard chest pressed against my back and hands squeezing at both of my exposed breasts. I gasped at the sudden second presence and grabbed at his hands. "Tell me you love me." He demanded in my ear.

"I love you." I whispered back to him as he pressed the front of his pants against my bare bottom.

"Do you trust me?" He whispered as he bit at my ear. I nodded my head slowly not exactly sure where this was going. "Strip me." I gulped before turning and pushing his shirt up over his head. Then I worked at the belt that was around his waist before pushing both down his hips and to his feet. "Good girl, now turn your back towards me and give me your hand." Gulping in breath I did as I was told and before I could protest around one wrist was a handcuff. A hand between my shoulder blades pushed me under I was bending over in front of him, little did I know the other cuff was going around the same sided ankle. I stood mortified that I was in this position as he kneeled behind me before his hands gripped my thighs. He pulled me back to him so that his knees were in between my legs before he further pushed mine apart. From the position he was in and the way my head was angled I could see right up my own legs and if I looked forward his cock was in my face standing at attention. I was spread eagle and fully on display. "You have a free hand if you need to balance yourself or to touch me." He looked down at he spoke. "I'm ready for some desert." He smirked before two fingers spread my lips even further apart. I moaned without meaning to. "If you make too much noise my cock's going in your mouth to keep you quiet." Without another word I watched as his mouth went up to my core and I felt him latch on, his tongue flattening against me. I wanted to scream as he licked me and then moaned. "You taste amazing." He whispered against my core. His tongue going to circle my bundle of nerves before going down to my opening.

"Oh my god." I gasped as he continued his assault. My free hand came up and braced myself against the wall. I was somewhere between loving every second of this and hating it. He was clearly enjoying himself and when my eyes weren't on him they were on what was between his legs. He pulled away from me as soon as I started to build and sat back on his heels, looking down into my eyes. Now I really hated him. "You've got to be kidding me." Something soft crossed over his eyes and all of a sudden he was unlocking me from the cuffs. I stretched out and turned towards him. He was still on his knees before I sunk down in front of him. My fingers brushed his cheek as he looked at me.

"You make me feel like I'm burning alive on the inside." He sighed. "And I love every second of it. Yet, here I am. I haven't even fucking kissed you yet and I'm already attacking you." He grunted at himself.

"Then kiss me." I breathed out breathless. His hands came up to grab both sides of my face and pull me towards him violently. I crawled into his lap and his lips attacked mine and his tongue invaded my mouth. The taste was one that I still couldn't tell how I felt about, it was myself and him mixed together. My legs straddled him which put his manhood directly between me. Slightly, as not to disturb the kiss that had turned gentle, I began to move against him. I push my hips up and down his length as my hands tightly gripped his thick neck. My head fell back as I exposed my chest to him and his lips attached to one of my collarbones. A deep moan that sent chills down my spine escaped his lips as I sped up.

"Fuck baby, how can it feel this fucking good?" A hand crept down to an ass cheek before he clenched it to the point it may bruise. I nodded my head, not knowing the answer myself, before looking up at him. His eyes were droopy, like he was forcing them to stay open, but couldn't fully manage. My eyes widened as he leaned back on the palms of his hands, his torso stretching so every muscle was defined. He spread his knees apart to support my weight better and one of my hands pressed the door between his shoulder and head. "Show me how good I feel, baby." My hair fell over my shoulder to cover one side of me as he spoke. "I wanna watch as you rub yourself against me, so show me how good I feel."

Fuck...

I'd show him alright and I'd do so without shying away this time.

~

I woke to kisses being showered over my shoulder blades and traveling down my spine. My eyes slipped open as a lazy smile graced my face when I caught his over my shoulder.

"Hi, baby." His morning voice was always the same; husky.

"Hi," I smiled and turned my body over towards him which earned a hissed fuck at the sight of my bare chest. "How'd the meeting go?" He had gotten a call late last night from a friend of his that keeps an eye on his mom. So, he had left to deal with that and I was left to fall asleep on my own. I glanced at the clock to see that it was around 4 in the morning.

"It went," he smiled before trailing kisses up my stomach, between my breasts and to my face. My legs wrapping around his waist as I felt him push his pants down. "How was your rest?"

"I had the weirdest dream..." I had, it was intense and I was still working through if I liked it or not.

"Oh yeah?" His teeth latched onto my ear lobe and gave a slight pull.

"Yeah," I blushed unsure of if I should tell me what happened.

"Was it dirty?" I could hear his deep chuckle rather than see it as he latched onto my neck. "Are you gonna tell me or am I gonna have to force it out of you?" His boxers slipped off and set him free as I felt him hot against my center. He pushed in between and then up so his head hit my bundle of nerves. A moan slipped past my lips as he repeated the action. "Do I have to put you over my knee?" He came up so his lips brushed against mine and looked into my eyes.

"It was about you." I started as he pushed against me. One of his hands slid in-between us as I felt his tip push against my entrance before slipping in. At the same time he let out a grunt a loud moan came from my mouth as he began to move inside me.

"Yeah, baby, what about me? Was I doing something to you?" he asked as he made eye contact again.

"Yes," I breathed out as I thew my head back, returning my gaze when he told me to look at him.

"What was I wearing?"

"Nothing."

"What were you wearing?"

"Nothing."

He grinned, "Where were you, I want details. Did I have you on your back with your pussy on display for me? Or where you on top of me with my cock between you?"

Fuck it was hot in here, I shook my head. "No," I couldn't tell him. It was too embarrassing.

"Tell me." He demanded as he pushed harder into me. I shook my head, but his hand latched onto a breast and squeezed.

"It was my butt." I screamed out as I came and he hissed as he released. His eyes closed, for a moment I thought that he hadn't even heard me and I was going to have to say it again. My hands flew up and covered my red face from his, but his hands came up to bring mine down. I turned away from him and shoved my face in a near by pillow.

"Baby, look at me." His voice was soft in my ear as he kissed the side of my face. His hand came up and gently pulled my face so I was looking at him. He gave me a soft smile before leaning down and gently placing his lips on mine. His kiss was gentle and soft and when he pulled away he rolled to his side and pulled me into his chest. "So, your butt." He chuckled softly. I covered my face and told him to shut the fuck up.

"You gonna tell me what I was doing to your butt?" I shook my head.

"I wanna know, come on babes, we gotta be open about this shit together. If we're gonna do shit I need to know where your head is so that I don't do something to upset you."

"Nothing really, just a finger. I could have sworn it was real."

"So, you want it up the butt?" I smacked his chest as he rolled onto his back and starting laughing so hard that he had to hold his stomach.

All laughing stopped when we heard a bang come from downstairs. Robert jumped up and threw a pair of boxers on as I rushed to pull his shirt over my head. I found his sweats on the floor and pulled those up my legs before grabbing his hand and following him quietly downstairs. He released my hand and held his gun in a position ready to shoot.

"It came from your moms room." I whispered to him as he nodded his head. Her door was closed , but that didn't mean shit to Robbie. He flung the door open only to loudly curse and turn towards me. The slapping of skin sounded around the room and moans filled the air before all stopped. Robbie was standing facing me with his eyes scrunched closed when I peaked around his body. Two men and Robbie's mom were all in the same bed with nothing to block our view and both men were in her. I closed my eyes and slowly shut the door leading him back into his room.

"I'm going to bed and never waking back up."

I laughed as he stripped and hauled himself into bed with me following.

Chapter Thirty

C atalina's POV

I woke to an empty side of the bed, it was cold, telling me he hadn't been in it for a while. My stomach was off once again, but I pushed the discomfort to the side and slipped on some shoes and pants. The house was quiet, as if it were empty and a small part of me panicked.

My feet pitter-pattered against the hard wood as I scuffed myself out of a sleepy state and towards the kitchen. Voices were coming from the living room and I made out a very unhappy Reaper among them. "They've been in this fucking house the entire time she's been here. Couldn't you be normal and fuck some random dude who's probably ten years your senior!"

"Robert, this is none of your business." His mother defended softly.

"This is my fucking business, I sent her here to keep her safe. I sent her here away from me for a month because I trusted you enough to know who was coming in and out of your home."

"I know who's coming in and out of my home."

"No you don't, mom. They're part of a club, one of them was lurking around. They all knew who you were because they know me."

Stacy didn't respond to that, maybe I should go in there but my attention was drawn to the kitchen. "I'm getting her and we're leaving, today. If she's not gonna be safe here she might as well be unsafe in her own home, in our bed."

I made my way into the kitchen to the two men from last night staring at me. A yelp was trapped in my throat as a hand came over my mouth and something cold pressed into my side. "If you don't think I'll blindly kill you youre wrong, don't move and no one gets hurt." I could hear the footsteps from the other room coming towards the kitchen. A certain heavy pair were heading towards the stairs but stopped short. My eyes locked with his as he took in the situation, his mother behind him.

"Do as we say and I don't pull the trigger on her."

His eyes stayed locked on me, turning cold as the men ordered him to his knees. Against my wishes he dropped as he was told and yanked his shirt front his body. His chest gave one heavy heave as he looked towards the man that was behind me.

"Hello Reaper," his breathe whisked my hair from beside my face. "Now, I've been sent here today by this lovely lady's little father."

"Figured as much," he scoffed as his eyes flashed back to me.

"I have strict instructions, but I'm a reasonable man so I'll give you a choice." I watched Rob's eyes squeeze shut for a millisecond before his blazing blues were searing back into the man. "Someone must be branded, but I'm also aware that you wouldn't be able to go to a hospital here Reap-"

"You know my answer."

"It'd be so much easier if you chose he-"

"You know my answer and I won't repeat myself, do it before I gain control of the situation." he spit back at the man. Why wouldn't he be able to go to a hospital. Branding? Out of a duffle bag on of the men behind Robert pulled out an iron cross, the size of a back. My breath caught in my throat as I watched them heat it.

Rob braced himself as his eyes fell from me to the ground, his knuckles white against the tile. His mother squeaked in the corner and she was smacked.

"No, No!" I screamed, thrashing in this mans arms. "Brand me, brand me! This is my fathers punishment and I'll carry it not him! Brand me!"

"Catalina, no." Robert seethed from his knees. The man released me as I straightened and walked so he could see my face; his own plastered with a smile as he glanced between Reaper and I.

"Whatever shall we do?" The sick bastard was having fun with this, watching us each fight to inflict harm upon ourselves instead of the others. This was my cross to bare... literally. My fathers sick, twisted sense of revenge was going to land Rob in the hospital or worse and I wouldn't let him get away with it. What sweeter way to have him bite himself in the ass than for me to get branded instead of the man he hates.

"It's me, you're branding me." Robert seethed from the floor. "If you lay a hand on her I'll slaughter all of you and make sure it's fucking slow. You're branding me and thats final. "

"Robert, no."

"Catalina." His warning was slipping off his tongue. The beast was roaming free at the moment, I could sense him in the air. The tone of his voice, his eyes, he had slipped into Reaper mode and he was itching to rip someone apart. This side of him had a soft spot for me, but that didn't mean he still wanted me to kneel to him if he were to order. My mouth went to open once more before he silenced me with a look.

My eyes flickered to Stacy's who was sitting on the floor slightly behind him with tears already running down her cheeks. As I watched a tear slip to the floor, my own began to cascade down. One of us was walking out of here with a cross branded down their back and it wasn't the person of my choosing. Father would pay for this.

His knuckles went pure white as they pressed against the tile floor of his mothers kitchen, sweat beginning to pour down from his body as his teethed gritted together and his eyes squeezed shut. Burning flesh filled the air and made me sick to my stomach, I almost didn't recognize my own voice as it screamed to him, at them, for god.

He wasn't listening.

As my Rob dropped to the floor unconscious, I couldn't find it in me to drop with him. My hands grabbed a kitchen knife that was so carelessly left beside me and the hand of the man who was doing the ordering.

He hadn't realized what was happening, hadn't seen me or my rage coming straight for him. As his hand hit the table, the knife went down and pushed away. Deep red blood squirted out and onto the cherry oak table. His thumb unattached to the rest of his body.

I shoved him away picking the severed limb from the table and held it up to him. It was as if the world had frozen, the other men did nothing but stand and gap at me, while the monster clutched his hand to his chest groaning. As my feet moved me to stand over The Reaper with the knife ready to attack, I threw this mans finger back at him. My eyes remotely drifting down to Robert who was withering on the floor, trying to gain strength to get up.

"Tell my father I'm coming for him."

Hi everyone, I'm so sorry for the wait. I had updated this chapter a little while ago and absolutely hated it so I took it down and began again. Then in the middle got complete writers block and have had some medical issues that needed my attention first. No excuses though, hope you enjoy this version better.

Chapter Thirty-One

T he Reaper's coming...

I love you...

You belong to me...

The Reaper's coming...

I sprung up from bed in a cold sweat, my mind trying to wrap around my dream. The vision was pitch black, but I got the message... I couldn't run from Robert forever. My heart still ached remembering the last time I saw him. It had been one-hundred and twenty days since the last time that I had laid eyes on him, since the night that I knew I had destroyed him. I hoped that he'd be able to see why I did what I did. The plane ride home I almost lost him, the next three weeks I watched him get an infection, scream in agony as they cleaned his wound, and almost die too many times for me. The only way for this to stop was to do what I was doing.

The right side of the bed stirred and my eyes slowly drifted to it, Alex was stirring during his slumber. I hadn't slept with him, couldn't bare to do it but we were sharing a bed. I knew that my parents were two rooms over fast asleep. The house was quiet, but I could feel him coming. It was pumping through my veins, he's closer than he was before.

I'd run home, spinning a story that made it seem like I had left on my own free will instead of trying to keep Robert safe. Yet, that still wasn't good enough and my father pushed Alex onto me for comfort. In the safest way possible and not to raise suspicions I'd allowed myself to fall back on Alex, but not actually. He was the safest way to keep Robert off my fathers mind. I'd kept in touch with what was going on with the Devils Disciples, the violence had gone down since I'd come to my parents.

I love you.

My heart swelled as my throat tightened, my feet coming out from under me to swing to the floor. The pads of my feet made their way down the hall and to the kitchen were I grabbed a glass of milk and Oreos, something Robbie and I always ate in the middle of the night. He still haunted me, after this time I still needed him craved him. Still hoped that when he did hunt me down, he'd forgive me. I still needed him to forgive me, I was doing this for him. After my midnight snack I went back upstairs and climbed into bed. My body as far away from the other as possible and slowly drifted off to sleep with Robert's eyes haunting my mind.

~

"So, have you guys done anything yet?" Rose asked me as we sat for our Sunday morning coffee states away from each other. We hadn't returned to our home yet and I wasn't sure when we would.

"No Rose, Jesus stop asking." I grumbled as I shoved a spoon full of sugar into my mug.

"Cause you're still in love with him." She mumbled from the other end.

I scoffed and pushed my mug away from me, "Rose, stop right now-"

"I saw him the other day!" She blurted out before I could stop her.

"I don't want to know." Lie after lie. I wanted- no I needed to know. What did he look like? Was he letting his beard grow? Did he still take up an entire isle in the grocery store because of his body mass and the amount of space he emotionally takes up?

"Yes you do, he looked a mess. Still like he should be constantly banging someone on the big screen for all to watch, but a fucking disaster."

"What do you mean?" My eyebrows scrunched together, worry taking over me.

"He was in CVS angrily staring starring at a tube of chapstick that was on sale. He clearly hadn't shaved in weeks, his hair was a disaster, he was wearing jeans and a t-shirt that were covered in dirt and grease, and clearly packing. He had a blunt behind his ear and was just casually walking around with it. I walked up to him to say hi."

"What'd he say?" I was biting my nails. I needed to stop biting my nails.

"He looked at me and grunted like an animal. I asked him why he was starring at the chapstick and he told me he found yours in his drawer the other day and then threw it away. Then he was pissed and went to one of his fights and then to CVS to get another one."

"He's fighting again?"

"Yeah, for money I guess. He asked how you were."

"What'd you tell him?"

"That you were doing great. He told me to tell you that he's still in love with you and he wants you to come home."

"What did you say to that?" I love you too, please tell him that I loved him too. I wouldn't be home until I went back there. My leg was shaking uncontrollably and I had to place my free hand on it to stop it from moving my entire body.

"I told him I'd tell you. Then he told me you had two weeks or he'd come and get you and bring you home himself even if he was dragging you kicking and screaming."

The Reaper's coming...

I knew that he was coming, had felt it in the wind. The air shifted when he got closer, I was more alert, more there. My pulse quickened, I had known that he was coming. Yet, I didn't know what type of rage would be awaiting me when he arrived.

"Did anything else happen?" I shuttered at the thought.

"I told him you were with Alex and your parents." I spit out the coffee that was in my mouth. "And he turned as white as a ghost and then red as a fire truck. He crushed whatever the hell he was holding and told me that you belonged to him and only him."

"Is that it?" I wiped a stray tear that was rolling down my cheek without my knowledge.

"He threw everything he was holding and stormed out. You broke him, babes."

"Don't say that." I huffed as I took another swig of my coffee. As I was swallowing Alex walked into the kitchen in his grey sweatpants and nothing else. He leaned down and briefly kissed me before pouring himself a mug of coffee.

"Morning, babe." He smiled. I gave him a small smile and pointed towards my phone.

"Is that Alex?" Rose asked from the other end after hearing the exchange.

"Yeah it is." I admitted quietly. "You know I don't believe that bull story you've been telling."

"I know Rose, I know but you're going to have to. Look I have to go, I love you."

"I'll make sure to tell him that."

"Rose, I was saying that to you."

"I love you too, Cat. Take care of yourself and come home soon. The girls miss you." I ended the call and brought my mug back up to my mouth. Alex was standing against the counter watching me closely. "What is it?"

"I never thought I'd get you." He sighed as he took another sip smiling to himself.

"What do you mean?" I questioned, he was making me nervous.

"Nothing, love. I'm gonna go into town for a little while would you like to come?" I shook my head. I shouldn't be going into town with him coming for me.

"No I think that I'm gonna have a relaxing day here by myself. I'm not feeling that well."

"You know that your parent's are coming out with me right?"

"Yes, I'm aware. Maybe I'll come out later and join you guys but for right now I'm not feeling too well. I don't want to get myself sick." He nodded his head and walked back up the stairs with his coffee. My feet brought me to the front porch where I stood staring at the long road that led to civilization from this house.

I love you.

You belong to me and only me.

The Reaper was coming...

Hi everyone! The last chapter was trash so I got back to work and rewrote it the way I originally wanted it. I'm sorry if this causes confusion for anyone, but disregard the last chapter you read and read this one instead! Lots of love!

Chapter Thirty- Two

R eaper's POV

The angry scar glared at me in the reflection of my bathroom mirror, It was something I looked at every day. A deep, fucked up part of me wished that I could regret placing it on my back but I knew better than that. The mer thought of the iron cross getting pressed into her skin makes my skin crawl. It was something that I couldn't handle picturing, it made my scar worth it. My mind swirled as I tried to stand upright, I knew that I shouldn't of had those drinks. The medication that Doc had put me on to keep this thing from getting another fierce infection didn't mix well with booze.

"Jesus man, it looks like you took a fucking bus to the ribs." Jess almost dropped his drink on the way in. I'd been in the hospital for far too long. I still felt as if I needed to boil my skin to get the smell off me. "Don't tell me man." Jess trailed off as his eyes scanned my battered rib cage, "You've been fucking fighting."

I glanced at him once knowing that no matter what I said I was going to get a lecture from him. "You're unbelievable, you died. I don't mean close to it, I mean Doc pulled you off that fucking plane and you had no vitals.

We barely were able to get you back, you aren't even fully recovered and you're already letting some hyped up scum take swings at you?"

"Makes good money." I countered as I tried to reason with him. "I win every time, makes good money."

"No, it makes you physically feel how you feel emotionally. "

"Don't fucking do that, this isn't about you." I seethed as I whipped around. "Everyone's better off with us apart and everyone fucking knows it. I should have gotten rid of her sooner, hell right away. Hit it and quit it just like I normally do."

"You're in love with her."

"She's with Him!" My rage had reached an all time high. I couldn't stand the thought, It made me want to take my own insides and rip them apart.

"And what are you gonna fucking do about it Reaper? You've been dropping bodies left and right, but I still don't see her here with you."

"I'm gonna drag her home even if it's the last fucking thing I do or else her little boy toy, father, anyone I want will be six feet under."

He huffed, "I'll believe it when I see it, but so far all I see is a man wallowing in self pity."

I could have snapped his neck, would have if it had been anyone else but I didn't. A sigh left my lips as I pushed past Jeff and left my own room to go to the kitchen.

- We need to meet. ASAP.

I sent the text before he followed me and threw my phone onto the counter, pouring myself a mug of coffee while I waited for a response. It came quicker than I had planned for, maybe she was expecting one from me. Maybe she was just as desperate as I was...

- Give me a time and a place.

- My house. 7 pm. I'll order a pizza.

- I'll bring the beer.

Jeff eyed me as I handled my conversation and when I was done questioned it. I brushed him off and grabbed my jacket, I needed out of this fucking house. Everything in it reminded me of her here and it was becoming overwhelming. "All I'm saying Reaper is that that girl wants you to come and get her. She didn't leave to go and be with him, she left for a reason. If I know anything about her she's got a plan and she's patiently waiting for your sorry ass to fall into your role and do what you're suppose to do."

"How does that work, she hasn't told me what to do."

"Maybe she can't have you knowing that she has a plan, maybe she needs you to react like you would if she actually was leaving."

"I would have followed her lead! I would have acted like she needed me too! I just needed her to tell me, but she up and fucking left!"

"Reaper, that woman's in love with you! Why can't you see that?"

"Then why is she with him?"

"She has a plan, I can feel it."

"I would have pissed away everything for her, fucked it all. Why wouldn't she at least tell me that she had a motherfucking plan!" I could feel my chest beating a mile a minute, feel my face heating up. The tell tale signs of me loosing my temper, but what I wasn't ready for was the constriction in my throat. It felt like someone had put a bowling ball down there. "I'm going for a drive, lock the door behind you."

~

The delivery man shakily handed me my change and all but booked it to his car. Little Bitch. I slammed my front door shut and walked into the kitchen, she was at the high top awaiting the food.

"Smells good." A smile crossed her face before the tip of the bottle hit her lips. Of course it smelt amazing, it's pizza. No greater meal on a night like this than pizza and beer. My eyes glanced towards her for a quick second before going back to the box in front of me. A small part of me hoped that she'd forgive me for what I was going to do at the end of the night. The larger part of me knows that I have to do what I have to do. It was all for the greater good or that was what I was going to tell myself. It wasn't going to be that big of a deal, I'm sure. I rolled my eyes to myself, no one was going to be happy about what was going to go down.

"So, what'd you wanna meet about?" She asked me as she shoved her face with a pizza.

"Yeah about that," I trailed off as I rubbed the back of my neck preparing to make my move. "You're not gonna like it."

You're doing this because you have to.

Chapter Thirty - Three

Catalina's POV

It had been two weeks. Rose hadn't called or texted since then. I was beginning to worry, but being so far from home was hard. I had called all the girls expecting for them to tell me what was going on, but none were able to. In fact, I think they may have even been avoiding me.

So, I did something that was completely unplanned. I called Reaper.

The phone rang...

And rang...

And. Rang.

He had ignored the call and the call after that. On the third call he just completely declined it. As I looked at my phone, I felt a small part of my heart shatter off the rest completely. He hated me and I was madly in love with him. Tears were streaming down my cheeks before I had the chance to catch them and a hand was at my stomach. As I wiped them away I walked upstairs and grabbed a suitcase from the closet. Throwing clothes into it as quickly as I could, I wasn't in the mood to have someone walk in. As the thought crossed my mind, my mother walked by my door and stopped in her tracks.

"Sweetheart, what's wrong?" She looked concerned and in that moment something clicked. Half of me hated her. The hatred that burned within you. I knew deep down that I would never love her again unless I was out of this place.

"Somethings wrong with the girls, I have to go." I zipped up my suitcase. Something crossed her eyes and she turned to walk out the door. I should have known.

A heavier set of footsteps came up the stairs with the light patter of hers. Alex's head popped into the doorway as I was hauling my suitcase off the bed. "Where are you going?"

"Somethings wrong with the girls, I have to go"He was shaking his head and moving towards me.

"You're going to see him." He was closing in and my heart was racing. I was shaking my head no, but couldn't get the works out. "Prove it."

"What? How"

"You know, I slept beside you all this time and never once made any sort of move. Never felt the soft skin of your spine against my chest. Never felt the smooth skin of your inner thighs against my leg. Never the poke of your nipples after I've played with them so they're hard or how your breast would fill my hand as I cupped it." He was backing me up. The backs of my thighs were hitting the edge of the bed and I was forced to sit. The door was shut and I doubt my mother had stuck around. "Never tasted you on my tongue as I sucked at your clit. Never felt the tip of my dick in the back of your throat. Never felt the warmth of your cunt around me as I fucked you. And never the tightening of your ass as I loosened you with my fingers." He was panting, his hard on all but busting through his pants.

My stomach was in my throat. "So prove to me you aren't going back to him."

I was shaking my head, but stopped myself. "I'm not forcing." He spoke softly as he came down to my level and gently kissed at my collar bone. His hands were rubbing my inner tights, lightly brushing my center and my thin leggings weren't helping. I could say no and a large part of me knew that. He wasn't going to force me, but he would tell my father. My father would think I was going back to Robbie and he'd send men after him. "What do you want?" I gulped.

"I want a taste." His eyes were blazing into mine and he got onto his knees in front of me. He leaned over as he spread my legs wider and put his nose against my core and took a sniff of it. His other hand was working at undoing his pants to free himself. Out of all the things this man was asking to do he wanted to lick my pussy.

I ran; Swung my other leg over him, grabbed my keys and booked it out the door and to the car with my phone. I typed in the location of the house and tossed my phone out the window. I needed to know what was wrong with Rose and I needed to know right now.

The drive was something else, I hadn't realized how far I was from home so when I saw the sign welcoming me my foot hit the gas. I wanted to be there and I wanted to be there now. The rounds were done and I began to panic when none of the girls answered any of their doors. What the fuck was going on. So, I drove to the only other place that could tell me.

I was let in with a second glance and when I walked in the door most stopped what they were doing.

"Oh shit." Rose was shoving popcorn into her mouth with all the other girls around her.

"What the fuck is going on? Why didn't a single one of you answer your phones." I threw my shit down and walked over to shut the tv off on them. "What are you guys doing here? I want answers and I want them now!" All eyes shifted to the stairs and I felt a tightening in my chest.

Robbie had come down the stairs of the clubhouse and was standing in a pair of jeans and boots. The t-shirt in his hand was drenched in an unknown substance and he was holding it like it was sticky. His eyes were glued to me and something told me he wasn't expecting to see me anytime soon. "Hi." I shrugged my shoulders at him. He nodded his head once and turned around to go back upstairs. My eyes drifted to the girls who were watching with bug eyes. And then Rose smiled.

My feet were off the ground in seconds and I was face to face with Robbie's jean covered ass. I looked up at the girls who were giggling as I was dragged up stairs. Once we were in his room in the clubhouse my feet hit the floor and he locked the door behind us. "Take your clothes off." He was circling me, like a predator tracking his prey. Mindlessly, I striped down to my bra and panties. Robbie walked up to me and ripped my bra off before turning me around and ripping my panties off. I was bent over rather forcefully so that my hands were on the bed. "Spread em." He demanded from behind me.

"Rob, please." His hand came through the air harder than I had thought it was going to. A moan instantly escaped from my mouth. He was beside my head in seconds with handcuffs. Using the metal poles at the corner of his bed, he cuffed each of my wrists to the one closest to him. The side of my face hit the mattress as I was stretched out. "I'm not gonna fuck you, but you're gonna fucking get it." I nodded my head, ready for whatever he was going to give me. I heard the zipper of his pants, his shirt drop to the floor as he stripped himself. He was walking around opening part of his dresser. I felt his tip as he brushed it up against my center. A moan rushing out of me as he rocked the tip of his cock against my bundle of nerves.

"You know your word." He grunted from behind me. A cold metal pressed against my clit harshly before the bulb entered me slightly. He tugged and pushed a few times barely fucking me with it. He pulled it out and slid the cool metal behind my entrance. "Robbie," I whispered as the pointed tip of it pressed at my back entrance.

"You're fine, relax." He whispered to me as I watched him from the corner of my eyes drop to his knees. I could feel his breath on my core, but panic was increasing as the freezing metal tip pressed at my rose bud. "Tell me everywhere."

A tear trickled down my cheek, I had hurt him so much. I shook my head, "No where, I didn't let him touch me. If you still wanna take me there it's okay, but start with you not metal."

"I need you in a new position." He grunted to himself as he began to un-cuff me. I was flipped onto my back as he spread my legs open and handcuffed my ankles to each to different posts of the bed. I was fully exposed to him and at the perfect angle when he shoved a pillow under my hips. "Fine, no metals... yet. I wasn't prepared for his fingers inside me or how he put them into his mouth after. He slid them over my entrance before going behind it and applying slight pressure. "Hold yourself open." He grunted go me as he placed one of my hands on a cheek. His finger began to slip in as an uncomfortable pressure washed over. I bit my lip to stop from making and noise, and then he was pulling out and adding another digit. There was a new pressure as my eyes stayed closed, this one cool at my actual entrance. I opened my eyes as he slipped the hard rubber into, the arm at the end of it directly landing on my clit. A slow vibration washed over me when he slightly twisted the end of it. He pulled his fingers from my back entrance as he grabbed the bulb of cool metal. I whimpered as he pushed it fully into me and stepped back.

"Maybe now you'll learn your lesson." His icy blue eyes caught mine as he turned to go into the back room. His angry scar glaring at me before the door closed and I was left alone.

Chapter Thirty-Four

C atalina's POV

    I awoke to a sore body laying in the coziest bed, a bed that smelt of a man who made my head spin and my heart pound. A black sweatshirt, that didn't belong to me, had been placed on my body at some point in the middle of the night along with a pair of boxers. I vaguely remembered Robbie coming back in and relieving me before I passed out, my body was so tired.

I was in his room engulfed by his bed, but he wasn't in it with me. We hadn't talked. Yet, I knew that he wasn't ready to and the fastest way to get him to listen to me was to do as he wanted. The girls had no real idea what was going on, but here they were in this clubhouse. How did they get here? Why were they here? Why the fuck had none of them told me what was going on either? There was a soft knock at the door before it creaked open. Half of Roses face was gently looking inside and once she saw what state I was in she came in.

"How'd it go?" She whispered as she sat down beside me? I shrugged my shoulders, I didn't know. "I mean at least you're here." I nodded, at least I could see him.

"What time is it?" I questioned her as I sat up in bed. "It's a little past midnight. Robert told me to come and see her before I went to bed." I scrunched up my face, what was going on with them? She shrugged her shoulders at my facial expression. "He seemed like he was worried about you."

I nodded my head, my mind blurred with thoughts running through it. "Where is he?" I would find out what was up with them later, right now I just wanted to see him. We had so much to talk about in so little time.

She shrugged, "He's never here at night." My breath caught in my throat... he never stayed here at night. Where did he go? I suppose it was only fair for him to be with another women; after all, he thought that I had been with another man. That didn't mean that it didn't feel like a tiger had just bit down and ripped apart my chest. "Last time I saw him he had come down about forty-five minutes after you guys went upstairs, was down for about an hour and then went back up. The next time I was him was about a half hour ago and he was heading out. He told me to check on you before I went to bed. What the hell happened that required me to check on you?"

I shook my head, "It's not important. So you have no idea where he went?"

"Nope, try asking Jess." I crawled out of bed and quickly changed into a pair of leggings and threw sneakers on, his sweatshirt I was keeping. I had desperately been waiting to be engulfed in that scent again. "Are you going to bed or are you coming?" I asked her as I stood at the door. I guess I'll come.

I walked to Jess' office door where I assumed he'd be and knocked, but it swung open on its own. He looked the same as when I left him, but this time stress was written all across his face. His eyes flickered up to me and froze. "Well well well, it's about fucking time." He rose from his seat and opened his arms. I booked it into them, it was the first warm welcome I had gotten since arriving here. "How have ya' been little one?"

"Been better..." I nodded my head as he looked me over. "Happy that he's alive and moving." Jessie nodded his head in agreement, "It was pretty uncertain there for a while." Trust me, I remembered. I couldn't get the sound of him screaming out of my brain.

"I was wondering if you actually knew where he was?" His eyes drifted to Rose for a moment before continuing.

"He's gone out for the night. He should be back around dawn."

There was that ball in my throat again, this time it was bigger. This time it was lodged and I didn't know if I was gonna be able to get it out. "Is it the same one every time or does he switch it up?" Tears were welling behind my eyes and I needed this conversation over before they spilled over.

"Same one, says it helps him work his feelings out. I've been trying to get him to stop it for a little while, but he won't listen to me. I just recently found out about it." He closed his computer and gave me a sad smile.

"How long has it been going on?"

"Since he healed up and was able to move."

Tears swelled in my eyes and one spilled over. I quickly wiped it away, "What is she like?" I'm sure he had met her. Jessie was like a brother to Robbie. His eyebrows scrunched together in confusion.

"Oh my god, Catalina. I'm talking about him fighting again. He hasn't been with anyone else but you. It's easier if I just show you, would you like to go?"

Relief washed over me, maybe there was still some hope. I needed to see him as soon as possible. I nodded my head, rubbing at my eyes and sighing in relief. "It's not gonna be pretty." I knew that.

"I need to know."

~

It was a popular restaurant that we walked into and it took me off guard. I wasn't sure what I was expecting, but it most definitely wasn't this. Jessie walked up to the guy that was seating people and told him he needed to be seat at table 43. I turned to Rose with confusion written all over my face. The man nodded and lead us to the back of the restaurant near the kitchen where he opened a door to stairs leading downstairs. Jess looked back at me before heading down them with me on his heels.

It was fight night once you hit the basement.

There were so many people that you had to shove your way through the crowd. The bright LED lights were blinding, but I could clearly see the iron cage with the mat inside. There were two men in it, one puerto rican and another white. I recognized him instantly, his angry scar covering his back. As I made it towards the cage, the air wasn't making it to my lungs. Robert was in the cage in a pair of shorts and boxers. Bare fights and blood covering the two men, I went to run up to it but a hand caught me. I turned to Jessie as he shook his head no.

"Make it stop, get him out of there!" I seethed as my eyes flashed back to him. I watched as the other man smashed a fist into Reapers ribs. My body hunched over as I felt the air get knocked out of me.

"You can't stop it, people have money bet on this. Down here, no rules apply." He brought me back closer to him as some of the men around began to eye us. I looked towards the cage once more, the men had switched positions. This time, Rob's back wasn't to me, but his chest was. His icy blue eyes caught mine in the crowd and he stopped in his tracks. His hands fell to his sides as his breathing slowed. I held his gaze as his opponent took the opportunity to sock him one to the face. When he got back up, all hell broke loose and in a moment the other man was on the ground tapping out. He walked towards the opening of the cage as the crowd went wild and headed towards me. Bloody and sweating, he walked up to me and grabbed my waist and dragged me to the exit. Jess and Rose were close behind as we exited a different way than we came in.

It brought us to a poorly lit room with some lockers and a bench. "Why the fuck is she here?" Reaper seethed towards Jess as he washed himself down. He pulled his shorts down his legs and threw his jeans on his body. He looked me up and down as he pulled his shirt and jacket onto him.

"She was looking for you. I decided to show her what you've been up to."

"She didn't need to come and see this." He grabbed his shit and walked up to Jess. "Grab Rose, we're leaving."

I was all but dragged back up out a different door that lead to the cars outside. Robbie put me into the passenger side of his car and sent Rose and Jessie to the other one. Once we were on our way back to the club house I turned towards him. As I was trying to begin the conversation, my phone rang.

I looked at the caller, Alex's name popped up onto my phone. Before I could stop him from seeing it he spoke up.

"Go ahead, answer lover boy. Why don't you put it on speaker for me too." My eyes drifted towards him as I answered the phone. "Don't make a sound." I warned as I placed it on speaker and said hello.

"Hi honey, I was just calling to check in." Alex's voice filled the car. My eyes darted towards Rob who looked at me with a burning expression. He snickered silently from behind the wheel.

"What's up?" I questions as tears swelled once again.

"How are the girls?"

I looked down at the phone, "They're doing fine. I ran out to get food and am on my way there now."

"When are you coming home? I miss you." Reapers knuckles turned white on the wheels as he balled one into a fist. When his eyes locked with mine again, tears dripped down my cheeks.

"I'm not sure yet, I have to do some things. I'll let you know though, it should be soon. Look, I gotta go it's raining pretty hard here and I wanna use both hands on the wheel."

"Okay baby, text me when you get back with the girls safe."

I nodded my head, "Will do." I hung up the phone. When I looked back at him he had one had on the wheel and the other was on the window holding his head up. He wouldn't look at me, but his face was covered with pain.

"Robbie, I need you to hear me. I didn't sleep with him. Nothing happened between us."

"I don't want to hear it." He whispered as his foot hit the gas petal.

"But you need to, I had a plan. It wasn't good enough for my father that I was home, he pushed Alex onto me. Nothing ever happened between the two of us."

"Why did you go home to begin with?"

"To protect you!"

"You weren't protecting me, you left me. I don't need your protection from your little father. I needed you."

"I would have killed you."

"And it wouldn't have fucking mattered because I had you." He was screaming at this point and I was crying so hard that I could barely see him. "You were mine," His hiccup caught me off guard.

"I still am, Robbie I never let anything happen. I love you!"

We pulled up to the house as he got out of the car and walked over to my side. "Then tell me you're staying. You are the only thing that I've ever needed. It matters if I fucking come home when I have you. So prove it, tell me you'll stay."

"I have to go back, they'll know that I'm with you if I don't go back."

"Let them know!"

"Then I'll never be able to find out what is going on!" I screamed back as I got out of the car and stood in front of him.

"That's not your concern, I have an entire club to do that."

I shook my head, he just didn't understand. My father would never stop. He wouldn't stop until he was dead. He had gotten to us before, what would stop him from getting to us again? I shoved at his chest. "He won't stop."

"I'll fucking kill him!" His face was red as he clenched his fists yelling. As I was standing in front of him my stomach jumped to my throat, "If you go back to him, I'll marry her."

I all but hissed, my fists hitting his chest and then recoiling into my own body. My feet moved away from him in shock. My mouth dropped open as the words processed. "What did you just say to me?"

"I said, if you fucking leave me again, I'll marry her." Calm had washed over him as he stood defeated with his arms by his sides and all color drained from his face. "I will marry her..."

Chapter Thirty-Five

C atalina's POV

The night that Robbie announced to me that he'd marry her if I left, I snapped in half. I wasn't sure if it was in rage or heartbreak, but I let him turn his back to me and walk out of the pouring rain. I stood there for god knows how long before finally finding it in me to move my feet one foot in front of the other.

My hands shoved open the offensive wooden door that stood between the two of us as I entered his bedroom unannounced. "What the fuck did you just fucking say to me?" I hissed as he turned, stoping in the process of discarding his soaked clothes.

I watched his eyes glaze over with that beautiful rage I had come to know, "You fucking heard me." He seethed as he all but ripped his clothing in two to get it off his body.

"No. No, I don't think I did. What I just heard was you telling me that after everything you were gonna marry some fucking bitch. Let me remind you, that she's the reason we're in this mess to begin with!" My chest was rising and falling rapidly as I closed in on him. Never before had my own rage been so prominent. It was like an animal had been released inside my body after years of captivity.

"No, the reason we're in this godforsaken mess is because you walked away Catalina, you!" He ripped the towel from the back of his door in order to dry himself. It was senseless to put different clothing on when he was as wet as he was.

"I was protecting you! What part of that don't you fucking understand." My head was shaking in disbelief, how many times was I going to have to say this.

"No, don't pull that bullshit. You know that I'm fully capable of being able to handle myself. I don't need anyone to fucking protect me. What don't you understand, Catalina, is that I could have ripped your father apart with my bare fucking hands from the beginning! You know it, but you're too fucking scared to admit it to yourself. You were too scared to have to choose between the two lives that you had found yourself stuck between." He had inched closer and closer to me with each step increasing his level of rage. There was a beast in front of me and I wasn't smart enough to back down.

"What two lives?" I hissed up into his face. "Enlighten me on how I was scared."

"It was all too real. Finally, finally you were able to make your own fucking decisions on what you wanted to do. There was no reporting to mommy or daddy about what to do with your life. Nothing was certain anymore, you were taking all sorts of risks. Yet, you knew what you wanted but it was a danger to your family because you had to take them for what they were. With me, you couldn't ignore the abusive, power-hungry, asshole that is your fucking father. You had to acknowledge that your mother practically sold you to some rich fucking doctor because it pleased your father enough not to fucking beat her for a moment." His chest was heaving as he screamed towards me. "And when I got fucking hurt and you almost lost me things became fuzzy. What was the point in staying here away from everything if you couldn't be damn certain that I was gonna be there. You were fucking terrified because deep down you knew that your father was fucking livid and all the barrels of his god damn guns were pointing straight at us."

I was shaking my head as my rage subsided to agony, no it wasn't true. "You fucking abandoned me because it was easier than you feeling like it was your fault if something happened. Everyone that got hurt because of your father, you put on your own damn shoulders. What do I have to do in order to show you that I'm here. In order to show you that I'm not fucking going anywhere and you can fucking unpack."

Tears were already cascading down my cheeks as my eyes met his. His breathing was labored, but his rage was gone and with it my own. How could I be mad at him. "You don't know what you're saying." I whispered as I wiped away at the salty tears.

He shook his head, "But I do because I know you better than the backs of my own damn hands." I shook my head at him, he couldn't. "You wanna know why?" I shook my head no, please don't tell me because it may break me. "Because I didn't have a single reason to wake up in the morning before you. Nothing mattered to me before you. If I lived or died didn't matter, if it happened it happened. There was no point in living and there was no point in dying, but I was such in the middle of both. I was breathing, but inside I was cold and bitter. I fought because it made me feel that the decision on if I continued to breathe was in someone else's hands beside my own. Instead of getting outta the M.C., I continued with it and allowed the monster inside of me free roam, why the fuck not? Until you."

I hugged at my own body, the confession making my head spin. How did I respond to that when I needed to say so many different things? "Your ass accidentally sat on my lap as I planned to fucking drink myself into a coma and all of a sudden I couldn't remember why I was drinking at all."

The lump in my throat was going to suffocate me if it didn't dislodge itself some point soon. "Why are you telling me all this?" I whispered to him as I took a step away from his body. I couldn't breathe, but I didn't know if it was because I needed to flee or because I needed him in order to get air into my lungs.

"Because I'm begging you to not give up on me, not you." I looked up into his icy eyes alarmed as the words left his mouth. How was I giving up on him? I never gave up on him. Everything I did, I did for him.

"I never did." I hiccuped back to him taking a step back into him and suddenly air was finding my lungs again.

"Yes you did, the second you walked out the door without even telling me. I just woke up, fighting for my damn life and all of a sudden the reason I was doing it was gone. I tried to fucking give up and Jess wouldn't let me." He sat on his bed, the only thing on his body was the soaking pair of boxers he had been trying to escape from. Now, it seemed, that he didn't even realize they were still on him soaking through his comforter.

"Every second of every single day I thought of you, I cried over you. I physically ached being away from you." He looked up at me from his slouched position over his knees before quickly looking back to the ground. "Everyday I wished that I was waking up next to you and every night I wished to be falling asleep in your arms. It hurt thinking about how safe you made me feel because of how scared I was. Every time I missed you and looked at my father I heard you screaming in agony from your back. I saw you on the floor dying in front of me with that fucking cross branded onto you." More tears began to fall as I moved closer to his hunched, sitting form.

"If you leave me again, I'll marry her. It won't be because of anything other than me finding a means to an end for my club. It'll stop the war. I will pack up that big ass house that has your ghost smeared all over it and leave it. Every ounce of my money will be divided between you, my mother, and Jess. And then, I will finally cease to exist." My stomach flew to my throat at his words as I kneeled in front of him between his knees desperately trying to find his face as it looked at the floor. My hands placed themselves on his knees. "Because I know what it feels like to live with you and then without you and I won't do that again. I won't live with that agony inside my body because I won't have the strength this time. I won't live without you again." His face looked down to mine when he was finished. I hadn't realized that I had wedged myself between his legs so I was under his head.

I expected rage filled eyes to cast me a warning, but all I was met with was a pair of blue eyes that were so glossy they looked like glass. I could see the little pools of liquid that was gathering at the bottom of them, solely being held up by the lid under his eyes. His eyes and the feeling of his body trembling under mine was enough to feel my whole existence rip into two.

You did this, Catalina, you.

All of this is your fault.

I sniffled as my hands found both sides of his face and my thumbs wiped under his eyes. Never in my life had I seen such an intimidating, large, strong man cry before. To have me be the culprit of it all was even worse. This hatred bubbled in me as I realized it was pointed at myself. This man was the world to me and for some reason I thought that it wouldn't affect him if I wasn't in his. My arms wrapped around his neck as he pulled my body into his embrace. His face finding the nook of my neck as my own face disappeared into his. "I love you." I whispered into his skin as I felt him squeeze at me. His grip was so tight that if he went any tighter surely my body would break.

"Then stay." His broken whispered from behind my hair sent another round of tears to my eyes. He didn't realize that I belonged to him and nothing was ever going to change that. "But I need you to decide, not right now either. Not while you feel guilty because of my own emotions. Just know, that if you decide to go that's it and if you decide to stay you're never leaving me again."

~

Reaper had wanted me to wait three days before considering the decision that I wanted to give him. Three days to decide if I was staying or going. Those were needed because my mind couldn't stop all the scenarios that were popping up in my head. We had been sleeping separately, per his request, due to the fact that I hadn't decided yet. He had told me that he didn't want to remember what it felt like to sleep with me in his arms. The girls and I were camped out in the living room area of this huge mansion due to everyone else being in their room. The girls had grabbed parts of the couch, but due to the fact that I was the last to arrive I was on an air mattress.

Alex had been blowing up my phone telling me that it was time to come home because he missed me. There was a huge storm coming and if I waited any longer to get traveling than I was going to be stuck here for god knows how long. My father was missing in action so far, I hadn't heard from him. My mother on the other hand was begging for me to come home. She called me about three times a day pleading with me to return. So far, I had done an okay job of convincing them that I hadn't gone back to Robbie; although I wasn't sure if they were just pretending to believe me.

A strange thud came from below the floor, that was funny. The club house had a basement, but it wasn't big enough to reach under the room I was in. I rose from my mattress and made my way to the basement door that was behind the stairs. The cement floor was cold against my bare feet and sent a shiver up my spine. At first glance, there was no door down here to lead to another room, but I could still hear the very faint thudding. I moved to the wall that it was coming from and as I placed my ear against it a small sliver of it cracked open. My spine straightened as I adjusted Robbies T that was covering my body and my boy-shorts. I wasn't sure why I had come down here, but I had needed to know.

Curiosity killed the cat was the saying and I definitely wasn't ready for what was behind that secret door.

Chapter Thirty-Six

I slipped into the darkness that was the hideaway room in the basement to be met with a long candle lit hallway. Rooms lined the hall on either side with shut or cracked doors. There was one room at the very end of the hallway that was cracked with a light on. For some godforsaken reason I advanced towards it. Jess' name caught my eye on the door, that was weird.

My eyes were met with a women's wide open legs. There was a large pink diamond filling her entrance and visible juices covering her womanhood. When my eyes traveled up her, her head was in between another women's legs who was straddling her face. Jess was above her face also taking the middle women from behind... in her ass. My hands flung to my eyes as it was all too much to look at. When I tried to flee a hand grabbed my biceps and pulled me back.

"Catalina what are you doing down here?" Jess voice was concerned as if I hadn't just walked in on him.

"A noise woke me up, I was curious." I mumbled from behind my hands.

"Have her join us." One of the women's voice met my ears. I started furiously shaking my head no, I was all set with that.

"I'm just gonna go back upstairs." I went to run again and Jess grabbed me.

"Catalina, you cant. Let me call Rob and he'll come get you."

"It's fine I can just walk myself back upstairs!" I peaked at his face from behind my hands. The phone was already to his ears and he placed it on speaker.

"What's up?" Robbies sleepy voice filled the room and I couldn't stop myself from picturing his furrowed eyebrows and grumpy face from being woken.

"I need you to come get Catalina from the basement." I heard the covers fly off him and his footsteps as he exited his room. Jess hung up his phone as he sat on the edge of the bed.

It took him maybe a minute before he was in front of me. His eyes briefly looked over my outfit as mine landed in his boxers and bare chest. "Did you see anyone else down here?" He looked around the room at the other people before bringing me closer.

I shook my head no "Nope, just way too much is Jess.", I shivered as the visual came back to me. That was something I wasn't going to be able to get out of my head. Robbie nodded as he looked me over once more.

"Okay, were gonna go back upstairs."

"What is this place?" I glanced out the door and into the hallway before I was yanked back.

"Curiously killed the cat, Cat." He hissed as he tugged at his shirt that was on my body. "Maybe I'll just carry you." He whispered almost to himself.

"Listen to me, do not look anywhere but the ground when we walk back out there. In fact, keep you eyes entirely closed and look to the ground."

"Why?" I scrunched my eyebrows together.

"I'll explain when we get upstairs." I nodded my head as he grabbed my hand and glanced out the doorway. He told me to close my eyes as I allowed him to lead me out into the darkness.

"Go quick." Jess ordered as we exited the room.

The hallway was quiet and I could all but feel the darkness of it on my skin. Robbie had my hand in a death grip as he led me away from Jess room. Yet, I didn't listen and I opened my eyes and glanced up.

Almost immediately a hand from behind was tugging at my shirt. I yelped and jumped closer to the protection I had. Robbie instantly turned and brought me into his arm as the other shoved at the hand. "She's not open, fuckhead. Piss off." He hissed as he shoved the other man away from us. With one large swoop, his arm was under both my knees and I was in the air. My arms instantly locked around his neck to make sure my body had some support. His heavy footsteps stormed up the stairs and roughly kicked the door closed behind him.

A yawn took over my body as he walked up out of the room and up the flights to his own. I was gently placed on his bed before he released his grip on my body. "I'm sorry," he began as his fingers gripped at the back of his neck. "You weren't suppose to ever find that place."

"What is that place?" I mumbled as I shuffled myself into the warmth, whiskey and chocolate smelling, sheets. They smelt of him and it made my heart flutter as I took in deeper breathes to breathe in more. He shook his head at me, his universal sign of him not about to open up to me. "You don't get to not tell. I was just snagged by some strange man I couldn't even see because of this sketchy place."

His jaw tightened as he looked down at his hands, coming to sit beside me in his bed. The expression of his face was one of shame and it had me questioning if I really wanted to know what that place actually was. "It's for the Dominants and Subs, you don't go down there unless you're planning on taking on the role of one or the other. Normally, people don't go down there and come back up without either getting fucked or fucked."

"So, it's some creepy sex dungeon." Even more shame washed over his face as he quickly glanced at me. He nodded his head as he swallowed whatever was stuck on his throat. "Your name was on one of those doors, Robbie." I whispered to him as I tried to catch his eye. He wouldn't look at me and I couldn't pinpoint why. He nodded once more as he sighed.

"Every guy that wants one has his own room, but you have to first be accepted in. There's a contract involved and rules. Any women that walks down there is pretty much fair game unless she's claimed by someone. If a guys in his room he can snag whoever walks down there."

"What if you don't want to do anything with who you get snagged by?" My skin began to crawl, I had been snagged when he was with me and it still wasn't the easiest to get out of. I had walked down there, taking my sweet time, the first time by myself... what would have happened if I had been snagged then?

He shrugged, "Most women don't really care who they get snagged by when they walk down there. New comers get a bracelet so the men know that they're in the process of joining. There's rules for those types of things, but a women without a bracelet down there tells the guys she doesn't care who snags her. Each room has a color. If women go down there only looking for a certain guy or so they wear their colors. If a women goes down there and she belongs to one guy, she wears a special collar given to her by the guy. If a women down there is wearing a collar and you want to snag her you have to get permission from the man who's collar it is."

"So I was-" I was gonna freak out.

"You were open season down there on your own." He glanced at me from under his lashes as he grabbed at my hand. "Catalina, this isn't a house you just go exploring in. There's many levels of this club, some of which you do not belong on." He sighed as he pushed my hair out of my face.

"Why was your name on the door? Why haven't you tried to bring me down there?" How many women had he had in that room? Why hadn't he wanted to bring me into that room before? Why hadn't I at least been made aware of it?

"Baby don't," He looked away from me. I wanted to know, no, I needed to know.

"Tell me." My back straightened as I waited for whatever his answer was going to be.

"I used to use my room down there." He whispered out. "I haven't even touched it since I met you."

"How many women have you had down there?" This was the only man I had even been with and I was just finding out that he had taken part in some sec dungeon shit.

He shrugged his shoulder, "Not an alarming amount. There was clearly regulars."

"Did you ever claim anyone?"

He shook his head, "That wasn't what I was looking for when I went down there. It was to blow off steam and shit. It never meant anything to me and all the women knew that."

"Why haven't you ever brought me down there?" I whispered to him, did I want to know the answer? "If this is apart of you, why haven't you tried to involve me in it?"

"Because you mean more to me than what happens in that room. That room doesn't deserve to see what we have together. That part of me isn't a man that deserves to have you. I don't want to be that person with you..." He trailed off. "Even if you wanted to go down there, you couldn't."

"Why?" My eyebrows scrunched together. What was so wrong that I couldn't do that for him. Clearly, it's what he likes.

"You aren't trained, you aren't allowed to be down there unless you sign something saying you're being trained."

"Have you-"

He nodded, "Yes, I've trained subs before."

"Candy?"

"She was one of my regulars."

"So the video of the girl that some of the club wanted you to marry?"

"Yes, I would have taken her down there."

"So you would have taken her, but not me." I wasn't questioning it.

"Cat, that women would have never slept in my bed. Any physical inter-action I had with her would have been in that room. She wasn't mine and never would have been. Since getting that room, I haven't slept with anyone outside of it besides you. You either want my bedroom or that room. You can't have both. Those are two very different people. I didn't even go by that name when I was in that room. Hell, I was gonna give that room to someone else."

"But those are both versions of you." I was trying to understand.

"Come with me." I grabbed his hand after I slipped on the sweatpants that he had handed to me. He lead me back the way we had previously come and into the darkness. Before fully entering it he popped open a drawer of a desk that was in the room and slipped a black bracelet around my wrist. I looked over to see all the bright colors shinning through the drawer, why was his black? "It's because I train and if they had wanted out they had to safe word. They thought I was one of the most aggressive and strict."

A women was coming up and out of the door when she walked in on our conversation. "Black bracelet, good luck sweetheart. I heard he reaps your body, mind, and soul in that room." I glanced between the two of them. Slowly, I moved closer into his side as he grabbed my hand and opened the door to lead me down the stairs. I saw a hand reach out before stopping in mid-air. They had seen the bracelet and the man with me. Something told me no women was worth taking on the beast beside me.

With a sigh he unlocked the door that read 'Reaper' and pushed it open for my eyes. A gentle hand on my lower back pushed me into the darkness of the room before him. He must have not wanted me in the hallway by myself. I heard his footsteps move closer behind me before dim lights flickered on. As the objects in front of me came into view my breathe got stuck in my throat. My arms protectively wrapped around myself as I took in the room. Structures with chains and leashes, ropes, objects, all things that I had never seen. This man had Christian Grey beat by a long shot. There was no bed, no carpet. Everything was cold and hard. This room held no love whatsoever, it smelt of sex and anger and dominance. The atmosphere was so heavy that in the dim light I was even a little afraid of the man that I loved. His entire demeanor had changed since we stepped into this room and even he was a little unsteady with it.

"I don't like seeing you in here." He whispered from behind me. "You're too good to be down here." He grumbled as he grabbed my arm and pulled me towards the door. I watched as the lights flicked off and he locked it behind us. I watched in shock as he grabbed the slides of the name on it and pulled until it fell to the floor. He walked me up the stairs and cut the bracelet off of me. My eyes followed as he threw it in the trash, shoved the keys in his pocket and walked away from me.

My feet quickly followed him back up to his room. When I walked in he was sitting on his bed in his boxers again. The sweatpants that he had thrown on were on the floor beside him. I shut the door behind me quietly as I met his eyes. "I need you to decide now, I can't wait any longer. I want to know if you belong to me or not because if you don't I need to try and figure my life out."

"My father-"

"Cut the shit, do you want to stay with me or not?" I moved towards him as he pulled at my waist. I grabbed at the sides of his neck and leaned down to gently kiss him. He pulled away from me, his eyes on my lips before flickering up to mine. "What do I have to do to make you stay with me?" My eyes drifted shut as I put my forehead to his.

I could hear him rummaging through something close beside us, but I was too focused on how I could tell this man he didn't have to do anything to keep me. I was already his and he didn't understand that. I just couldn't live with him hurt and it landing on my shoulders. He nudged me with his nose against my own before I opened my eyes. They caught his before traveling down to both his hands between our two bodies. My breathe caught in my throat as I took in the little velvet box that he was holding open for me. Sat perfectly inside of it was the most breathtaking diamond ring...

Chapter Thirty-Seven

C atalina's POV

How long had he had that thing for? Was he just showing me this thing that could be my future or was he being serious? Why would he want to marry me? "Make me mean something more than just some rugged biker. Make me have a home to come home to, a family. Make my life worth it by being the center of it. Make this fucking cross of my back worth it and be my wife. If it takes your father covering my body in scars then I'll do it and I'll enjoy every second of it because I'll come home to you. Let me protect you, sleep beside you, take care of you. I can't offer you much, in fact I don't really know how we got here to begin with, but I'll keep you safe. I'll do my best to keep you happy and healthy, I'll give you as many rotten kids as you want from me. There's so many reasons for you to say no to me right now and I know that, but I'm sitting here in my underpants asking the women of my dreams to be my wife because I don't want to wake up or fall asleep beside anyone else. I want my life to mean something and you're that something to me. You're the only women I've ever loved and with the few times I've tried the only one I ever will. I can't live without you, so please, be with me. I love you, Cat. Will you be my wife and stay with me?"

I wondered if he could feel my hands shaking against his neck or see the tears that were welling in my eyes. I watched as he licked his lips and gently bit down on his bottom one, his chest heaving and falling. His eyes were desperately searching mine and I couldn't find the words to describe to him how much I loved him. My eyes couldn't look away from the ring and I didn't know how much time had passed, but I panicked as I felt him slightly move away from me and his fingers go to close the box. "You're gonna close it before putting it on my finger?" I whispered between us. His chest fell completely as my eyes went to meet his. "Put the thing on my finger so I can say I'm gonna be your wife." I smiled softly as his eyes closed and he pushed against my face until he was kissing me.

"Say it." He whispered as he pulled away from my lips.

"Yes Robbie, I'll marry you." My hands shook as he slipped the ringer onto my finger and pulled me so I was straddling him. Icy blue eyes sparkled at me as a smile broke across his face, "I thought you were gonna say no." He whispered to me.

I shook my head, "My fathers gonna skin you alive."

A devilish smile broke across his face that was almost sinister like he enjoyed the idea of being skinned. This man was something else, "I'd like to see him try." I nodded my head, oh I'm sure he would.

My hands slipped down his bare chest as I looked over every aspect of him. His hands were on my hips as he slowly turned us around so that I was laying under him. Rough fingertips traced my skin as they pushed every article of clothing off of me. His lips followed the path of his fingers before he came up and met my mouth. "I'm so in love with you." He whispered to me as he pushed his way in filling me to the brim. I gasped as I looked into his eyes, "I love you too." He was slow and sensual tonight. I suppose it had something to do with popping the big question and getting the answer he wanted. There was no rushing, just the two of us and not another care in the world.

I was getting married. I was engaged to the only man that I had ever allowed inside of me and he was going to be the last. I never thought that it would end up like this. I looked him over as he kissed over my collarbones. He was mine and I couldn't believe it. He was perfect, everything I had been looking for without even knowing.

I came as I felt his hot seed shoot into me. His eyes came to meet mine and he brushed my hair away from my face. He pulled out and rolled to his back side me pulling me into his side to nuzzle into him. My eyes were slowly shutting as I looked over at the clock to read that it was four in the morning. His fingers were running through my hair as his stomach grumbled. "I'm gonna go get something to eat, do you want anything?"

I shook my head no as he quietly slipped out of bed and threw some sweatpants on. As I heard the door shut behind me, my hand came up before my face to examine my ring. It was oval and the entire thing sparkled as it moved different ways. The entire band was covered in small diamonds that individually glistened.

My hand fell down to the pillow I was resting my head on as I left my eyes close and I quickly drifted off to sleep.

~

The next morning I woke up to Robbie sleeping deeply beside me. His chest was bare and the sheets were covering him from the waist down. The morning sun caught my ring and brought my attention back to it. My breath caught in my throat. This was really happening to me, this was real and it wasn't a dream. I brought one of my hands up and lightly placed it on the cheek that wasn't against the pillow as Robbie faced me fast asleep.

Slowly, I slipped out from under the sheets and headed into the bathroom to take a quick shower before going downstairs. I threw on the same clothes that I had on the night before and made my way to the kitchen after my shower was done. Reaper was fast asleep in bed after I had gotten out and I decided to let him sleep.

The girls were sitting around the table having coffee when I walked in in my sweats. All heads turned towards me as I entered abruptly. I sent them a small smile as I poured myself my own cup of coffee and added cream and sugar to it. Heavier footsteps walked into the kitchen before I had the chance to turn around. Strong arms went under my arms to wrap themselves around my torso and squeeze me. "Hi baby," A hot whisper hit my cheek as Reaper kissed at my ear and neck. I turned in his arms and placed my hands on his chest to give him a good morning kiss. My skin pressed partially against warm skin and a cold zipper of his sweatshirt. He kissed me good morning before getting himself his own cup of coffee.

My fingers wrapped around the warm mug as I turned towards the beaming girls at the table. "Oh my god!" Rose jumped from her seat and quickly moved towards me. Grace grabbed my coffee mug from me as Rose grabbed my hand and put her face to it. A smile breaking across my face as the girls squealed and jumped around with each other. The warm smile of Robbie greeted me as I looked towards him glowing. "You guys are getting married!" Grace looked towards me with tears in her eyes. I nodded my head furiously as my eyes drifted between my ring and my friends. All of this felt like a fairy tale.

All the gushing settled down quickly as Reaper went to go have a meeting with Jess in his office and I sat down with the girls for breakfast. "How are you going to tell your parents?" I shrugged my shoulder. I didn't have the answer to that yet, but I knew that I would eventually have to break the news to them. The questions came one after the other before the phone in my pocket starting going off. I took it out of my pocket without truly looking at the I.D and answered it.

"Hello?" I beamed into the phone.

"Catalina." Alex's furious tone send a shiver down my spine. The beautiful bubble that I had been in was just officially popped and I didn't know if I was going to get it back.

I gulped as I answered, "Alex, hows it going?" Instantly, the girls went dead silent as they all shared a glance. The bubble that they had been in had also just been busted and they knew that I was in some deep shit. Rose glanced towards the stairs that Robert had disappeared from before her eyes were back on my phone. Grace mouthed to me to put it on speaker so they could hear what he was saying. My eyes rolled as I took the phone away from my ear and placed it on speaker before resting it on the kitchen table.

"I'd be a hell of a lot better if my women was home where she belongs with mc." He all but seethed through the line. The mere thought of him near me made my skin crawl. There was no way that he didn't suspect something going on by now, I had been gone too long. "You need to come home, now."

"I know that and I am soon, I just was so worried about the girls..." I trailed off as I looked up at the table for some help. What was I suppose to say to him. There were no more excuses that he'd believe and he was already pissed.

"Don't give me that, Catalina. Your father is riding my ass about me getting you home so you need to come home now. Get your shit, put it in your car, and get on the road now. I can't give him anymore excuses as to why you aren't here yet." His pacing footsteps from the other line were heavy enough that I was able to hear them. "Cat, I'm trying here my love." The girls faces scrunched up as they listened to him speak. "I know that you're going through your own thing and I'm trying to give you the space that you need, but understand that I need to draw some lines. I promised your father that I would take care of you and I can't do that if you're this far away from me. Please babe, come home."

I felt his presence before I saw it, even the girls shifted in their seats before they could figure out why. He came in like a predator stalking its prey. I didn't even know that he was there until he was in front of me gently taking my face into one of his hands as he crouched in front of my car. He was silent as he listened to another man beg me to come home to something that wasn't mine. The girls all eyed him widely as they awaited his next move. Ever so slowly, his other hand tapped the screen of my phone so that he could see the options and hung up on Alex as he was mid beg. Once the line was dead he grabbed the other side of my face with his now unoccupied hand.

"Let me make one thing clear, my love, he's gone. This game that you have been playing with him in order to keep your father happy is over." I nodded my head as he brought my face to his and gently laid a kiss on my forehead, nose, and lips in a line. The phone on the table rang once more and 'Alex' popped up on the screen. Rose licked her lip to try and hide the smile that was crossing her face. Little did the girls know that Robbie couldn't hold the beast back any longer. I sat quietly as he clicked answer on my phone and then hit speaker.

"Catalina, did you just hang up on me?" Alex was fuming on the other end.

A sinister smile crossed Reapers face as he leaned over the phone. His knuckles whitened as they pressed against the table, his frame towering over all of us. "No, she didn't."

"Who-"

"This play is over. The women that you call your own and beg to come back to you doesn't belong to you and never has. Catalina is mine, you must be pretty dense considering you haven't gotten that through your head yet. She won't be coming back to you. Every moment with her was a lie and you were just too fucking stupid to realize it. Now, listen to me very closely. You're going to go get her father and you're going to put this phone on speaker." His ice blue eyes dashed towards me as he moved closer to my side.

"This is for you." We all heard from the other end.

"Hello?" My fathers deep voice seeped through the phone as filled the room we were in. It made me nervous as I glanced up at my love.

"Let me make myself clear. Catalina is with me by her own free will and here she will stay. In fact, I've just made her my fiancé. I'm sure that just tickles you pink doesn't it?" My father stumbling over his words from rage was evident. "You can send all your men, you can give me everything you've got, you may even make some leeway, but you will never win this. Catalina is mine and I'll make sure that doesn't change if it's the last thing I do. Be prepared to loose whoever you send after us because you are never going to get t her."

"I'll kill you." My father threatened as I tightened my grip on Reaper's arm. He meant it.

"I'd like to see you try. The choice is yours. You can do as you please, my men and I will be ready with whatever you decide." Robert smiled from ear to ear, some part of him secretly loved this. He loved the hunt and the satisfaction of the kill.

"You better-" He hadn't gotten anymore words in before Reaper cut him off.

"Oh and I'd bring a bigger cross this time." He clicked the end button and shoved the phone across the table away from us. Worry laced through me at his interaction, it was out in the open. There were no more games, they knew that I had gone back to him and they were going to react to it. They had come after us before and nothing was going to stop them from doing it again. My fingers gripped Robbie's sleeve as he rose to his full height. The girls were just gapping at the two of us.

"Rob-" He cut me off as he looked down at me, my face between his hands.

"There is nothing to be worried about, baby girl. He can give it all he's got, he won't be able to touch me this time or you. You are mine and no ones gonna take you away from me." His lips brushed mine before he rose and left the room to go and find Jess, he needed to be aware of what could be coming.

My attention turned towards the girls who were either looking at me or looking after Robbie. "I think I just wet my pants." Rose mumbled to the room.

"He's not bad, he's not that scary typically either." I grumbled.

"Oh no, don't take this the wrong way, I wasn't scared. I'm saying I think I just came in my pants." I shook my head at her as I looked towards the now empty stairs. What had just been started? My eyes caught my ring once more as I looked towards it and the girls directed their attention to it. Holy shit I was getting married.

Grace spoke this time, "Jesus girl, you're getting fucking married."

Chapter Thirty-Eight

Catalina's POV

It had been three months since that phone call and I had been on edge ever since. Besides that, things had calmed down a significant amount. Robbie and I were trying to decide if we would be moving out of the clubhouse anytime soon. It was a difficult decision with the girls still staying here due to safety reasons. Personally, I think that they had just started to like it here and didn't really want to leave.

I was sitting in the kitchen as Jess cooked dinner, he was talking away as he added mushrooms to the stir-fry. It was almost instantaneous, as soon as the sizzling oil hit the mushrooms and the smell of the them wafted into the air I was on my feet and moving. My palm covered my mouth as I b-lined it for the nearest bathroom. Robbie happened to be an object that I went rushing by on the way and before I could protest he was on my heels. My hands grabbed the toilet bowl as I kneeled down in front of it, my hair being caught in a big calloused hand. The contents of my stomach emptied themselves into the bowl before I could try and keep them down. A soothing hand rubbed circled around my back as they allowed me to finish before a damp wash clothes was wiped around my face and I was lifted from under the arms.

Rob secured my balance on my feet before turning me around and giving me a head to toe once over. "You look fine, do you think you're done?" I nodded my head as I went under the sink to grab the mouthwash that was stored under there. The swishing in my mouth made me dizzy before I spit the blue liquid into the sink and rinsed out my mouth with cold water. Robbie grabbed a dry towel from beside him and handed it to me before brushing my hair to the side. His eyebrows raised in question, the only response I had for him was to shrug my shoulders.

Instead of returning to the kitchen, we went to the living room to sit on the couch and watch a film before dinner. My mind was racing over the fact that I had gotten sick and was trying to pinpoint why exactly that it had happened. Rob sat dozing beside me before we were called to the kitchen to eat what had been prepared for us. I had seated myself before any food was placed in front of me with Robbie's hand on my thigh under the table. Again, it was instant. As soon as Jess walked into the room with the food in his hands I was on my feet and lunging towards the bowl again. Reaper was in the exact same spot and we repeated the moment in the exact manner. This time when I was finished and wiping my mouth dry Robbie leaned against the bathroom door, "What's the deal? Was it the same thing twice?" I nodded my head at him, "Those mushrooms man, they really got to me I guess." He nodded his head as we both got to our feet and moved out of the bathroom, "Maybe you're just getting sick..." He trailed off as his eyes nervously flashed towards me.

The rest of the night was quiet which was something I was thankful for. The days following also were. I couldn't place my finger on it, but my skin was crawling for some unusual reason. Something was about to go down and it was like I was waiting for the other shoe to drop. My feet quietly pattered back into the bedroom to find Robbie still fast asleep in the early morning sun. The rays reflecting off the snow covered ground made the room extra bright this morning. The bile taste in my throat was still bothering me as I went over and looked at myself in the mirror. Nothing seemed off, but I still wasn't feeling myself every since those mushrooms. Maybe Robbie was right, I was just coming down with something and it was slowly fucking with my system.

I walked down to the girls as they sat around the kitchen table as they always did. The only one that was still sleeping here was Rose, Robbie had set the other two up in an apartment close by. For some odd reason, Rose had stuck around and was very serious about staying in the club house. Robbie had made the decision to buy another house instead of going back to the previous one, he wanted one that was ours and one that I had a say in. Personally, I think it had something to do with the fact that other M.C's knew that it was The Reaper's house. A sigh escaped my mouth as I leaned agains the counter and faced the girls, a full coffee mug in my hand. They were talking about the couple that we had all went to the wedding for, they were now expecting their first child.

"No," I trailed off as I looked down into my coffee mug and placed a hand over my stomach. No, it wasn't possible. We had been safer than that. My eyes glanced at my ring as it all fell into place. I wasn't coming down with anything...

"What's up?" Grace glanced at me as I dumped the coffee down the sink and leaned back into my original position.

"Nothing, I just need to run to the store. Anyone want to come with?" I shrugged my shoulders as I grabbed my phone from my pants. It was a text from my mother begging me to come back. Immediately, I tucked it away.

The girls shook their head and told me that they were planning on heading home soon. I nodded at them as I walked back up the stairs to the bedroom. Robbie was sitting up in bed when I walked in and instantly my body heated at the image. Boxers and bedsheets covered him as the rest of his body stayed exposed to the morning air and I. The second I walked through the door a sultry smile washed over his scruffy face and I was moving towards him. "I don't like waking up without you." He huffed as he shuffled to the other side and rested on his knees, pulling me in and up onto the mattress with him.

"I'm sorry, I was downstairs with the girls." I whispered the white lie to him as his mouth caught mine. What woke me up this morning was bile rising up my throat and me rushing to the bathroom, what I did afterwards was go see the girls in the kitchen.

"Excuses," He teased as he flipped our positions and pinned me under him. My heart rate rapidly rose as the excitement washed over me in a wave of heat. Hands were pulling at my pants before I had anything else to say to him and I was engulfed in the pleasure that rushed through my body. His mouth was on me, hot against my skin as he lapped between my legs. Teeth nipped at my lips before he sucked me into his mouth, my back arching at the intense feeling.

"Robbie," I hissed as his tempo sped up as I got closer. My fingers knotted themselves in his hair as my body snapped for him. As my vision came back to me, he was still between my legs and nipping at my inner thighs. His crooked smile was looking up at me as he came up my length to kiss me.

"I'm gonna jump in the shower." He kissed me before getting up and discarding the rest of his clothes.

"Wait!" I begged at him, what did he mean? "Where are you going?" I leaned up on my elbows to get a better look at him.

Once again, he flashed me his smile. "Decided that I haven't heard you beg me in a while and decided I needed to." His shoulders shrugged as he went into the bathroom and got into the shower without another word. I threw myself back onto the bed as I squirmed, I wanted more of him. My eyes closed as I prepared myself for how he was going to be pushing my body. This game he played with me always had me in a soaking wet mess begging for him to fuck me. My eyes rolled as I told myself that was exactly what he wanted. Fine, two could play at that game.

"I need to go to store." I called into him as I put my pants back on and straightened myself out.

His voice was muffled from the shower, "I'll come with you." I went to tell him that it was alright and I'd go by myself but he spoke first, "I mean it Catalina."

I waited on the bed patiently for him to be done and get dressed so that we could go. The nearest store was a ways away, but when we got there I sent him to go get some other things while I got what I needed alone. I didn't want him to know. This was something I had to do on my own until I knew for sure. It took some convincing, but after a few moments I convinced him that nothing was going to happen to me while I was an aisle away.

The cashier glances at me as she held out her hand for money, I quickly handed it to her and shoved the thing in my pocket. I went to find Robbie in food section looking over the miniature white powdered donuts. "They didn't have what I was looking for." I whispered as I walked into his side. He nodded his head as he walked away from the food and we headed out of the store.

I scurried off when we got back to the club house and headed into the bedroom. Jess caught Robbie's attention on the way and the two headed off into the office to discuss club stuff. The girls were no where to be seen so with the little time I had to myself I was going to do what I needed to.

I waited ten minutes before looking and something washed over me that I wasn't prepared for...

They everyone, I'm sorry for the wait. This chapter is shit but I promise the next one will be better. I kind of just wanted this chapter to be over with. Let me know what you guys think she's up to.

Chapter Thirty-Nine

C atalina's POV

Two little blue lines.

Panic was washing over me as I stared at them. My eyes couldn't pull away from the stick and I wanted to run. I wanted to run until my legs gave out and let my body fall into the ground. There was no way, this wasn't happening. I wanted my mom.

He was going to be pissed, this wasn't what he wanted. Hell, I didn't even know if this is what I wanted.

Tears rushed to my eyes and fell down my cheeks as I wrapped the stick in toilet paper and threw it away under the sink. I looked up into the mirror and wiped the tears from my face and pulled myself together. How long could I keep this from him?

The noise coming from downstairs had me turning around and exiting the bathroom I was locked away in. Heavy footsteps were running up the stairs when I was out of the bedroom door and Robbie's running figure came into my vision. He grabbed my bicep and rushed me back into the bedroom where he locked the door. I went to open my mouth before his hand came over it and he whispered to me, "Your fathers sent people to come and get you." My eyes bugged out as I looked up into his blue ones. This wasn't happening.

"How are we gonna get outta here?" I whispered once he removed his hand and let me speak. "What's happening downstairs?"

"The guys are holding down the fort." He whispered back to me. "They aren't going to get in here and if they do, I'm gonna get you out."

Another pair of footsteps came booking it up the stairs to bang on the door. "Reaper, you gotta go now!" Jess' urgent voice came through the wood. "They're gonna get in here and we can handle it, but they aren't gonna leave without her." I watched panic rush over Reaper's face as he looked at the door.

I looked down at the shoes I was wearing, thankfully sneakers. I had a feeling I was gonna have to run. Robbie looked back over to me and nodded as he grabbed my hand and pulled a gun from his waist band.

"They're here for me, people are gonna get hurt because of me." I hissed as he opened the door and Jess was waiting outside. He was holding a pair of car keys and motioned for Robbie to follow him. "Back staircase, the cars waiting."

I didn't realize something was off until it was too late.

We were already down the stairs and in the car when I looked outside to Jess and saw his body jolt. His left leg giving out as a bullet whizzed through it. "Somethings wrong." I whispered and when I looked to the driver seat Robbie had his eyes closed. I gulped as I looked to the back of the driver headrest to see a gun directly against it. The older gentlemen from the club was sitting behind Robbie on the other end.

"Bobby, you don't want to do this." Robbie warned as his hands gripped the steering wheel.

"I gave you plenty of warning, I tried to convince you to marry her." I looked between the two.

"Just let me take her somewhere safe and then the two of us can handle this."

"Drive." Robbie shoot his head as he put the car in drive.

"So you're a rat." Robbie seethed as he glanced in the rearview mirror.

"I wouldn't say that." Bobby hissed back to him.

"You're working with the other club then if you want me to marry her. That makes you a rat. So tell me, what does this have to do with Catalina? Let me bring her somewhere and then we can handle this between the two of us, she has nothing to do with this!" I couldn't stop my body from shaking as the two argued back and forth about this.

"Juan has a place he asked me to take her."

"I thought this was about her father coming!" His face was redder than I'd ever seen. This was going down hill fast.

"Her father will be informed that we have her." Bobby responded as he continued to give Robbie directions to wherever we were driving. My eyes stayed locked on his face as I tried to read his emotions. He was beat red and breathing heavily as his eyes went in and out of focus of the road. I'd never seen him this way before; for once, Robbie was panicking. There wasn't enough time to figure out a plan and he was cut off from all communication to his club. As far as we knew Jess was still bleeding on the gravel.

His eyes caught mine as he tried to get my attention. The flickering of his eyes to the handle of my door was confusing. What did he want from me? My eyes followed his hand that was closest to the door and he gently grazed the door handle and the lock. The car was locked, but if he pulled his it would unlock all the doors. My head scrambled as it tried to keep up with his nonverbal instructions, what did he want. His eyes widened as he glanced at my own door and me.

He wanted me to jump.

The Reaper wanted me to tuck and roll out of a moving vehicle going way too fast.

Little did he know...

He nodded once at me. A command. He was telling me to do it, it wasn't an option. I began shaking my head, he didn't understand. He thought I was just scared, but he didn't understand what he was asking of me. My eyes shot to the entrance of the freeway that we were heading towards. As we advanced up the ramp our speed slightly increased.

He nodded again.

And once more.

His eyes were begging me as he refused to merge out of the right hand lane. Bobby was getting agitated in the backseat as he told him to get into the fast lane. "Catalina now!" he screamed towards me as my hand grabbed the handle and I braced for the impact of the concrete.

The screeching of tires filled my ears as the cars that were behind us came to stop in order to avoiding my rolling body. I could feel the warm liquid of blood beginning to rush down numerous parts of my body. Maybe I was in shock, but when I rose from the ground and put my hands in front of me to brace for the impact of getting hit I didn't really feel anything. An older women got out of the passenger seat of the car that had almost destroyed me and quickly rushed me. As her hands grabbed my shoulders my knees buckled and I dropped to the floor. My vision as black as I vaguely saw the driver come to my side and put his phone to his ear.

"Car." I mumbled to them as I saw the SUV stop miles ahead of us.

The women looked up confused as she began to panic. "Get her in the car honey, quickly." She rushed her husband as he lifted my shattered body into his arms and rushed me into the backseat. They immediately got into their spots and ripped into the left lane in order to avoid the man running towards us. I was able to see out the window when we drove past the SUV. Robbie was still in the front seat, but this time he was covered in blood and his eyes were shut.

Chapter Forty

R obbie's POV

My vision came to as my eyes took in the room around me. Metal was biting at my wrists from the sides of me and I realized then that my hands were chained. The room was wet and cold as I kneeled on the ground, my shoulder throbbing as the muscles were stretched. The bullet wound would heel, but they had done a shitty job wrapping it.

"Fuck," I whispered under my breath as I looked at my figure solely clad with boxers. Panic suddenly surged through me as I scanned the room for Catalina. She was safe, she had jumped like she had been told. For once, she actually followed my order without giving me any lip.

The door swung open as the same man I had had a meeting with entered the room: Juan. "Did you really think I was gonna let you get to her?" I snickered as he circled my body silently.

"Very bold order you gave her, her jumping from a moving vehicle." He chuckled as he came before me and kicked at my knees.

"I know what she can handle and what she can not." I hissed up to him, venom seething into my voice.

"I'll be sure to tell her father you had her jump; I'm sure he'll reprimand her when he finds her."

"You'll never get that close to her again."

"Neither will you." He spit into my face, his daughter walked into the room and immediately began to whine, "Daddy, I told her to be gentle with him." She advanced towards me to move my hair from my face.

"My daughter here still wants you to wed her, I will give you once more to answer." I could feel her fingers drifting down my chest to my torso. They moved to my back and drifting gently across my scars as I squirmed away from her touch, it was nothing that I'd ever want.

"He has a cross." She gasped as she took in the appearance of the burns, it was most people's reaction. Most seem to think that it was on purpose, Catalina's the only one who looks at it with sadness in her eyes.

"I will never marry your daughter."

He sighed as he took in my position, "I was hoping that you were going to be smarter than your brother."

My eyes shot to meet his as I took in his words, "What did you just say about my brother?" A smirk cane across his face as he shrugged his shoulders and headed towards the door.

"Someone will be in shortly to see if they can change your mind."

"Let the torture begin." I seethed towards his back as he exited with his daughter in tow.

~

Catalina's POV

The nice couple had taken me directly to the closest hospital, but once the car was stopped I booked it away from them. I didn't have time for that and there would be too many questions. Hell, they might even try and involved the police and I couldn't let that happen. My phone was shattered, but I walked into a nearby store and asked them if I could use the phone. Thankfully they were nice and didn't care enough to question why I was in the state I was in.

Rose got here as fast as she could and then headed back towards the club. I wasn't exactly sure what I was getting myself into when I went back there, but it was the only place I knew to go. It was the only place I felt safe at this point. Plus, the club doctor would be able to look me over and make sure nothing was seriously wrong... maybe find out if I was still pregnant.

When we pulled up to the gates everything seemed to look intact, the guard was where he was suppose to be, and there were no firing sounds around. "Catalina, aren't you suppose to be with Reaper?" The guard leaned into the open window and looked me over with concern written across his face.

I nodded my head, "I need to see Jess." He nodded his head and opened the gate for us to get through. Once the car was parked we walked in and I headed immediately towards his office. The room was empty, but I noticed something that was slightly moved on the wall... the basement. I had never been to the clubs doctor before but Reaper had told me his place was one of the safest in the clubhouse because only club members knew where it was. If I had to guess, I would assume it was somewhere within the basement.

I walked behind Jess's desk to look through his drawers; the bracelets had to be in here somewhere and I wasn't going to venture down there without them. "What are you doing?" Rose asked from across the room.

"We can't go down there without bracelets." I grumbled as I got to the last drawer and they still weren't there.

'Why not? Go where?" Rose walked towards me.

My eyes glanced at the door and with a sigh I decided that it was more important to go find Jess than find bracelets. Wherever Jess was the doctor would be because of his leg. My eyes glanced to Rose, "You shouldn't come. Stay in the chair and I'll come back up and get you if I find what I'm looking for." She shrugged her shoulders as she went to sit behind the desk and I headed towards the basement. God help me, this needed to go smoothly.

It was pitch black per-usual, when I started to walk down I noticed that multiple rooms had a few lights on. Almost immediately, there was a hand grabbing my forearm and a hiss escaped my mouth. The adrenaline that was coursing through me was beginning to fade and I was realizing how badly my body hurt.

My eyes raced to the strange mans that was dragging me into his room. "Let go! I'm looking for Jess! I'm looking for Jess!" The man chuckled at my remark and continued to move my body. "I belong to Reaper!" Instantly, the grip on my arm dropped and he was looking at me directly.

"Go, please don't tell him that this happened. Jess is the last door on the right down the hall. It's right beside Reaper's."

I scurried away from him and booked it down the hall to Jess' room before anything else could happen. When I barged in he was laying on the bed with nothing but boxers on and some man was hovering over his wound. "Catalina?" His voice trailed off as I looked at him and dropped. My vision turned black and a buzzing noise in my head took over before I was out.

When I came back around I was in a different room, this time it was familiar to me, The Reaper's room. I looked around to find the same two men from before everything went black. Jess rushed to my side when he noticed my open eyes and grabbed onto my hand, "What happened?"

"Bobby was in the backseat. He's a rat and was working with Juan's M.C. Robbie made me jump from the car in order to get away. When we drove past him Robbie was covered in blood and his eyes were closed." As I spoke tears pooled in my eyes and slowly fell down my cheeks. Was he dead? If he wasn't dead, where was he? Jess nodded as he gently wiped one away and turned to the man behind him. "This is the clubs doctor Henry. He's gonna be taking care of you. I think it's safest to keep you down here until you're feeling better. I'll stay here with you." I nodded towards him as Henry gave me a small smile. Jess was down here because of his leg, but now I'd have to be down here too?

"How are we gonna find him?"

"We'll find him." He reassured me as he looked towards the doctor. "Go to sleep Catalina, you need to rest." I nodded my head as my head fell to the side and something washed over me.

"Hey Jess," I called to him before I was out again.

"Yeah?"

"I'm pregnant." I whispered as I let my eyelids close completely and sleep take me over.

~

Our hands were tied, there was nothing that we could do besides sit back and watch. Yet, nothing was getting accomplished because there wasn't really anywhere to start. I had began to heal enough that I could move around, but with his newfound knowledge of my condition, Jess wasn't letting me do all that much. He was unable to really move around because his leg was still healing, but against doctors orders he was walking around on it. I had been moved back up out of the basement and into Robbie and I's bedroom at the clubhouse. Jess was barking orders to try and have the other members find Robbie, but he was itching to do it himself. He had replaced my phone with a new one, keeping the same number incase anyone tried to reach me.

I was tired of waiting and knew that wherever he was, he wasn't safe. I walked over to the bedroom door and closed it before heading into the bathroom and doing the same. Scrolling through my contacts I found who I was looking for. Robbie was going to be livid with me...

"Hello?" His voice came through the line as I suddenly lost all my courage. "Catalina, I know it's you baby."

My mind scrambled, suck it up you're doing this for Robbie. "Hi," I whispered into the line. "I need you to come and get me."

"Where are you I'm on my way?" He sounded delighted with what I was asking of him.

"Only if we make a deal." My thumb twirled at my engagement ring on my finger as I waited for his answer.

"What's the deal?" I could hear his footsteps pausing.

"You come and get me and don't tell anyone you're doing it. You tell my father that you want him to get Reaper for you. Reaper gets moved to my father and mothers house where he's gonna stay untouched. Then you bring me to their house too and I come home." This was what needed to be done.

"What's in it for me?" I could hear the smile in his voice. I swallowed as the question came to my ears. What was in it for him? What would make this worth his wild?

"I get to come home to my father and mother and I'll talk to them about what needs to happen." I repeated.

"What's in it for me, Catalina? I'm not gonna come get you and bring you right back to your love. We have him right where we want him."

"What do you want Alex?" I hissed through the line.

"You." His voice sounded sinister coming through the phone.

"Do what I've asked and I'll send you my location when I have proof that it's done." Tears swelled in my eyes. This was the only way that I was going to get near Robbie. The M.C would never let the Devils Disciples get to him, they'd kill him before they let him return home. I needed to handle this myself. I should have known that they would never let me be with him. I should have protected him when I had the chance. I didn't even want to think about what they were doing to him right now. If nothing was being done then he would have been able to get away and get back here. The fact that he wasn't able to get himself out was a bad sign.

"Do we have a deal, Catalina?"

My eyes squeezed shut as I made a deal with the Devil. "Deal." I whispered into the phone as my fingers crossed over one another. Lord, let this play out as it has in my head.

Chapter Forty-One

Catalina's POV

When we arrived at the house my mother was waiting at the door. She held it open as she embraced me into a hug. Instantly, her eyes caught my ring finger and they looked to have began to water before she pulled herself together. The hug was one sided, at some point in time I had disconnected myself from this women and didn't want anything to do with her. How could this be? Alex's hand found the small of my back as he guided me into the house and shut the door behind him.

"What made you decide to come home?" My mother asked me as she up-downed my disheveled figure. "Did you realize you missed home?"

"No," I stated bluntly. I could feel how empty my stare was when I made eye contact with her. "I have never missed it here and never will. I'm here for one reason only."

I knew that I was about to break her heart and I couldn't find it in me to care. "What's that?" She asked meekly.

I swallowed as I looked around. "To end this." She nodded her head as she looked down at her hands.

"Well I'm happy you're home, I haven't seen you in so long. Your father will be thrilled when he gets home."

"It should have stayed that way." I huffed as I turned to Alex. "Where is he?"

"Here."

"I need to see him." The glare that was directed towards him was something that was out of my control. "Make sure you held up your half of the bargain." Alex glanced towards my mother before nodding his head. I followed him as he headed towards the basement, my mother on my heels. Numerous codes were typed in before we were even allowed access to the stairs leading down there. It was a maze in order to find the room that he was supposedly inside and when we were at the door I couldn't help the pit in my stomach. I wasn't ready for the rage that I was about to face at the fact that I was going to be standing in front of him.

"As you wish." Alex snickered as he unlocked the door and stepped inside of it. The room was filled with LED lights that made it painfully bright. It felt to be below freezing and it was wet. When my eyes found the center of the room he was there balancing his weight on the tips of his toes. His arms were tied tightly to the walls beside him and he looked to be stretched to the max. Yet, his head was held high as he looked down his nose at me. As soon as my face registered in his vision his head fell.

My feet were moving before I was able to even think about it and I was before his boxer clad skin that was caked in blood and sweat. Tears rushed to my eyes and quickly fell over once I placed my hands on his chest and peaked up from under him. Tears were seeping from his scrunched eyes as he tried to calm his breathing. My hand went to his cheek as I turned towards my mother and Alex, "Take him down now!" I seethed towards the two.

Pure joy was written across his face when he looked at me shaking his head. "Nope, he gets to stay exactly how he is. That's how your father wanted him."

"Do it or the deals off!" His eyebrows furrowed as I all but hissed at him. "Now." He shrugged his shoulders as he went to slightly lower the ropes so Robbie wasn't on his tippy toes. "All the way, let him sit."

"He goes right back when you're done here, but if it makes you happy princess." Alex went and stood back beside my mother who was silently blubbering.

Robbies knees buckled under him as he crashed to the floor, a groan leaving his mouth as his arms fell beside him. "You can't be here." He whispered to me as I grabbed his face with both hands and forced him to look at me.

I nodded my head, "I need to be. It was the only way to get to you."

I could see the rage slowly building within him, I had been expecting it. "You were safe. You should have never come here I would have been fine."

"No you wouldn't have, look at you." I whispered to him as his voice slowly began to rise.

"None of it mattered, you were safe and sound and they weren't going to be able to get to you. You don't get it Catalina, this isn't about me making it it's about you!" His chest was heaving as he leaned towards me. "You put yourself exactly where they wanted you to. What fucking deal did you make with him? Huh?" I lowered my eyes away from his, "Look at me." I couldn't. "Catalina, I gave you an order."

My eyes met his as his dominance raced through me. "I had him bring you here and in return I let him come and get me." My voiced trailed off and I shrunk as I waited for his response.

"You are mine." He seethed.

I nodded my head, "I know and you are mine and I couldn't get to you."

"That doesn't matter. How did you get Jess to allow you to leave?"

"It does matter! You are mine just as much as I am yours and you're in this because of me." His anger decreased as he took in my tears. "Look at you!" My arms rose up from his chest and wrapped around his neck as I buried my face in his neck. A sigh left him as he accepted the embrace. "Jess knows I'm here, we couldn't get to you." I whispered into his skin so that only he could hear. "Don't do anything okay, we just have to wait now." His head turned into my neck as he laid kisses from my ear down to my shoulder. "I thought it through this time." I whispered to him.

"That's enough." Alex huffed as he started to tighten Robbie's ropes again. As he began to stand I held onto him, he needed to know.

"I'm pregnant." I whispered before Alex grabbed me by the back of my shirt and yanked me away from him. His eyes were wide as he seemingly ignored the fact that he was currently back balancing his mass on the tops of his toes. The exit wound of his bullet being pulled and agitated as his arms were stretched. I could see the question in his eyes, not having to vocalize it in order for me to know what he was thinking. I nodded my head as another tear dripped down my cheek and the look of shock washed over him.

Alex slammed the door shut and shoved me back the way we came. My eyes glanced back towards it and then towards my mother who had tears streaming down her cheeks. Once we were back on the main floor of the house and the basement was securely locked the tears stopped. This was my plan and it was going to work. Alex pointed up the stairs, "Go to the bathroom and shower that piece of shit off of you." Do I obey or disobey? I didn't know which path would be the best bet. I wanted to keep the smell of him on me, but I looked down to notice that I was soaked in his blood. I grabbed my bag and headed up the stairs to what was designated as my bedroom, where Alex apparently was also sleeping. The bathroom door was securely locked before I even considered taking off my clothes. Once I was standing naked in front of the mirror my hand laid itself over my stomach, he knew.

He knew that I was pregnant and he couldn't react the way the would have in a different situation. I wondered if he would have reacted differently regardless. If he was possessive before I wondered what me carrying his baby would do to him. I made my shower as long as possible in order to try and avoid seeing anyone. My father was MIA, but I was sure that he'd be turning up at some point soon. The diamond ring on my finger glistened as I held it up against the light in order to look at it. There wasn't a shot that I was taking this thing off. What I wasn't prepared for the most was the grunts coming up from the vent. They had placed me in a room where I could hear them torturing him.

My feet pattered against the hardwood floor as I made my way back downstairs to the main level. My mother was alone in the kitchen cooking dinner, "Where's Alex?" I questioned her as I stood by the kitchen table.

Her shoulders tensed as she bowed her head. "He's busy."

"Busy downstairs?" I hissed towards her.

She nodded her head lightly before trying to return to her prep. "I pegged you for a better women." The venom in my voice was so thick that I also couldn't hear myself through it. A small sob exited her body.

"I can see it on you you know." She whispered over her stew.

"See what?"

"The glow." she turned towards me ashamed. "You're pregnant." My entire body tensed at her statement. She was just trying to gage my reaction she didn't actually know. "A women who has had a baby knows when another women is going to have one. I suggest that you somehow convince Alex it's his."

My eyebrows furrowed. "Excuse me?"

"You father will kill any offspring that is that mans downstairs, but he won't kill Alex's."

"Over my dead fucking body will your husband get anywhere near my baby. This baby is Robbie's and no other man is ever going to step foot in the role of father for it. You'll have to fucking kill me."

"It's for the best sweetheart, I understand what it's like."

She had tried to brush over this, but I caught it. "What do you mean you understand?" I advanced towards her. She shook her head and turned back towards the meal. "Who is that for?" I asked her.

"Us, love." She smiled towards me. I would bring up whatever she had said later on.

"Make me a bowl and I'll bring it down to Robbie."

Once again, she tensed. "He won't be eating this." She whispered as she served me some.

"Then what does he eat?" She shook her head, "You haven't fed him? Move!" I shoved by her and grabbed the full bowl and walking towards the door. "Open the door." I seethed towards her as she shook her head no. "I'm not asking."

She typed in the code and opened it for me, I walked down and retraced my steps to find his room. Banging on the door, Alex swung it open to reveal the room. Fresh blood was dripping down multiple parts of Robbie's body and Alex was livid that I was here, "What do you think you're doing?"

"I'm feeding him, get out."

"Who do you think you are coming here and barking orders at me. You should be kneeling to me." Alex's face was inches from mine as he spit at me.

"She will never." Reaper's voice filled the room with certainty.

I pushed by him and moved towards his strung up body. "Put him down." Within seconds, Robbie's body was lowering down. "You need to eat." I whispered to him as I lifted the spoon towards his mouth.

"You need to get out of here." I nodded my heads towards him.

"We both do." I continued to feed him until the bowl of stew was empty and there was nothing left for him to eat. Some dripped down his chin and I wiped it away with my thumb before gently laying a kiss on his lips. "Soon." I whispered.

"You need to go back upstairs before your father gets home." He whispered to me. "Get some sleep."

"I'm not gonna leave you down here."

He nodded his head, "Yes you are. You're going to go upstairs and eat some dinner, take a bath, and then you're going to bed and get some rest." I nodded my head. "Catalina, if I had known..." He trailed off as he glanced to the wet ground.

"I know, baby." My fingers grazed his cheeks as. "You were only trying to save me."

"I didn't hurt the baby, did I?" His voice was mumbled as to not let anyone else into our conversation.

I shrugged my shoulders. "I don't think so. Don't think about it too much, you need to sleep." I kissed his forehead and rose to my feet before turning towards Alex. "He needs to sleep. At least let him rest without hanging." My fingers entangled into his hair as his head hung. From behind Alex's shoulder I spotted my mother who was silently crying as she looked towards Robbie.

"No-" Alex was cut off by my mothers voice.

"Yes. She's right."

Alex rolled his eyes as he allowed Robbie to stay on the floor and took me by my arm, dragging me out of the room. "I love you." Robbie shouted before the door slammed shut.

I yanked away from his grip and rushed up the stairs and to what was suppose to be my bedroom, but my mother was following me. My body spun around to meet her as tears rushed down my cheeks. "Tell me! Tell me how you understand any of this."

She nodded her head as she went to sit on the bed."I understand because your father isn't your father."

My eyebrows scrunched together as I looked at her. "What are you talking about?"

"I was in love with your father, but I was drunk and had met someone one night. It was a one night stand, but I ended up pregnant. I knew what your father was like because I knew who he had run around with. He had always run with motorcycle clubs, so I knew that I would have to convince him that this baby was his. I was able to, but I ran into the man that is your father one day and the next day he was dead. Your father had killed your birthfather. When you were born I made him promise that we would never be involved in anything with the club, that you would never know. So he kept his promise, until the club that he was apart of killed someone else son."

Chapter Forty-Two

Catalina's POV

It had all fallen into place. This was why my father hated Reaper from the very beginning. My father's M.C had killed Reaper's brother, wife, and child; in return Reaper burned the M.C's club house to the ground with everyone in it but one. Although, clearly it was more than just one because my father was alive and Reaper remembers who he thought was the only one to survive. This entire time my father has been trying to kill him in order to get back at him for what he did. The cycle was just continuing over and over again.

My mother had rushed out of the bedroom when she heard the front door open, my 'father' was home from whatever he had been doing. I searched for my phone in order to contact Jess, he had to be slightly close by now. Unfortunately, he wasn't able to even begin getting close until we were already gone. Alex would have been able to know if we were being followed and he wouldn't have brought me to Robbie. Footsteps came into my room as my phone was in my hands and I quickly deleted the messages. Alex's frame crowded the doorway in a much less intimidating and sexy way that Robbie's did. He was smaller, less muscular and it really showed at this point in time.

"I didn't bring him here for you to be tending to him. I brought him here so that Juan and his men wouldn't kill him like you asked. That doesn't mean you two get to play house while he's tied up in the basement." My eyes met his as I nodded my head, be smart about this Catalina. He's baiting you.

"How do you expect me to not tend to him? I would tend to anyone in the situation that he's in." I shrugged my shoulders and looked over my shoulder out the window in order to avoid his eyes meeting mine.

"Well, I guess we won't have to worry about it for much longer." He mumbled to himself. My head shot to his direction.

"What is that suppose to mean?" My skin has goosebumps covering it and I felt paralyzed.

He shrugged his shoulder as he advanced into the bedroom and shut the door behind him. "You're father's home, did you really think he was going to last much longer?"

I couldn't breathe, panic was washing over me in crashing waves and I didn't know if was going to jump and run or pass out. "W-when?" My voice stuttered as a smirk came over his face as he sat beside me.

"Probably tomorrow, I don't really know." He gestured with his hands before laying back. "Not really my problem, I'm ready to have him out of my way." His hand on my back send chills up my spine in the worst way possible, he was skin to skin with me and I felt like I needed to crawl out of mine. "Shouldn't matter to you anyway, you promised me you. Maybe if you treat me kindly I'll ask your father to make it quick on him."

There was nothing around me, I didn't have anything that would work to my advantage. I needed out of this room and I needed it fast before I did something that would get Robbie killed tonight. My eyes searched for his before I spoke, "I suppose I should go and say hi to my father." He nodded his head.

"I suppose you should."

"Then I'll go and say goodnight to my mother before I turn in." I was nodding to myself, I needed something from the kitchen.

My feet pattered down the stairs as I skipped over every other before I was in the kitchen. I knew that my father was in the living room watching a late night show. In order to not look like I was up to no good, I'd have to go and see him first. Sure Catalina, go hug the man that isn't actually your father, but thinks he is and is going to kill the father of your unborn child. Great.

"Hi." I whispered as I stood in the arch of the doorway. I wasn't exactly sure how he was going to respond to me being here after all this. Would he react with anger and hit me? He did have me kidnapped.

He placed his beer on the side table and looked me up and down before a smile crossed his face. "I'm so glad you finally realized what you should do." He motioned me to come and sit next to him. I did as I was told. "Alex is going to make an amazing husband, child." I nodded my head, not knowing any other way to respond. "I'm sure you're a little upset right now, but it will pass and you'll be glad that it happened this way."

I was gonna be glad about something that was for sure. "I'm sure I will." What I'm gonna be glad about and what you'll be glad about are going to be two different things. "I just wanted to greet you, I should get going to bed." He nodded his head and tapped me on shoulder before I made my way to the kitchen.

His foot steps behind me were silent, but I should have known that he was going to follow me. "What are you doing in the kitchen?" I jumped at my fathers figure standing behind me.

"I was just trying to get some water before bed." He nodded his head as he watched me closely.

My mothers room was cold, but she was snuggled up under the covers reading a book before she dozed off. When I opened the door and walked in she seemed taken aback like she didn't remember that I was here. "I don't want to sleep in that room with that man." I whispered towards her. She nodded her head and held open the covers for me to climb in next to her. I never planned on falling asleep, but something about the comfort of knowing that the person next to me wasn't going to touch me in any type of way made me feel safe. Just before I was completely out her hand came and brushed my hair away from my face. "I've never loved someone the way I love this man." My whisper cut into the air like a knife. "I would rather die with him than live without him." I heard her silent sigh before I glanced up at her with tears in my eyes. "No matter what happens, I will never choose what happened to me to happen to my child and allow them to be stuck in my same position." I closed my eyes and drifted asleep before I could stop myself.

I woke to my body being yanked awake by someone and I could hear my mothers voice pleading. "You're fucking pregnant?" Alex screamed so loud that spit was flying out of his mouth. My eyes immediately looked to my mothers. She had told them? My father was no where to be seen, but something told me he already knew. Robbie... "Answer me you fucking whore!"

I shook my head, I didn't know if lying or the truth would be best. "Alex be gentle with her!" My mother sobbed from behind me, her robe wrapped tightly around her.

"Lets go." He seethed as he flung me over his shoulder and began to march down the flights of stairs. When he threw me to the ground, I was beside Robbie who was barely staying conscious. Instantly a squeak came out of my mouth and I was crawling toward his face that was pressed against the floor. I didn't know which part of him had the most blood coming out, but his eyes fluttered open at my touch.

"Run." He choked out to me before Alex swiftly kicked him in the ribs.

"Stop!" I screamed as I moved my body over his. I was banking on the fact that this man still believed that I was his daughter and that he wouldn't physically harm me.

"Catalina, go." Robbie's voice was muffled as he tried to speak through the wheezing. I shook my head frantically.

"You're pregnant with his child!"

At this point I didn't know who was talking to me, but I'd answer. "Yes! Yes!" I was covering his head with my arms.

When the room went silent my eyes raised to the man that had helped raise me, he was completely silent, but Alex was cleaning a gun behind him. Panic washed over me as Alex turned towards us and raised his hand. "Stop! Stop!" Think Catalina, you need to think. "I'm not your daughter!" I screamed up to him as my eyes pleaded.

His head cocked as his hand raised to stop Alex. My mothers head dropped to face the floor as my father raised his eyebrows at me. "What do you mean?" His hiss sliced my ears.

"You aren't my biological father." I cried as I hugged my body to Robbie's. "What does it matter who's baby I carry if I'm not even yours!"

"It doesn't, but he still burned down the clubhouse and killed the M.C."
I shook my head as my eyes went to plead to him. My eyes scrunched together as a gun shot was fired and I waited for whatever had just happened
to hit me.

"Catalina!" Jess' voice filled my ears as I looked up to see Alex on the floor.
My father scurried to grab the gun that was on the ground near his feet as
I rushed to mine. The knife on the table that was used to torture Robbie
had my fingers wrapped around it as I shoved it into his stomach. There
were no thoughts that crossed my mind before, just the animalistic need
to protect what was mine. When I yanked the weapon out of his body he
dropped to his knees slowly as Jess came up to grab the gun that was in his
hands.

More figure's rushed into the room as I stood staring at the man that was
bleeding out before me. One of the men grabbed my mother who squeaked
in response, but Robbie interrupted it all. "Don't, she'll regret it later."
He whispered out. The man holding my mother dropped her and then
proceeded to stand around waiting for a different order.

Henry walked into the room and immediately went to Robbie's body. "He
doesn't have much time, let's move him."

They had the back of a van set up so that Henry could take care of Robbie
on the way back to the clubhouse while I sat beside him. The ride would be
long and we'd be lucky if we got him back to where we needed to get him.
I had no idea if my mother was following us or not, all I knew is I told her
I didn't care what she did when we left. Maybe she would follow us back
to town to try and be close, but either way I didn't feel the need to know.

Once we were back to the clubhouse Robbie was immediately brought
down into the basement and to his room. I wouldn't ever understand why
the doc insisted on doing his work down here, but as long as he fixed
Robbie I guess I didn't really care. I knew that the healing process was going

to take time and right now the only thing they could do would be to get him stable.

The palm of my hand found the side of his head as his eyes fluttered at me. I knew that he was fighting sleep and it was getting close to winning. "Robbie, I don't know if you know or not, but my fathers M.C. were the ones that killed your brother." I swallowed the lump in my throat as he searched my face.

"You aren't his blood." His voice was shaky as it left his mouth. His eyelids barely opening as he tried his best to continue to look at me. I rubbed at his cheek as a comfort as my head nodded. "That isn't your burden to carry."

"Rest Robbie, you're safe."

The corner of his lip turned up in a smirk as his eyes began to close and the muscles in his body relaxed. "Don't leave." He whispered before sleep overtook him. I brushed his hair away from his face and kissed him gently on the forehead whispering, "I'm not going anywhere."

I turned to look towards the door as Jess' shadow came into view. "You need to go and get yourself checked out." He nodded his head towards me.

My head shook no before the words could vocalize it. "I'm not leaving." I whispers to him as my eyes looked over Robbie's naked torso.

"I'll stay with him. You need to go get someone to check on that baby of yours." I nodded my head as my hand my stomach and I rose from my seat. I needed to make sure I was still pregnant.

Chapter Forty-Three

- -

Catalina's POV

Rob slept for what felt like years. His body was taking its sweet time in repairing itself and I was beginning to feel like this was never going to be over for him. I sat in the chair beside his bed as my hand grazed over my flat stomach, I would have been entering my third trimester.

Sunlight peaked in between the curtains hanging over the window as I gently touched at his twitching arm. I knew that he was having another nightmare, he didn't need to tell me what he was thinking about.

Catalina now!

We hadn't been ready for a baby anyway, but Robbie blamed himself for the loss. When his eyes fluttered open and caught me in his eye sight they immediately looked down to abdomen. Just as quickly as they were there, they were gone. He pushed himself into a sitting position with a great sigh as he found my eyes again. The sheets fell to his hips as he reached out to me.

"It's not your fault." I whispered to him as my legs trapped his hips between them. He nodded his head as he looked down to my zip hoodie.

"You wanna distract me?" His fingers found the zipper and gently pulled at it.

"This early in the morning?" A small smile came across my lips as I glanced at the clock. It wasn't even seven a.m. yet.

"We've got this big ole house all to ourselves." He shrugged his shoulders. "Because we haven't christened our new home yet." His hands had undone the entire zipper and were now pushing the fabric off my shoulders to expose my chest to him. A hiss left my lips as his thumbs brushed over my hardened nipples sending shocks down my spine. My head nodded, "Yes." I whispered as he began to massage them.

"Strip. Now." He pushed at my hips as I stood up on the bed and quickly discarded all clothing that was on my body. I was standing over him completely naked as I waited for another order. "Get on your back." He ordered as his body shifted out of my way. I quickly landed on my back in the bed as he kneeled at the bottom. He pulled me so my bottom was hanging off the end of the bed and then pushed my legs so they were closer to each post near them. I walked as he walked towards a dresser and came back with three ties. Each of my feet were tied to a bedpost and my hands were then tied together above my head. I felt like a pretzel with my bottom dangling in the air and my legs beside my head.

"Pick a word." He hissed to me as his hands grabbed at my cheeks. His thumb coming up to rub my clit in circles.

"Reaper." He nodded his head as he dropped to his knees. I heard him drag something hard alone the floor from under the bed. He blew gently on my center before his tongue came out to lick me. His mouth covered my clit as his tongue swiveled out to circle it. My body arching in response to the pleasure. His tongue dropped lower and pushed into my entrance before he pulled back.

"Look at this." I briefly opened my eyes to see that he was holding something hot pink. My head fell back, I was in for it. The little pink vibrator brushed over my clit before I could protest and send my spine arching before he moved it to my entrance and shoved it inside of me. He fucked me with it until I was dripping wet and then pulled it out of me. I felt him drop lower as some panic washed over my body. "Relax." He ordered as he pushed two fingers into my soaking entrance and pushed them in and out. They poked at my walls as I clenched around them before they were removed. My eyes were closed as he pushed himself inside of me before the tip of him was poking at my back entrance. As my eyes flung open and I looked at him he slowly pushed an inch inside as he shoved the vibrator back inside of me. "Relax baby, you trust me?" I hesitantly nodded my head. His cock pushed deeper into my back entrance. The pain was burning though me as my body tried to accommodate to the foreign object entering it. "I needed to take that virgin ass too." He hissed as he pushed further in as tears started to brim my eyes. "Talk to me baby, tell me how it feels."

"It hurts." I whispered as he pushed further.

His hand beginning to push the vibrator in and out of me. The little arm hitting my clit every time it reentered me. "How about this?" His eyes shot up to mine. I nodded my head, "Good."

"Good." He grunted back to me as his body began to work into mine. I couldn't wrap my mind around what he was trying to focus on, but all I knew was that as time went on it didn't hurt as much. My fingernails slowly started to retract from his skin and he was kissing me intensely as I felt my body tighten. Before I knew it he was releasing onto me and I was laying back with my eyes closed.

When my eyes fluttered back open his presence was gone and it had just dawned on me that I was still tied in a very compromising position. Where had he gone to? My eyes scanned the bright room as I searched for him, but came up short. When he came back into my sight his body was dripping wet and he aggressively untied me from my position before sitting on the edge of the bed. "Why did you leave" I whispered as my body pounded. It felt as if everything below the belt had a heartbeat and I wasn't sure if that was a good or bad thing. His shoulders shrugged as he turned to look at me, but couldn't meet my eye.

"I need to go to the club for awhile, I'll bring back lunch." My mouth gapped as he got up and threw clothes on before walking out the door without another glance my way. I heard the front door followed by the roar of his bike before my ears were filled with silence. Before I moved to try and clean myself tears slipped from my eyes and down my cheeks almost instantly. I didn't even know what I was feeling in that moment, but I knew something was sitting on my chest and it felt as if I was going to curl up in a ball and cease to exist.

Hours passed before I moved any part of my body to try and clean up the mess that had been left behind. I practically crawled to the bathroom to put myself in the bathtub. The epson salt calmed my sore muscles, but not the one sitting in my chest. He had pulled that outta no where, all of a sudden deciding that we were going to try anal for the first time and then he just ups and leaves. It hadn't been all that bad besides the fact that he took my other virginity and then walked away as if it had never happened. My hand came down to cradle my flat stomach as I longed for it to be a watermelon. Once more tears trickled down my cheeks before my eyes closed and I finally rested.

Robbie's POV

I hadn't meant to, hadn't meant to get carried away and spring that on her. All I could comprehend was my urgent need to have all of her. To take everything that she could offer and be her first in every aspect of the word. For some reason, in that very moment, I needed it more than I've ever needed it before. I should have prepared her more for it, taken more time, been sweeter about it. It didn't feel like I was in my body, or bedroom had morphed into somewhere else and I knew that I wanted to claim her before she left me. She would leave me. I had been preparing for it for days now and a part of me just wanted her to get it over with already. I prepped for her to hand the ring back and tell me she couldn't take it anymore, for her to tell me that this was all my fault and she didn't love me anymore.

I was the reason our baby was dead. I was the reason she miscarried.

I burst into Jess's office as he sat behind his desk. "I fucked up." I grunted to him as I plopped myself into the opposing chair. His eyebrows furrowed as he looked over my appearance.

"You reek of sex, tell me you were with Cat." I rolled my eyes at him.

"Of course. I would never do that to her." I grunted as I looked to my feet, no I do worse.

"Okay so you didn't cheat, how'd you fuck up." His hands fold in front of him on the desk. I had to be careful with this one, I knew the odd friendship him and Cat had formed over all this time. I knew that if I worded this any worse than it actually was that he'd beat me into the ground.

My eyes found the ground. I needed to voice the words so that way I could deal with them properly instead of however the hell the voice in my head was gonna tell me to deal with them. Jess was more sensitive to women and wasn't shy about the fact that he loved himself some anal. "We were fucking and I don't know what came over me, all of a sudden I was in her ass." His eyebrows rose as he looked at me, not prepared for that to be what was wrong.

"Taking into consideration that Catalina was a virgin before you, I'm assuming she had never had anal before." I nodded my head at his statement as I leaned back in my chair to look at him. "How tight?"

My muscles tensed. "Jesus Christ, you can't even imagine."

He licked his lips before nodding his head. "How slow were you?"

I shook my head, "Not slow enough."

"Had you guys ever discussed having anal before?"

I shrugged my shoulders. "She had had a few dreams about it and she knew that I wanted all the virginities that she could give me, but I don't know if she was ready for it today." I whispered.

"You're telling me you didn't slowly work her up to your size?" I shook my head as my fists tightened.

"I don't know what happened Jess. I was slow for the most part. She didn't tell me to stop." My hands came over my face as I recalled the look in her eyes. I knew that I had slightly hurt her, but she told me she felt good. "I know that she was confused." I admitted. I could see the question in his eyes. "I stuck a vibrator in her while I was in there." He nodded.

"No blood afterwards?"

I hadn't checked... I left.

"Reaper, tell me you checked on her after you were done." I swallowed hard, my head shaking as my eyes welled up.

"I panicked, I didn't know what came over me and then it was just done and I got up. I was so upset with myself that I came here."

"Reaper, you aren't fucking small in the dick department man. Do you know how drastic of a change her tight ass is gonna be to your fucking dick?" He was upset. "You need to go back there and make sure there's no tearing. Put some fucking cream on her and make her some damn food. She's not gonna be able to walk for a fucking week, let alone sit on her bottom."

I panicked the more that he spoke until I was on my feet and moving towards my bike. Jesus fucking Christ. If she wasn't gonna leave me before she would probably leave me now.

I made it to the house within the hour between driving and picking up the lunch that I had promised. Flowers would help. I grabbed the biggest thing of those that I could find in the process and hesitantly entered the house. Her car was still here which meant she hadn't left yet. She wasn't on the first floor so I made my way up to the second. I knew that she'd probably be in the bedroom, but when I opened the door the bed was empty. Panic set in me as I made my way into the bathroom and found her in the tub with her eyes closed. I rushed her as I pulled her up and out onto the ground in my lap. Her eyes opened quickly as she looked around before her eyes landed on me. Her breathing steadied as she looked me over before sighing.

"What the fuck were you doing?" I hissed as I pushed her wet hair away from her face. Her head being cradled between my chest and my hand as I looked over her naked body.

"I was taking a bath." Her voice was meek as she looked towards the tub. "I must have fallen asleep."

"You could of drowned yourself." I scolded her as I grabbed the towel closest to me and wrapped it around her small frame. My body relaxed as I brought hers closer into mine before I lifted her up. A small hiss left her mouth as I walked us over to the bed to place her down. Beside her I spotted the red mark that was on the sheets as my hands pulled at it to inspect the size. I had made her bleed. I swallowed the lump in my throat as my eyes found hers also looking at it, tears quickly welling up before she closed them all together. "I'm so sorry." I whispered to her as the pounding in my ears heightened. "I never meant to hurt you. There's no excuse for my actions." Her eyes found mine. "I should have never taken your ass."

Tears dripped down her cheeks as she searched my eyes for something she clearly wasn't finding. "I knew that you wanted to try it. I was okay with trying it with you. I knew that it was gonna hurt, I've felt what your dick feels like entering my pussy where it's suppose to be, let alone someplace it isn't." She hiccuped. "What I wasn't okay with was that you took apart of my body that I was only willing to share with you and left afterwards like I mean nothing to you. I have no idea if what I feel or how my body is reacting is normal or not because I'm new to this and you aren't. I needed your help and you left like I was some one night stand."

I felt the wetness of my cheek before I could stop it. I grabbed her face in my hands as I looked at her, "You know how much I love you."

"Do you?" She cried back to me. "Because leaving me in that state is not love." Her voice broke at the end. I nodded my head. I knew that.

"I do. More than you could ever know. I panicked. I panicked that you hadn't wanted that, that I had hurt you and you would hate me. I panicked that this was just gonna be another reason that you leave me."

"Leave you?"

"Yes." I hissed out.

"Why would I leave you?" Her voice was rising.

"Because I killed our baby!" I couldn't look her in the eye as I confessed. I couldn't stop the shaking of my body or the tears that were steadily rolling down my cheeks. I had never felt like this in my entire life. I had killed my baby and lost the love of my life all in one swoop. Her hands were on the side of my face before I could tell her differently and she was resting her forehead against mine.

Her voice had turned softer than it normally was as it invaded my ears. "You didn't kill our baby." She whispered to me as her thumbs wiped away my tears. "If anyone killed our baby it was my father and Jose. They were the people that put us in the position that made me miscarry. It wasn't you baby. I know how much you wanted that baby. I know how much you already loved that baby. You did not kill our baby."

"I'm the one who made you jump." I whispered back to her.

"I'm the one who didn't tell you until it was too late. I'm the one who jumped anyway. I didn't have to jump then and there. I could have told her I couldn't, that I was pregnant. If anyone killed our baby it was me." Her voice broke at the end as I felt her tears drip down her cheeks. I was shaking my head no. She wasn't to blame here. I'm the one with the fucked up life that put us in this position anyway.

She grabbed my face and kissed all over until she found my mouth. My hands reached out to her waist as I pulled her further into me, my teeth grabbing her bottom lip and pulling it into my mouth to taste her. A whimper left her lips as I grabbed at her ass. Reality coming to smack me in the face as I pulled away from her. Her eyes looked worried as she rested her hands on my chest.

I pulled the shirt that I was wearing over my head before placing it on her body. She instantly brought the collar to her nose to sniff as I brought her to the foot of the bed. "Face down, baby. Let me look." I whispered as she hesitantly stuck her bottom in the air for me. I spread her bottom open further as I looked at her. She was red and slightly swollen, but I couldn't see much. I went to the bathroom to grab a wet grab and some ointment before returning to her. The white towel was a light shade of pink when I pulled it away from her. From what I could see there was no area that was bleeding or agitated, but I put ointment on my finger and spread it around regardless. A soft grunt left her mouth as I made contact with her. "Maybe we should try something smaller next time." She whispered from her position. A slight giggle leaving her mouth as I shook my head.

"Are you asking me to use more toys on you?" I whispered down to her playfully.

She shrugged her shoulders. "Ya can't knock it till you try it, right?"

Chapter Forty-Four

Catalina's POV

The next week or so following the incident was odd and off. Robbie was distant from me and from us, it felt as though I was walking around this big new house and it wasn't mine. I wasn't sharing it with the man that I was suppose to marry. Jess was unusually cautious around me and I was beginning to snoop around for answers. When I was at the club house I'd walk around silently hoping that I'd be able to overhear something about what was going on, but I was kept in the dark for the most part. It wasn't until I was outside of Jess's bedroom that I finally heard what I was looking for.

I could all but smell him in there. "What am I suppose to do? How do we plan a wedding when I've got an M.C. gunning for her head on a stick? How do I send out invitations with her without it causing problems?"

I heard a sigh come from the crack in the door, getting a glimpse of Jess as he paced in his bedroom. "I don't know. You send those things out and then all of a sudden there's a chance that he's gonna get his hands on them. I don't think you'd be particularly happy with Catalina being gunned down while she's walking down the aisle. I don't know what to tell you, Reaper."

"It's gonna spark too many questions about her father and where he is."
I heard a chuckle, deep and throaty come from him. "For all I know, her
mother's already reported it to the police. I have no idea what her state of
mind was in when we left."

"You were the one that wouldn't let us kill her."

"I know, what did you expect me to do? At the end of the day it's still her
mother and she's not the one that was causing the problems." Jess went
out of sight as Robbie came into it, his fists shoved to the bottom of his
front jean pockets. My chest was tightening as the conversation went on.
I really didn't know what my mother planned to do. People were going
to ask questions eventually. I had just figured that they would clean it up
afterwards.

"Our clean-up crew was there. They disposed of the bodies, but eventually
someones gonna realize that they went missing. If her mother was smart
she'd drop off the face of the earth so no one can question her."

"If we were smart, we wouldn't have left loose ends." Robbie whispered as
his eyes met the floor.

Jess's voice was on the other side of the room. "What are you gonna do
about this engagement?"

I watched Robbie's shoulders shrug as he looked up at his best friend.
"How am I suppose to get married without putting her in danger and
raising questions we don't have the answer to? The only easy way out of
this is to tell her we aren't gonna have a wedding."

"You're calling it off?"

"Do I have any other choice? She wants a wedding, a real wedding."

My hand came over my mouth as tears started streaking down my cheeks. I didn't know any other way to react then move. My feet were light as I moved away from his room before running down the stairs. I had no where to go. My father was dead, my mother was god knows where, the love of my life was changing his mind on marrying me because it'd be too difficult and I was stuck here. I snatched my jacket as I moved out the front door with my phone in my hand. The keys to his car were in his pocket and at this very moment I didn't want to be anywhere near him.

I headed through he cold wind towards where Rose lived, knowing that if I hurried I'd get there before dark. I wasn't dressed for the weather, didn't have on the proper shoes to be trudging through slush. When I showed up at her front door my fingers were blue and I was sure my toes were too. Without question she ushered me into her apartment and immediately made me a cup of tea. Hey eyes searched mine as I sat in front of her fireplace quiet. "I don't want to talk about it." I whispered to her from the floor. "I just need to crash here for a little while if that's okay with you."

She nodded her head as she left me to myself and went into her bedroom. My phone went off as I was sitting there and Robbie's face popped up on the screen. Instantly, I declined the call only to have him call me again. This happened three times before I decided to text him.

- I just need some time alone. I'm fine. -

- You can't just run off like that I've been looking for you. I thought something had happened. Where are you? I'm coming to get you and we can go home. -

- I just want some time alone for a while. Things are just getting to me. -

- Where are you. It's not safe for you to be alone like this. -

- I'm fine. -

I ignored the new messages that he was sending me and turned my phone off as my attention went back to the fire. A few hours passed peacefully before Rose came out of her room worried. "Are you gonna tell me what's going on?" I shook my head.

"It's too complicated to explain. I just wanted a safe place." Her eyebrows furrowed as she took in my appearance.

"Where's Robbie? Why aren't you home? Is everything alright between you two?"

I nodded my head, what I needed was for her to not ask any questions. "I'm just gonna nap."

She sighed as she looked at me once more before turning on her heels. I knew Rose and even with how worried she was she wouldn't involve herself. At the end of the day if she felt it wasn't her business she didn't think too much about it. She knew that I'd eventually tell her what was going on.

There was a gentle knock on the door before Rose came out of her room in her PJ's and answered it. I couldn't hear the mumbling, but when she stepped back to let the person in Robbie's presence filled the entire apartment. He seemed calm on the outside, but I saw the fiery flashing in his eyes and he was fucking livid.

"You called him?" My own fiery was directed at Rose who just shook her head.

Robbie interrupted before she could answer, "She didn't need to, I called her." I rolled my eyes before looking away from him. "Get up, you had me fucking worried sick and now you're gonna sit there and roll your eyes at me like you didn't know that I'd fucking find you."

"I'm not going home. I told you I wanted some time alone."

"You are going home. If you don't want to be near me that badly then I'll go to the clubhouse, but you're intruding on Rose's home and privacy."

"It's really okay, she can stay if she wants." Rose corrected as she sent him a smile that wasn't met. She shrugged and looked towards me with wide eyes.

"See." I shrugged my shoulders towards him as his eyes bore into mine. He was loosing his patience.

"So help me God I pull put you over my fucking shoulder right now." I shook my head no as I stayed seated on the floor. "What is going on right now?" He advanced towards me as he crouched down to put me between his thighs. He was face to face with me and I couldn't look at him. I knew myself too well to know that if I looked into those icy blue eyes that I'd crack. With a shaky hand and his words replying in my head I took my engagement ring off my finger and held it up to him. I heard Rose gasp and shift her weight. "Baby, don't do this. Just talk to me. We'll figure it out." I didn't have any words left so I didn't give him any. I heard the jiggling of his keys and then cold metal against my other hand. He closed the key into my hand before speaking, "The house is yours, I don't want it without you. Give me an hour to gather my things at the house and then it's all yours. I've leave the extra key on the kitchen counter." My eyes quickly glanced to his and instantly regretted it. A stream of tears was falling down one of his cheeks as he looked between me and the ring. He rose to his feet and turned back towards me once he was at the door. "Do what you want with the ring, it was only ever meant to sit on your finger."

I watched with my own tears swelling in my eyes as he turned towards Rose, unashamed of the tears rolling down his cheeks. He slipped his jacket off and handed it to her. "She's gonna need it to get to the car." and with that he walked out the door and shut it behind him.

Chapter Forty-Five

- -

Catalina's POV

Tears streamed down my cheeks like a dam had let go as I starred at the door. Rose starred at me for all of five minutes before she burst into a fit of laughter, "You're a fucking idiot you know that?" She laughed through the tears on her own face. "Give me one good reason you just basically told the man you're in love with to go fuck himself."

"He was calling off the wedding." I whispered to her as my eyes looked to the ring and set of keys in my hand.

"He just evicted himself for you and you think that he was gonna call off the wedding." Another fit of laughter broke through her. "You're dumber than I thought."

"You wouldn't understand." I hissed towards her. "You don't get it!"

"No, maybe I don't Catalina. What I do get is the scariest man just looked me in the eyes with tears coming outta his and all he could think about was me making sure that you took care of yourself. He's so fucking in love with you it's not even funny. He asked you to spend the rest of your lives together and you just gave that promise back to him without any explanation."

"He'll figure it out." I whispered.

"Maybe, but in the mean time you're gonna spend the rest of your life regretting that."

"The decision had already been made, I just ripped the band-aid off." I tried to justify my actions. I didn't come here with the plan to break up with him. It just happened as he was speaking. I couldn't unhear him saying that he was gonna call it off.

"That was not a man that was gonna give up on you otherwise he would have never shown up here." She crossed her arms over her chest and walked into her room slamming the door behind her. I sat in silence as steady tears poured out before I turned my phone back on.

- Robbie's worries sick, where the fuck are you?- Jess's text message said. -Alright enough is enough, you're gonna give this man a heart attack.-

I had one from Grace, -Rob's looking for you, give him a call please.-

Stacey had sent me one. -Hi sweetheart, Robbie's looking for you, please contact someone soon so that he can stop worrying.-

I scrolled to the top one, -I love you.-

More tears poured out as I read it over and over again. The messages that I had chosen to ignore and the last thing he's gonna say to me is I love you. He had found me after that message and I was sure that I wasn't gonna get another one.

I woke the next morning from the floor when there was banging at the door. Panic washed over me as I took in my surroundings. I had never meant to fall asleep, I had meant to do something else. Rose stumbled out of her room in her bathroom and rushed to the door, "Hold on, Jesus Christ, I'm coming." She swung the door open without another thought and Jess was standing in the hallway, panic over his face.

"Is Reaper here?" He hadn't laid eyes on me yet. "I can't find him or Catalina anywhere and he's not answering his phone. She hasn't contacted me whatsoever since before she left the club house yesterday."

"She's here right." Rose stepped out of his line of sight and he took in my appearance.

"Where's Reaper?" I shrugged my shoulders as I looked over his panicking state. "What do you mean?" He copied me and shrugged his shoulders. "His stuff is gone."

"What do you mean?" Rose took the question out of my mouth.

"He never checked in last night. I went to the house to see if he had found her and all of his shit was gone. I went back to the club house and it was gone there too. He emptied his clubhouse room in the middle of the fucking night and his shits MIA. I called his fucking mom and she's panicking."

Jess's eyes flashed between the two of us as he waited for someone to fill him in even the slightest bit. "Catalina called off the engagement last night and broke things off." Rose spilled out to him as his eyes all but popped out of his head.

"You heard us didn't you?" He immediately looked towards me. "He was calling off the wedding to keep you safe, not leave you!" He seethed in my direction. "We were panicking until we thought of something else to do!" Panic began to sit in the bottom of my stomach and work it's way up my throat before I rose to my feet. Rose had an 'I told you so' look plastered all over her face. "I need a fucking cup of coffee." Jess hissed as he moved his way into the apartment. His eyes briefly looked over Rose's robe covered body before looking towards me.

"I'll make a pot and we'll help in whatever way we can." Rose whispered to him as she led him to one of the island stools. Jess sat down as I moved into the bathroom to change and fix myself slightly. I borrowed Rose's clothes knowing that it wouldn't bother her. When I came out of the bathroom they were both at the island and Jess's head was in his hands, Rose was gently rubbing his shoulder.

"What if he did something stupid." He whispered to her before their eyes found me standing behind them.

"What's the worst that he could do." Rose asked the two of us as Jess shook his head. So many things came to mind.

I shook my head unable to wrap my mind around the aftermath of last night. I never would have ever seen this coming. Rose poured three cups of coffee as she stood on the other side of the island across from Jess who was holding his head in his hands. "I'm gonna call Stacy." He whispered as he took out his phone and placed it on the island. It rang a couple times before she finally picked up.

"Hi sweetie, what's up?" Her voice came through the phone and filled the room. "Did Robert find Catalina?"

"Jess he found her." Jess glanced at me quickly before looking back to his phone. "We can't find Robert now." He huffed out as he took another swig of his coffee.

"What do you mean you can't find Robert?" Her voice changed in the slightest as she became worried for her only living son.

"He's gone. We have no idea where he is and he's not answering."

"He didn't answer my phone call this morning, I just figured they'd be sleeping." Her voice is even worse than before.

"Try and reach him and if you have any ideas where he might be let us know." Jess tells her through the phone as the call comes close to an end.

"He's a sentimental guy, think of places that changed him in some way or where important things happened."

All three of us nodded our heads as she hung up to go and make some calls. With a pen and paper in hand we wrote down all the places that we thought he could have gone to. The house, the club, a bar, hell even the fucking highway stop. Once dressed and ready to go we went together to search each of these places, but came up with nothing. He hadn't been anywhere.

I sat down at the lunch table as the waiter brought over our burgers. Jess had stress written all over his face and no matter what we talked about it stayed that way. His eyes found mine as I bit into my burger before he spoke to me.

"You really thought that he was leaving you?" He whispered across the glass patio table to me. We were in some weird greenhouse restaurant that made it feel like it wasn't zero degree's outside.

I shrugged my shoulders, in all honestly I didn't know what he was capable of after everything went down. I couldn't get a read on him for the life of me and he was trying to work on it, but was struggling. The loss of the baby was hitting him harder than I had expected it too and a part of me thought that he needed to get away from me in order to cope with everything in his head. "You didn't see how he was at home after everything Jess. He was heartbroken about the baby."

He nodded his head once before pushing his food away from him. Something was eating him up inside and I couldn't put my finger on it. It was as if he was feeling something that he wasn't going to let me in on. Everything inside of me screamed to get him to tell me, what if he had some clue that I didn't. "He's never been with someone like he's been with you Cat. His world starts and stops with you. You are literally the most important thing in his life, you're the reason he gets up in the morning. I'm not surprised about how he reacted with the baby situation, he wants nothing more than to be your forever and have something with you that no one else does. He told me about the incident that you guys had in bed..." he trailed off as his eyes caught mine. I looked away instantly embarrassed about the fact that Jess knew about that.

"I don't know what happened that day." I whispered to myself as Rose gave me a very confused look. "He talked to you about that?"

"That's where he went afterwards when he left you alone. He was panicking and didn't know what else to do." I nodded my head, I knew that he had panicked. Everything had happened so quickly and I wasn't really sure if I had liked it or not, but I knew that I didn't want him to leave.

"We're gonna find him, right?" I whispered to him as he scanned the room a couple times. He nodded his head as his hand reached over to me and gave mine a squeeze.

"Yeah, we're gonna find him Cat."

~

We called it quits when the sun was fully set and snow started to fall from the black sky. We brought Rose back to her apartment and thanked her for helping before he walked me back to the car.

"I was thinking," He broke the silence as his hands gripped the wheel of the SUV. My attention pulled towards him as I tried to fight the urge to fall asleep. "Maybe we crash in your living room? Nice little slumber party?" I raised my brows at him as his eyes glanced towards me. "Robbie would kill me if I let you stay in that house all alone. Plus, I don't wanna be alone with all my thoughts right now."

I nodded my head. "I think that's a good idea." I whispered to Jess as I looked back out the window, I didn't wanna be alone right now either.

"Are you sure you don't wanna go and get laid?" I chuckled lightly to him, he shook his head in response.

"Who am I gonna go and fuck, huh?" He chuckled back.

I scoffed at him, like he didn't have a fucking waiting list. "Rose would have been willing." I stated as I stole a glance towards him, he shook his head.

"I couldn't do that."

"Why?"

"She's gorgeous, trust me, but I'm not into the things that she'd be willing to do. If things went bad then that would make things weird between us and I'm not willing to take that chance." He shrugged his shoulders as he glanced over at me.

"You don't think he's done something super stupid do you?" I asked him.

"He's capable of a lot of things, but when The Reaper looses purpose he begins to do things without thinking of their consequences." I looked towards him alarmed. "I man with no reason to live is not a man you want to cross."

Chapter Forty-Six

Catalina's P.O.V

I laid awake for what felt like hours when in reality it was only a half hour. I was on the couch in the living room while Jess was on the mattress on the floor. As I was laying there it washed over me that Robbie would have loved the bar that we first met in. It's where everything started and if I was feeling sentimental why not go to the place that began it all. We had went there earlier and there was no sign of him, but why go to the bar in the middle of the day.

I dressed quickly as I threw on a black crew neck and some leggings with my snow boots. The note placed next to Jess told him not to worry that I was just going for a drive and then I'd be back. I slid behind the wheel and peeled off in the direction that the GPS instructed me to go. The drive was therapeutic as I thought over what I would say to him if he was there. My words were scrambled, what could I say?

I parked in front of the door unapologetic that it wasn't actually a parking spot as I took a deep breathe and pushed the door open. There wasn't a single female in this entire place, but I walked directly to the bartender as if I belonged here. His eyes caught mine as he stopped what he was doing and looked around nervously.

"Fool me once shame on you, fool me twice shame on me." He clucked as he walked over to where I was and leaned across to me. "I never expected to see this gorgeous face in here again."

"You remember me?" I gasped as I looked around to all eyes on me. The volume level had clearly gone down since I'd entered this place.

"Oh honey, of course I do. You don't see someone like you everyday in here and you surely don't forget the women who talked back to the Reaper. I heard you guys ended up together." I nodded my head at him.

"That's actually why I'm here, have you seen him tonight?"

He nodded his head. "He was in here about ten minutes ago, downed three drinks and then suddenly lost all interest in his favorite drink all together. Sat around the rest of the time and just observed everyone around him. Something was very wrong."

"Did he say anything to you? Like where he was going or staying for the night."

A hand on my hip jutted my hips out and then the one that landed on the center of my back pinned me to the bar. I gasped as hips roughly pushed against my bottom and the stranger had no problem whatsoever with what he was doing.

"Hey fucker, get your hands off her she's Reaper's." The bartender barked as he swatted at him with his rag.

"Oh yeah? Well where is he?" The strangers voice was higher than I had expected as he laughed at his own question. Clearly, he was impressed with the pair of balls that he had miraculously grown.

"Right here motherfucker." The hands instantly were off my body as there was a large thud on the ground. I spun around to lock eyes with Robbie as he moved over the body on the ground that was cowering away. Robbie took his hand that was being held up to him in a surrender and snapped it at the wrist causing everyone in the bar to fall silent and the man on the floor to scream. "You ever put your hands on what's mine again and your wrist won't be the only thing I break." He squatted over him to get in his face, "Do I make myself clear?" The venom that seeped out of his mouth had my entire body quivering.

The man nodded his head, "Yes."

"Yes what?" He grabbed him by the front of his shirt and brought him closer.

"Yes Reaper."

"That's right." He threw him backwards and stood up to look around the bar, everyone averted their eyes as he walked over to me and grabbed my wrist gently, pulling me towards the door. He walked me to what he knew was my car and put me in the passenger seat before putting himself behind the wheel. I didn't ask any questions as he started the car and drove out of the parking lot, I knew where he was going. The hotel that we had stayed in that first night, he walked me inside and into the elevator, he already had a room.

When we were up at the door he pushed it open and pushed me into the room first. "Do you know how fucking stupid it was for you to show up at that bar alone?" I nodded my head as he shook his. "Say it." He seethed as he turned to shut and locked the door behind us. We were in the exact same room from the looks of it.

"Yes Robbie." He shook his head as he went and leaned against the desk that was provided in the room. I on the other hand, didn't know what to do with my body so I just stood where I was in the middle. His eyes flashed to the engagement ring that I had placed back on my finger.

Instead of commenting on it, his icy blue eyes found mine with something in them that I knew too well. His beast was coming out to play. I nodded my head yes as my eyes stayed locked with his. "Strip, now." He demanded as he stayed where he was. I did as I was told instantly removing all articles of clothing that were covering my body until I was completely naked standing in front of him. "Bend over the bed, hands above your head."

I turned on my heels and bent at my waist, putting my torso onto the soft sheets and my face buried in the comforter. My arms stretched up above my head and I gripped the blankets. My feet were apart and my ass was jutted out for him. "Safe word."

"Reaper." My voice was muffled from the bed.

His hand came flying through the air as it connected to my bottom and repeated the motion ten times before it stopped. Tears were in my eyes but I couldn't deny how my body had woken up from the punishment. His fingered rubbed my bottom before moving down between my cheeks and gently entering me. "Soaking fucking wet." He hissed as he pumped his fingers in and out of me before I heard him drop to his knees. His tongue came out and flattened against my center as he ate me from behind. His teeth pulling my clit between them and nibbling on it hard enough to make me scream. The sounds of him slurping up my wetness had my cheeks crimson, but I couldn't stop my hips from grinding on his face. He jammed his fingers back into me as my body came aggressively above him. "Robbie." I screamed as I lost all control and let go.

He left my body and rose to his feet as he used my hair to pull me back into a standing position. I watched him as he discarded all of his clothes and then took the mirror off the wall and placed it on the chair in front of the bed. I was standing directly in front of it and could see the wetness all over my legs. He sat on the edge of the bed and instructed me to move the mirror closer before pulling me onto him so I was sitting on his lap facing it. "You're gonna watch." He commanded as he pulled me closer to his chest and put his feet on the edge of the bed so that his knees were bent and I was on-top of him. My legs were spread as I took in the image of my own center spread wide open in the mirror. His hand came over my body to rub at my clit as I watched before he aligned his cock at my entrance and slammed into me from behind. "What do you see?"

My breathe caught in my throat as he stretched me. "You and me."

"What am I doing?" He breathed into my ear as his other hand grabbed a fist full of my hair to expose my neck to him.

"Fucking me." I huffed as I watched him enter and exit me quickly over and over again.

He shook his head against my neck before hissing into my ear, "Who owns this?" He slammed into as he spoke.

"You." It was a mere whisper when it came out of my mouth.

"I didn't hear you, who owns this?" Another powerful thrust back inside of me.

"You, you, you!" I screamed louder and louder every time, unapologetic about who could hear.

"I what, baby girl?"

"You own this." I proclaimed aggressively as my body began to tighten.

"That's fucking right." He slammed into one last time before my body ripped open and I came aggressively all over him. His hand holding my head up as he made me watch. I watched as his release seeped out of me slowly before he laid back on the bed and pulled me with him.

"I-" I went to speak before he cut me off.

"Don't. Let me just have this for a minute. I just wanna be with you and pretend everything's fine." He whispered into my ear as I slid off of him and to his side.

I couldn't, "Robbie, I never wanted to call off the engagement. I misunderstood the situation and it was easier to break my own heart than have you break it." My voice got stuck in my throat as I looked at his furrowed eyebrows and scrunched up eyes. He wasn't looking at me and I didn't know if it was because he couldn't or didn't want to.

"Why are you wearing your ring again?" His icy blue eyes were glazed over as he turned his head to make eye contact with me causing my heart to shatter. It looked as though he was about to cry.

"Because I love you. Because I don't wanna be with anyone else, all that I want is you. Is it alright that I'm wearing it?" My hand laid on his chest and my eyes instantly caught it. How would I respond if he told me no?

He nodded his head as he turned on his side so that we were chest to chest and his lips pressed against my forehead as he crushed me to him. "You've always had me, baby." His words were mumbled against my forehead as I closed my eyes. "Sleep." He ordered as I let my body relax in his hold. As quickly as the command, my eyes fell shut and my body relaxed as the world turned black.

Chapter Forty-Seven

Catalina's POV

I hauled myself up off the ground, removing my head from the porcelain bowl and wiping my mouth on the back of my hand. My shaky legs dragged me in front of the sink so that I could rinse my body and splash water over my sweaty face. Throwing up is a funny thing, my body sweats uncontrollably before it happens. All of a sudden I'm soaking wet and shaking head to toe, that's when I know it's coming. Then my vision blurs and I try to make it to an acceptable place to put the contents of my stomach. During the entire process, as bodily fluids come back up I basically almost pass out.

I looked myself over in the mirror, noting that I look like fucking shit before removing myself from the bathroom to try and make myself look like a human. Leggings were pulled over my feet and I slipped Robbies sweatshirt over my head before heading to the kitchen to try and keep some food down.

Rose sat at the kitchen table holding my phone out to me as she looked me over. "You look like fucking shit." I rolled my eyes as I tried to pour myself a cup of coffee. "That's the third time you've puked this morning, what's going on?" I shrugged my shoulders before looking back at her, the mug to my mouth. Her eyes widened as I stopped mid sip and panicked. "Oh my fucking god, are you?" She trailed off, unable to say the word.

I slammed my mug to the counter, thankful it didn't shatter, and looked back at her. "Oh god."

"Do you wanna take a test?" I couldn't tell if she was getting excited or nervous from the way that she was speaking to me. "Is Robbie home?"

I shook my head, "No, he's with Jess somewhere handling some things." She nodded her head before a small smile creeped over her face.

"What if you are?" I almost didn't hear the statement.

What if I was? I swallowed the lump that was forming in my throat as I thought about the possibility. How did this make me feel? I was devastated when I lost the other baby. When did this happen? I thought back three months to the hotel room. The rough sex that we had had after he found me in that bar. How he came inside me and then made me watch his cum seep out of me. My body tightened just thinking about that night. How deep he had been, how hot it was to watch the things that he had done to me. I shifted uncomfortably, my body heating up at the mere thought. What if he had gotten me pregnant that night?

"I guess I should take a test." I mumbled to her as I slowly walked up to the bathroom. We had one from months back that I had kept. I didn't end up using it due to all the ones that I had bought when I was panicking before. Rose sat on the edge of our bed as I walked into the master bathroom to pee on a stick. I looked at the box and threw it in the trash as I reopened the door. "That ones too old, I think I should get a new one."

"Okay." Rose nodded eagerly as she stood in front of me.

"Maybe I should wait. Maybe I just have some weird bug. I should see how the rest of the day goes, if I get sick again I'm probably just sick with something." Or I was pregnant and I was too scared to find out. Too scared for it to be positive, but also too scared for it to be negative. I wanted to be and I didn't want to be. I was too nervous to find out for sure at the moment.

Rose and I left the bedroom to go back downstairs and watch some tv before we did anything. It was pouring outside and the storm was relentless, so the only thing that we could do was stay curled up inside. When the show was done, Rose was practically jumping out of her skin. She couldn't sit still and she couldn't handle not knowing my uterus status. "I'm gonna go to the store, buy snacks, pick up lunch and buy like five pregnancy tests." I rolled my eyes at her as she grabbed her keys and darted out the door.

My body sprawled out on the couch as I thought over the events of this morning. Maybe I was pregnant, which gives me an excuse to nap. My eyes drifted closed as I snuggled into the cushion...

I awoke on the floor. My arms were pinned above me and some man was sitting on me holding me down. A scream ripped through my throat as I tried to get them off of me, but it was no use. They were too strong and there was too many.

"Shh." He hushed me as his finger came over my mouth. My chest was going to explode as I looked around the house to see three other men, one of which was holding Rose by her hair as she kneeled in front of him. She had tears streaming down her cheeks as she silently sobbed.

"Reaper will be home any minute and you better hope that you aren't." I hissed up st him from my position.

"Oh trust me sweetheart, Reaper knows we're here and I'm sure he's on his way. As a matter of fact, say hi to him." My eyes followed his finger as he pointed to another man in the room who had his phone pointed towards me. I shut my mouth as my eyes found the man above me again, I had nothing else to say. A shiny silver knife came from his pocket and traced it along my neck. Rose sobbed once before a yelp flew out of her mouth. He dragged the knife down between my breasts, ripping through the sweatshirt in the process. I couldn't stop my chest from heaving, but I refused to make a noise as he barely cut me. "She doesn't wear a bra gentlemen!" He called to the room. "It's time to say goodbye Reaper. You'll find her when you get home."

The guy put the phone back in his pocket as my eyes darted to Rose. She was quiet as fear covered her face like a cloak. A phone rang from the one on top on me, he sighed before he answered it. "Juan." He answered. There was speaking on the other side that no one else could hear. The guy heaved a sigh as he looked down at me. "You're positive." More speaking. "I really wanted to know what the hell was so magical about this pussy, Juan." "It won't count if I take her in the ass." "Fine." He hung up as all the breath in my throat caught. "Big boss says no."

"What if I just stick it in once?" The guy holding my hands asked. He shook his head. "Her mouth?" He shook his head again.

"Reaper told big boss that he'd cut his daughters tits off and sew her cunt shut."

"When's that ever stopped him before?"

The guy sitting on me shrugged his shoulders. "Maybe she heard."

"What about her friend?" Rose heaved from the floor.

"Eh, I just wanted to know what the Reaper likes so much." He grabbed at my breast before standing. "Cut down the center of those pants, make

Reaper question what happened here." He ordered before walking away. Another man came over and cut down the center of my bottoms, skimming over my core, and in between my cheeks. He spread my legs open to look at me before looking back to the leader. "Sure is a pretty pussy." He sighed as he walked towards the door. "Let's go boys."

My breath was caught in my throat until the door closed after them and Rose clasped to the floor in tears. I scurried to the floor in front of the couch, grabbing the blanket that was on it and pulling it over myself. It was seconds before the front door burst open and a furious Realer barged through it with his gun loaded. I sat meek where I was as his eyes scanned the room and finally landed on me. "Cat," he whispered before bolstering his weapon and rushing towards me. His mass dropped in front of me as his hands pulled me into part, inspecting me from head to toe. I felt his eyes connect with my core before frantically searching my own. All that I could manage was to shake my head no. My eyes wondered over to Rose and his followed before he spoke. "Rose are you hurt?" She shook her head no as more blubbering exited her lips. He rose from his position in the floor and walked upstairs, I listened as the water starting running. When he appeared again he was walking down the stairs and to Rose.

He crouched in front of her before his hands hooked under her arms and he pulled her to her feet. "Come on sweetheart." He whispered as he led her gently upstairs and out of my sight. I blinked and he was back in front of me scooping me into his arms and allowing me to bury my face in the crook of his neck. He carried me upstairs before placing me on the counter of our bathroom. The water was running in here also and I knew that he was going to put me in the bath to calm me down. It was something that he always did. He undressed himself before gently undressing me and pulling us both down into the water. His fingers massaged my skin, trying desperately to knead the tension from it. "I'm so sorry, Catalina." His shaky whisper entered my ear.

I nodded my head, I knew that he was. What did he have to be sorry for though? This was the life that we lived and I was the one who chose him. So, in a sense, I chose the higher risks too. I let him hold me before he decided it was over and he pulled us outta the water to dry me. He placed me in his comfy clothes and for a moment I was alone in the bathroom. I peaked down at the little stick that was in the trash and closed my eyes at what it was telling me. Tomorrow, I thought to myself as I tossed it back and allowed him to tuck me into bed. As I drifted off to sleep I got the sense that he wasn't going to stay. Something in him was too unsettled to be in bed at the moment, but I couldn't keep my eyes open any longer to worry about it.

I awoke only an hour later to an empty side of the bed. My ears picked up on movement on the first floor before my eyes caught the white piece of paper on the pillow beside me. As I sat to read it, I heard the front door close.

Catalina,

I can't begin to tell you how deep my love is for you. It has taken over my entire body and made me into someone who wants nothing but to return it to you. And yet here we are, no matter how hard we seem to try there's always something. The thought of the possible outcomes that could have happened today isn't something my mind can wrap around, but I know what I could have been walking into. Thank you for choosing to love me, to see me, and to save me from everything. For a moment there I really thought that I could have you, but I was foolish to think that I could have something as amazing as you. So now I'm choosing you, I'm choosing your life and your safety... your future. No matter where I go it seems that you always end up in front of me. Maybe that's my fault or maybe it's yours or maybe both, but as long as you always end up in front of me you'll never be safe. You'll never be able to live the life you're suppose to live. We've tried to stay apart and we've tried to stay together and neither seem to work, so there's only one other solution. I told you once that I would never live in a world where I couldn't have you and I meant it. As long as I can have you, you'll be at risk, so it's time I do what I'm suppose to do and finally protect you for good. I'm no good for you baby, I was never suppose to be your happily ever after, but you were suppose to be mine. Thank you for making my life worth it. I love you more than words will ever begin to explain, but it's time you live your life safely. I love you, baby. Don't spend your life missing me, I got what I wanted... and that was you. All my love forever, Robbie

Epiloque

Catalina's POV

My feet hit the ground running as I grabbed my keys and threw on my shoes. The night air hit me in the face as the front door swung open and woke Rose who was on the couch fast asleep. My phone was to my ear as I dialed his number over and over again, where would he have gone? The pedal was floored as I made my way to the clubhouse. Jess has known him his entire life, he would know what to do.

As I was running in, he was running down the stairs with his phone to his ear. Fumbling, he desperately tried to get both legs into his sweats as his eyes locked with mine. "Get in the car." I nodded as I turned around and made my way back out the door. His phone went straight to voicemail as I tried once more to reach him. This fucking letter wasn't going to be the way this ended, not with his baby inside of me.

Jess threw himself into the driver seat and slammed the car into reverse before swerving off down the road. "What the fuck happened?" He screamed as his eyes desperately searched the road.

"Some men broke in, they had Rose and I. Nothing happened! I found this note." I hiccuped through my sobs as I searched Jess' face.

"He said goodbye to me." The whisper fell over the cabin of the car.

"Where would be go?" The shaking in my body was uncontrollable as I placed my hand on my stomach. He didn't even know. What if I was too late? What if we didn't get there in time? What if we couldn't find him...

"Jess, I'm pregnant." I heaved as my eyes tried to find his. Like a deer caught in headlights, he turned to look towards me. Without saying another word, the dial on the accelerator moved higher. "How do you know where he'll go?"

"A part of him died on that bridge with his brother. It's where The Reaper was born, it was the reason The Reaper was born. He'll want to finish it there. He'll make sure everything's come full circle before he's done." His knuckles had turned ghostly white as they gripped the wheel.

"He's gonna kill himself where his brother and family was murdered?" My fingers racked through my tangled locks as I tried to wrap my head around what was happening.

"He told me once that he had wished it had been him instead. That he wished he had taken his brothers place." More tears spilled down my cheeks as I pictured it. His face while he was trapped in that car. The panic that his brother had gone through with his family. I shook the image out of my head as I saw the road become curvy in front of us. "Where almost there. Prepare yourself, Catalina."

Air wasn't filling my lungs. I couldn't exhale. The inly thing that I could think about doing was throwing up. How could I stop him, would me being there be enough. I saw the bridge first, before I saw the black outline sitting in the side of it. Jess slammed on his breaks once we were at the entrance and I jumped out. My feet slipped on ice as I tried to catch my balance and I saw the gun to his temple.

"Stop!" My voice carried as I rushed towards him. He didn't look at me and for a moment I knew it was over. I knew that he was gonna pu the trigger. "I'm pregnant!" Well this wasn't how I had imagined telling him we were having a baby... The first thing I saw was the hesitation. It was a split second where it felt like the entire world had come to a standstill. A tear rolled down his cheek before he closed his eyes and steadied his hand.

"Are you gonna leave her alone in this?" Jess seethed from behind me. I hadn't heard him get out of the car, but I could feel his heat fuming a couple feet behind. "You're taking the easiest fucking way out and leaving her all alone to deal with the shit that's gonna follow?" I couldn't speak, couldn't tell him to stop yelling.

"They will never stop." His voice carried softly over to us. "They will never stop hunting her unless I'm gone."

"You're a fucking pussy." If I hadn't glanced back to look at him I would have thought that he had melted all the snow around him with his fury.

"Please, I need you." I hiccuped to him. "Robbie please, I love you. Don't do this. Don't leave me, don't leave your baby." I begged as I took a few steps closer to him. He hadn't lowered the gun yet.

It had all happened so fast. I didn't see it coming, didn't know what was happening. Jess had taken over the situation. I'd never seen him more that fast in my entire life. He had Robbie by the hoodie and ripped the gun out of his hands as it fumbled into the river. With a hard yank, Robbie was back on solid ground. He was laying in his back in the middle of the road with Jess's foot pressure into the center of his chest.

"You're a fucking asshole. What makes you think that you get to play fucking god? You don't get to take the easy way out because you're tired.

You don't get to leave me behind. You don't get to make your mother lose her final child. You don't get to abandon Cat when she needs you the most and make the baby fatherless before it's even a baby. How could you fucking say goodbye to me with a text message, you're my fucking brother!"

I watched gasping as I tried to comprehend the conversation. My body was shaking now that the gun was away from his face and I felt thatfor the most part he was safe.

"Just let me go, trust me. There's no safe outcome when I'm still in the picture." Tears we're streaming down all three of our faces as I watched Jess stand over the man I was in love with.

My heart dropped to my feet when Jess spoke. "You wanna did so bad? Fine, but you don't get to play god." He grabbed his gun from his waist line and aimed it at Robbie's face. It happened so quickly, I didn't have time to lung until it was too late. The scream ripped through my throat as Jess pulled the trigger.